Elinor Mead Buckingham

The revival of English poetry in the nineteenth century

Selections from Wordsworth, Coleridge, Shelley, Keats and Byron

Elinor Mead Buckingham

The revival of English poetry in the nineteenth century
Selections from Wordsworth, Coleridge, Shelley, Keats and Byron

ISBN/EAN: 9783337278601

Printed in Europe, USA, Canada, Australia, Japan

Cover: Foto ©Andreas Hilbeck / pixelio.de

More available books at **www.hansebooks.com**

THE
REVIVAL OF ENGLISH POETRY

IN THE

NINETEENTH CENTURY

SELECTIONS FROM

WORDSWORTH, COLERIDGE, SHELLEY, KEATS AND BYRON

WITH AN INTRODUCTION BY

ELINOR M. BUCKINGHAM, A.B. (RADCLIFFE)
INSTRUCTOR IN ENGLISH, ADELPHI COLLEGE

THE MORSE COMPANY
NEW YORK .·. BOSTON
1898

TO

𝔐. 𝔚. 𝔅.

IN MEMORY OF MANY SUMMER EVENINGS

SPENT WITH THE POETS

PREFACE.

This volume is an attempt to supply adequate and convenient means for a systematic study of early Nineteenth Century poetry. The authors here brought together, though widely separated in some respects, do nevertheless form a group by themselves in the development of English literature. They stand as exponents of that renaissance of poetry which marks our century, and they should be studied not only as contrasted with each other, but as marking a distinct era.

So far as the editor is aware, no good opportunity exists for carrying on this work in high schools. One of the poets is not represented in any of the ordinary collections of poems now in use as text-books, and no simple explanation of their position in the history of English poetry has been published. To offer such an explanation is the chief purpose of the Introduction in the present volume, which aims to give not only an elementary, but, at least for high schools, an adequate conception of the reawakening of the poetic spirit in this century.

In addition, it is hoped that the student will make diligent use of the lists of dates and of biographical material, which will throw light not only upon the five poets as individuals, but also and especially upon their mutual influence and common sources of inspiration. The selection of poems has been determined in part by the desire to rouse this personal interest, in the hope that the student will be stimulated to read more fully in the authors' works.

The reference lists are far from exhaustive. The intention is to restrict them to such books as can be procured in a good school or town library, and the works selected have been arranged, in general, in the order of importance. Many well-known essays have been omitted because it seemed unwise to spend time upon criticism which is unsympathetic, or which has been superseded by later and more accurate knowledge.

It is earnestly hoped that the teacher will require a much fuller general acquaintance with the poets than is to be obtained from these selections. Indeed, the book is intended to suggest lines of thought and of work in various directions, which the individual instructor can best determine for his own classes. No book is well used which is slavishly used.

The editor wishes to acknowledge the kindness of Professor Stockton Axson in reading proof, and of Miss Sarah W. Brooks in generously giving both time and thought to practical details.

INTRODUCTION.

English Poetry is generally understood to have died
with Milton and to have renewed its life only in this
century. Not, indeed, that no poetry was written during
the intervening century, but the current was neither full
nor strong. The poetic impulse, like every other faculty
of man, ebbs and flows through the ages, and there seem
to have been three periods of high tide in English poetry,
separated by times when men devoted their best intellect
to other concerns. The eighteenth century was one of
those times of low tide.

In none of these seasons of depression did men cease to
write verses, nor is it true that there were no poets of
genuine feeling between Chaucer and Shakspere, or between Milton and Wordsworth; but, so far as poetry is
concerned, both these ages were characterized by imitation of great men who had gone before, by care for the
manner and form of poetry rather than for the soul, by
feeble attempts of a few men to introduce a more healthy
style.

Each age, too, was followed by the sudden development of a free, natural poetry of the heart. In the reign
of Elizabeth this outburst was in part a result of the

immense widening of the horizon of men's thoughts consequent upon the discoveries beyond seas, and the life-and-death struggle with Spain for national importance and religious independence. In our century, the impulse came with the introduction into England of fresh trains of thought from the German philosophical writers, and also, most strongly, with the new interest in humanity roused by the French Revolution.

By the middle of the seventeenth century, the freshness of poetry, expressing the eagerness of human living and the keen enjoyment of the senses, had already faded; for the court of Charles II. there could be no return to natural simplicity. The same terms might be used, but epigram and wit took the place of genuine song.

Moreover, most men who wrote possessed only mediocre intellects, and, notwithstanding the work of Dryden, their verses displayed neither wit nor form; so that by the time Pope had grown to thinking years, he was right in asserting the necessity for a revolution in the poetic world. We should have either good matter or good manner, if we cannot have both. Most men had neither. Pope perfected the latter. His style is generally acknowledged to be faultless, in his favorite form, the rhymed couplet, which contains some witty or trenchant remark in every pair of lines, completes the idea at the end of the line and allows no irregularities of metre. In our day it is hardly possible to conceive how popular this form became, or for how long a time men considered it to be the standard by which to judge every other form. Goldsmith wrote his two best poems in this metre, and Dr. Johnson lamented the offensive irregularity of Milton's blank verse.

Aside from mere form, there was another characteristic of eighteenth century poetry. It was the fashion to ignore the country, and to live only in and for the town. This was indeed natural, when literary men as a class depended upon some rich patron for the reward of their labors, or when courtiers themselves wrote about the only life they knew. Furthermore, " from the deep things of the soul, from men's living relations to the external world, educated thought seemed to turn instinctively away; " and " to exult over the ignorant past, to glory in the wonderful present, to have got rid of all prejudices, to have no strong beliefs except in material progress, to be tolerant of all tendencies but fanaticism, this was its highest boast." [1] From these statements, we can see that poetry, as we understand it now, was well nigh impossible.

No doubt when the tide has again turned, when a school corresponding in materialism, in intellectuality, in worship of form, to that of Pope shall have come again, the age will enjoy his poetry and that of his school more generously than we are able to do.

Even before Pope died, there were a few spirits who revolted, perhaps in despair of rivalling the master, perhaps wishing for novelty. In particular, James Thomson (1700-1748), a Scotchman, who had grown up beyond the sphere of Pope's influence, and in a country where simple poetry and a love of nature had never died away, ventured upon two innovations. In the first place, he chose to write on winter, and described what goes on in the country in winter. He followed it by descrip-

---

[1] J. C. Shairp, " Studies in Poetry and Philosophy," pp. 91, 92.

tions of the other seasons. Here is one of his simpler passages:

> " Till, in the western sky, the downward Sun
> Looks out, effulgent, from amid the flush
> Of broken clouds, gay-shifting to his beam.
> The rapid Radiance instantaneous strikes
> Th' illumined mountain, through the forest streams,
> Shakes on the floods, and in a yellow mist,
> Far smoking o'er th' interminable plain,
> In twinkling myriads lights the dewy gems." [1]

This shows some of his faults as well as some merits, but especially it brings out the second innovation which he dared to make, the substitution of blank verse for the rhymed couplet. There is hardly a line in which the sense is not closely connected with the next. It is different enough from

> " Then flash'd the living lightning from her eyes,
> And screams of horror rend the affrighted skies.
> Not louder shrieks to pitying heav'n are cast,
> When husbands, or when lapdogs breathe their last." [2]

Thomson was not strong enough to break altogether with the old style. He made use of such hackneyed phrases as "effulgent" and " dewy gems," and he was not above employing the adjective form " instantaneous " when he needed an adverb. In common with other poets of his century, also, he used nature either solely to fill in a background, or to make a pretty picture in and for itself. He never showed nature as reacting upon man. A sense of the close communion between man and nature is the distinguishing mark of Wordsworth's poetry, and,

---

[1] " The Seasons," Spring, lines 186-193.

[2] Pope, " The Rape of the Lock," lines 155-158.

in varying degrees, of the poetry of this whole century, but few men in the eighteenth century thought of her as anything more than an element outside of man,—to be enjoyed externally and to be described sympathetically, but yet an entirely distinct and merely physical creation.

Slightly later than Thomson, Collins (1721-1759), in his short life, evinced a truer touch in his descriptions of nature than the poets who had gone before. Though brought up in the city, he loved the country, and unlike Thomson freed himself from the conventional poetic diction which with the elder poet often served to hide really original thoughts.

> " Or where the beetle winds
>   His small but *sullen* horn,
> As oft he rises midst the twilight path,
> Against the pilgrim *born in heedless hum*,"

is a homely bit of description, but close to nature, and wonderfully suggestive of the spell which evening casts over the open moor. Again, in the same ode, " To Evening," a few words express the feeling of nightfall:

> " Thy dewy fingers draw
>   The gradual dusky veil."

In the latter part of the century Cowper (1731-1800) continued the development of nature poetry and the practice of writing blank verse. To-day we can hardly understand the popularity of his poetry during his lifetime. Cowper was an over-excitable lawyer's clerk, who had several times fallen a prey to insanity, had been forced to give up his profession, and had found a shelter from the disturbing tumult of the world, with his friend, Mrs. Unwin. He was a somewhat sadly contemplative man, deeply tinged with a religious sense of his personal guilt and necessary damnation in the future world. This terrible belief brought about, or at least accompanied, his various fits of insanity. During his calm periods, when he could feel an interest in the life about him, he began writing poetry as a diversion, to distract his thoughts, and, in addition, as a means of teaching religious truth. He was fond of out-door life, of meditative winter morning walks, and he was a close observer of the landscape, the flowers, the trailing vines about him. He described them lovingly, for their own sake, but it is obvious that a man who consciously turns to nature and poetry as a relief from oppressive gloom, and who thus by accident discovers himself to be a poet, can hardly have the strong inspiration which effects reform. He was one of those precursors who herald a coming revolution. Only now and then did he rise to the real passion of poetry when, in the terror and anguish of his own soul, he wrote from the depths of his nature.

Undoubtedly the most genuine English poet of the eighteenth century was Thomas Gray (1716-1771). Gray was, however, in a sense hampered by his acquirements. He was a student, " perhaps the most learned man in Europe," and he saw in preceding literature so much beauty that he would fain reproduce it. He was classic in a different sense from Pope, for he went back to Greek as well as to French literature; he was versed also in Norse and in Welsh poetry, and everything he wrote showed not only the form but the spirit of the works he loved. It is true that the inherent quality of the old writers was much the same as that of the Nineteenth Century renaissance, and Gray himself had more of the modern attitude of mind than any other poet of his time. Consequently we have, scattered through his poetry, such indications of the dependence of man upon nature as

> " The meanest flowret of the vale,
>   The simplest note that swells the gale,
>   The common sun, the air, the skies,
>   To him are opening Paradise."

Nevertheless, the whole body of his poetry is so small that these passages are few, and made little impression upon his generation. To break the chains of evil custom, it needed a man with less reverence for the past, and more abounding confidence in himself and the future.

The doggerel that was still written by men whose poetic instincts were not so true as those of Gray, need only be read to be condemned. Compare, for virility, Dr. Johnson's

> " Turn on the Ant thy heedless eyes,
>   Observe her labours, Sluggard, and be wise; " etc.

with the original, " Go to the ant, thou sluggard, consider her ways and be wise." As for subject, " the idea of writing a poem about sheep or daisies seemed to the magnificent men of the Pope and Johnson era to indicate some incipient lunacy." [1] As late as 1800, Charles Lamb wrote of the versifiers, " Some of them are idolators and worship the moon. Others deify qualities, as Love, Friendship, Sensibility, or bare accidents, as Solitude. I have been able to discover but few *images* in their temples, which, like the caves of Delphos of old, are famous for giving *echoes*. They impute a religious im-

---

[1] Wm. Knight, " Studies in Philosophy and Literature." p. 300.

portance to the letter O, whether because by its roundness it is thought to typify the moon, their principal goddess, or for its analogies to their own labors, all ending where they began, or for whatever high and mystical reference, I have never been able to discover."

The poetry of Burns (1759-1796), which shows an intimate love of nature, lies properly outside the development of English poetry. His typical work, his poetry of the field and the moor, is essentially of Scottish growth, comparatively uninfluenced by English verse, and not in any true sense reflecting the temper of English poets. It had a profound influence upon Wordsworth, but it could not attain to the wide popularity of "The Seasons" or "The Elegy in a Country Churchyard," partly because, as the *Monthly Review* said, it was " composed in the Scottish dialect, which contains many words that are altogether unknown to an English reader," and even more because the English mind was so provincial as not to understand or take interest in " modes of life, opinions, and ideas of the people in a remote corner of the country."

There were, however, two tendencies in literature, which were gradually making themselves felt. A taste for romance was being fed—and vitiated—by such novels as " The Mysteries of Udolpho." A perception that nature is something different from the prevailing picture of her drawn by the poets, was indicated among others by Crabbe, a close student, who painted her with all the minuteness of diagnosis and all the truth of scientific observation.

In other directions, also, men's ideas were being quickened and stimulated. In politics the American Revolu-

tion had roused real passions and great energies; among
the nations, England was assuming the right of the most
powerful in India, and the stories of the wealth of the
East were as intoxicating as had ever been the dreams of
El Dorado in Elizabeth's time; in philosophy the new
German metaphysics was becoming known in England
and undermining the materialistic, utilitarian system of
Locke.

Altogether, the nation was beginning to wake from
the lethargy of imagination which had given scope only
for a hard, practical, worldly tone of thought, when it
was startled into vivid life and consciousness by the
French Revolution. Immediately there was a vital interest in liberty, equality, fraternity; there came that
quick interchange of emotion, that swift tide of stren-
uous feelings in which virile poetry is born. Wordsworth on his travels, and Coleridge still at college, both
caught the enthusiasm. One must read such outbursts
as Coleridge's sonnets of 1794 to appreciate how madly
passionate was the tension.

The two men did not meet during their college days.
Wordsworth was just leaving Cambridge when Coleridge went up. As early as 1794, during the eventful
year when Coleridge finally quitted the University, he
became acquainted with Wordsworth's " Descriptive
Sketches," and was struck by their originality; but the
two did not become personally acquainted till 1797.
Coleridge was then living with his wife in Nether Stowey,
Somersetshire, while Wordsworth with his sister was not
very far away, at Racedown. They met, and Wordsworth

was so impressed with Coleridge's personality that he moved to Alfoxden to be near his new friend. The result was the " Lyrical Ballads," and the evolution of Wordsworth's theory of poetry, which might very probably have taken a different form but for the influence of Coleridge. Though the famous preface to the " Lyrical Ballads " goes by the name of Wordsworth, Coleridge wrote some years later that it was as much his work as his friend's, being in fact the result of their walks and talks together. He added that he did not assent to all Wordsworth said there, and intended to study into the subject to discover the principles on which he disagreed.

To all appearances, the men were totally different, as well in body as in mind. Wordsworth was long and spare of limb, somewhat stern of countenance, reserved and shy; there was a certain awkwardness about him, both physical and mental. Though of a deeply poetic and impassioned nature, he yet possessed a mind and conscience which led him to restrain himself, to keep back his emotions till he had tested them, to reflect before he wrote or acted.

Brought up among the Cumberland mountains, where he had been allowed to follow pretty much his own way in reading nature rather than books, in playing games or rowing on the lake, he had grown up full of the sights and sounds of the country. The impression left upon his mind by the hill " statesmen " also tinged the character of his thoughts. These men really were what he afterwards imagined all unsophisticated men to be—self-respecting, upright, simple natures, with a certain elevation of character caused by their independence, their comparative isolation, and the silent influences of sky and mountain. While Wordsworth was growing up among them, he reflected little either upon them or upon the country about them, but the total impression they made upon his mind caused him in later years to write very differently from the ordinary observer of ordinary country people.

When, during his residence at Cambridge, the French Revolution broke out, Wordsworth began to be absorbed in men and affairs. After he left college, he travelled in France and wished that he might aid the revolutionary party to adopt a wiser course. When he returned to England, the French still, as he felt, made mistake after mistake. They showed themselves more and more to be under the control of passion instead of right reason. Yet all Wordsworth's sympathies were called out by the events which were happening across the Channel, and he went on hoping that the good sense of the people would manifest itself. At last, in 1793, when King Louis was beheaded and France declared war upon the nations, the shock of disappointment to high hopes threw him into a state of doubt and distrust which was torture to a mind like his. He was of too intense a nature to take any happiness or any trouble lightly, and the struggle with himself which ensued left its mark on his temperament.

It is generally said that the suffering of this period was the sharpest trial through which Wordsworth ever passed, and also that Dorothy Wordsworth by bringing him back to the love of nature, helped him to greater sanity in his whole outlook upon the world. All honor to his sister, but it may be that enough stress has not been laid upon his own strength of character. Wordsworth conquered himself. The fight was a stubborn one, and when his sterner, self-mastering will gained the victory over the softer, emotional spirit which would have laughed and cried with greater readiness, and which might have been more beloved by the world because of its very weakness, he both gained and lost by the conquest. It rooted in his nature habits which afterwards showed themselves in austerity of temperament and obstinacy against criticism, as well as in a command over his feelings which has deceived the world into thinking that he had few or insignificant sorrows. It also strengthened an inherent conservatism in his nature, which made him fearful of reforms, and too early deadened in him the creative power.

These later developments, however, did not show themselves at once. For the present, he was living with his sister, enjoying the country, and making tentative efforts at composition.

Coleridge, much weaker of will and more wayward in temperament, had undergone very different training. Though he had lived for the first eight years of his life in the country in pleasant Devonshire, he had really spent his boyhood in the city, among the crowd of seven hundred boys at Christ's Hospital, surrounded by the busy thoroughfares of London. His teacher, Dr. Boyer, was a severe but excellent critic of literature. Coleridge himself said that Boyer taught him to prefer Demosthenes to Cicero, Homer to Virgil, Virgil to Ovid, and in the school compositions never allowed a metaphor to stand unsupported by sound sense. Such training suited Coleridge's naturally reflective mind, and helped to form that wonderful critical judgment which he afterwards displayed. Unlike Wordsworth, who spent half the time in play in the country, Coleridge, during these school days, read all the books he could find, devoured whole libraries, and was fond of button-holing any chance acquaintance to discuss metaphysics.

Being a brilliant pupil, he was appointed by Christ's Hospital to an exhibition at Jesus College, Cambridge, where he would have special opportunities to study for the ministry.

Alas! his character was anything but ministerial. His letters during this college period are a sad mixture of light-heartedness and despondency, bounding spirits and miserable ill-health, industry so long as his friend Middleton remained in Cambridge, idling and running into debt when his senior was gone. It is impossible not to love and also to fear for this high-strung boy. In one letter, in good spirits, he winds up, " Without a swan-skin waistcoat what is man? I have got a swanskin waist-coat"; in another he is taking ether or laudanum to quiet pain.

The account of the year 1794 reads like a sensational novel, for the rapidity of its occurrences, and their re-action upon him. Falling into debt and perhaps despairing in love, he ran away to enlist in a company of dra-goons, but was so homesick that in less than two months he made himself known to his family, and in letters of the humblest self-abasement accepted his brothers' good offices in procuring a discharge. After a short time back in Cambridge, he visited a friend in Oxford, was intro-duced to Southey, and with him hatched the wild scheme of " Pantisocracy," by which a few congenial spirits were to go out to America, live in perfect equality by the toil of their hands, possess every thing in common, and im-prove their minds by conversation and reading. In September, in the midst of this scheme, he suddenly engaged himself to his future wife, Sara Fricker. In October he was writing a frenzied letter to Southey about Mary Evans, his friend in London. "I loved her, Southey, almost to madness," he says. "Her image was never absent from me for three years, for more than three years. . . . I have restored my affections to her whom I do not love, but whom by every tie of reason and honour I ought to love." He even made a final appeal in December to know if Mary Evans really loved another man. Then Southey carried him back to Bath and Miss Fricker. All this time he was writing sonnets to eminent men, and showing how ardent, if ill-considered, an interest he felt in popular affairs.

This year was the turning-point in his career, just as the same time was moulding Wordsworth. Unfortunately, in the case of Coleridge, the effect was wholly disastrous. Whatever hand Southey had in his engagement to Miss Fricker,—and Coleridge himself afterwards believed that he had given up Mary Evans solely through his sense of duty as Southey presented it,—it is certainly true that Southey inflamed his already heated imagination with the scheme of Pantisocracy. Perhaps, if he had never met Southey or Miss Fricker; if for the next few years his mind had not been kept in a perpetual ferment in consequence of Southey's gradual defection from the American plan: if he could have married Mary Evans, and been more sure of his friends, he might have enjoyed the quiet, loving sympathy which he above all men needed, and might have been strengthened by happiness to greater exertion of will in overcoming his faults of character.

As it was, the year was the most tumultuous of his life and only increased his flightiness. He married, it is true, in October, 1795, and wrote not long after, " I love, I am beloved, and I am happy." " The Eolian Harp " shows how peaceful his mind could be. He enjoyed something of love and the consciousness of love for a few years, and in 1797 the most lasting happiness of his life came to him in the friendship of Wordsworth.

Walking together over the Quantock Hills, these two young men of twenty-five and twenty-seven years discussed the faults of the prevailing mode of poetry, and decided that the diction ought to be simplified, while new thoughts and images needed to be introduced.

Wordsworth wrote in his preface to the " Lyrical Ballads " that, with one or two exceptions, not a single new image of external nature had been presented from the publication of " Paradise Lost " to that of " The Seasons." He might almost have added to his own time. Thomson, Cowper, and a few others were exceptions not followed by poets in general.

It must be acknowledged that English poets had been terribly hampered by the body of literature and of literary men close about them. It would have required a superhuman genius to cast off entirely the tricks and mannerisms not only of style but of thought in which they had been brought up. Thomson had been comparatively free from them, but he was a Scotchman, and did not come into the literary world of London till he had reached manhood. Cowper never belonged to the literary set. In 1782 he wrote, " I have not read more than one English poet for more than twenty years." Burns was the only true, fresh singer in these evil days, and he, too, was a Scotchman, familiar with the less conventional, more nature-loving poetry which, in Scotland, had never died. It is to be doubted whether Wordsworth himself, if educated in the artificial atmosphere of London, instead of on the wild hills of Cumberland, would have struck the note of simplicity which is associated with his name.

It was not only that men wrote in a stilted fashion, or that when Pope, for instance, settled down in his easy chair and described the moon as silvering the slope *behind* which she rose, the picture was accepted as beautiful without questioning its accuracy; it was not that they did not see nature rightly, but that they did not regard her at all. So remarkable a man as Hazlitt took a walk through Llangollen Valley " by way of initiating himself in the mysteries of natural scenery," before he visited Coleridge in 1798. At that time he was twenty years old, an age when, nowadays, we expect a man to be particularly susceptible to the picturesque, to enjoy consciously a fine sunset or a green forest road. But, that we are trained in a habit of sensitiveness to the beautiful in natural scenery, is partly owing to the influence of Wordsworth's poetry, and to the long train of successors who have taken their inspiration directly or indirectly from Wordsworth and Coleridge. Concerning this visit, Hazlitt relates that Wordsworth, looking out of the window, remarked, " How beautifully the sun sets on that yellow bank," and says that he thought within himself, " With what eyes these poets see nature." If ordinary men did not even look at nature, and such men as Pope did not observe her correctly, no wonder that poetry was the artificial, untrue thing it had become.

Of course there were a few spirits who did not yield to the prevailing fashion. Crabbe observed nature almost too minutely; the love of simplicity, started in France by Rousseau, had before the end of the century spread over the whole of Europe, and Blake wrote about children and children's thoughts.

The conjunction of Wordsworth and Coleridge was a most happy one for the crusade against prosy verse, and for purifying the two tendencies of naturalism and romance which were beginning to be felt. The passage from Coleridge's "Biographia Literaria,"[1] concerning the evolution of the "Lyrical Ballads," need not be repeated here. Wordsworth felt that simple, commonplace objects might be invested with an ideal beauty; or rather, possess such beauty only needing to be discovered, and that they might become subjects for good poetry expressed in the ordinary language of prose. Coleridge contended that the supernatural or romantic is also a legitimate theme for poetry, and that it could be so treated as to appear for the time being as real and human as incidents of common life. In other words, the ideality of nature as she really exists was to be brought out, and the purely ideal was to be made to seem natural.

Each poet took up the side that was congenial to him. Wordsworth produced " We are Seven," " Goody Blake," " Expostulation and Reply," " Lines above Tin-

---

[1] "Biographia Literaria," chap. xiv.

tern Abbey," and other poems. Coleridge finished "The
Ancient Mariner" and had begun "Christabel" and
"The Dark Ladie," but did not wait to finish them.
"The Nightingale" and two fragments were substituted.
The volume came out in 1798, with a simple advertise-
ment stating the views of the authors. It began with
"The Ancient Mariner" and ended with "Tintern Ab-
bey."

To tell the truth, it was so different from anything
that had appeared before, that the public hardly knew
how to take it. That it had a sale is clear, for a second
edition with a second volume added was printed in 1800,
and Lamb wrote, August 9, 1800, "They have contrived
to spawn a new volume of lyrical ballads, which is to see
the light in about a month, and causes no little excitement
in the literary world!"

This, however, is the style of criticism it received from
the *Quarterly Review:*

"'Simon Lee, the Old Huntsman,' is the portrait, ad-
mirably painted, of every huntsman who by toil, age, and
infirmities is rendered unable to guide and govern his
canine family.

"'Anecdote for Fathers.' Of this the dialogue is in-
genuous and natural, but the object of the child's choice
and the inferences are not quite obvious.

"'We are Seven.' Innocent and pretty infantile
prattle.

"'Lines Written near Richmond.' Literally 'most
musical, most melancholy.'"

Poor poets! What hope had they of moving the world
when a well-meaning critic in the best journal of the time
could say no more, and understood the spirit of the poems

no better than this? It is not strange that, in the second edition, Wordsworth felt it necessary to explain his theories fully; and in a few over-strong statements of the new preface lay the germ of all the future pother about the " school " of Lake Poets.

In this preface and in succeeding additions to it, Wordsworth gave expression to a great many truths concerning the nature of poetry, but among other statements he declared that the common speech of country people is the proper language for poetry, and that no words should be allowed in poetry which are not commonly used in prose. Very different this, from Gray's dictum that " the language of the age is never the language of poetry. Our poetry has a language peculiar to itself, to which almost every one that has written has added something, by criticising it with foreign idioms and derivations, nay, often with new words and invented terms of their own." This was exactly what Wordsworth complained of, for in that age " poetic diction " was often the only thing that distinguished a poet from a prose writer.

The source of trouble lay in the fact that Wordsworth over-stated his own theory. In these very lyrical ballads he repeatedly put language into the mouths even of his country characters which they could not have employed, and sometimes words which are peculiar to poetry: e.g., " My watchful dog whose starts of furious *ire*," or " Cottage after cottage *owned its sway*."

In addition to this, he seems never to have had a perception of how the pictures he presented might appear to other people. It is often acknowledged that he lacked humor, another way of saying that he had not a sympathetic imagination. If an incident affected him in a

certain way, that the same incident with all its details,
would, he supposed, impress others in the same way. If
his words expressed that idea to his mind, he did not understand that to others the effect might be different. The
swollen ankles of Simon Lee made part of the pathos of
the story, and he did not perceive that some details assume
a prominence out of proportion to their real value, if put
into words along with others more essential to the picture.
Why should not his readers take as he did,

> "For still, the more he works, the more
> Do his weak ankles swell,"

or the famous couplet in "The Thorn" about the grave,

> "I've measured it from side to side,
> 'Tis three feet long and two feet wide"?

Without the preface the public would have accepted
such defects as something which the poet would learn to
overcome, but when Wordsworth seemed to maintain that
this sort of thing was his ideal of what poetry should
be, and also attacked some of their cherished favorites,
then they began to fear and hate him, and defended
themselves by heaping ridicule on him and on everyone
who happened to be connected with him.

It must be acknowledged that, into the most beautiful
creations, Wordsworth would occasionally insert a trivial
or a grotesque detail. His "hebetude of intellect" shows
itself in several of the lyrical ballads, but we might sup-
pose that the criticism of friends—Coleridge and Lamb
were no mean critics—and his own natural affinity for
the essential beauty of nature would have helped him to
outgrow the tendency.

To some degree he did outgrow it, but as Hazlitt says,
" If Byron was the spoiled child of fortune, Wordsworth
was the spoiled child of disappointment." Such criticism
as came to him was mainly downright insult. The general public ignored him. The inherent charm of his
work could not immediately win recognition in a world
accustomed to something so entirely different. He had
to create the taste for his poetry, and comparatively few
men read it enough to acquire a liking for it. For years
he earned almost nothing by his writing. In 1820 he
complained, " The whole of my fortune from the writing
trade not amounting to seven-score pounds." He had to
live in the humblest fashion, trusting to the rightness of
his doctrine to conquer in the end. Naturally, however,
the very fierceness of the attack upon him caused a nature
like his to cling even more closely to his preconceived
theories; and, still worse, to cling to the bald statement
rather than to the essential spirit of them, so that he came
to insist more and more upon untenable principles, and
finally to develop a chronic commonplaceness from which
he might perhaps have been saved, had he not been
goaded into obstinacy.

A certain inability of his nature to perceive how an image would impress others caused an insistence upon trivial details which was rendered more emphatic by opposition; his inborn reserve and austerity of temper were increased by the battle with himself after his disappointment in the French Revolution. These two defects
caused the chief blemishes in his poetry; but the beauty
of the best portions of his work, and the far-reaching effect he has had upon the poets that succeeded him, make
it an ungrateful task to mention his shortcomings. His

own prefaces to the second and third editions of the
" Lyrical Ballads " state his theories. Coleridge's " Biographia Literaria," Chapters IV. and XIV. to XXII.,
discuss their merits. When Coleridge writes, " And I
reflect with delight how little a mere theory, though of
his own workmanship, interferes with the processes of
genuine imagination in a man of true poetic genius, who
possesses, as Mr. Wordsworth, if ever man did, most
assuredly does,

'The Vision and the Faculty divine,' "

we acknowledge that our feeling but corroborates the
statements of discerning criticism.

By 1802 Coleridge had lost his " shaping spirit of imagination." The fatal opium habit was already apparently his master, and he ceased to write poetry except occasionally. Wordsworth's power lasted much longer.
Most of his best poetry was written before 1808, but there
is a great body of composition, conscientiously increased
from year to year down almost to the very end of his life,
and until 1818 there are many gleams of the old light and
life.

Without any more writing, however, the two poets had
sowed the seeds of an inevitable revolution, in the volume
which began with " The Ancient Mariner " and ended
with " Tintern Abbey." They had pointed the way to
a simple, natural realism, and had shown that the romantic could be treated without sensationalism and without
vulgarity.

Much as has been written about Wordsworth, it is easier to feel his charm than to analyze it. Hardly any two men find the same elements in it; each one discovers special beauties, and having felt the attraction invents some theory to account for it. One man thinks his early poetry is strong in its appeal to the eye; others are persuaded that hearing was his most perfect sense. All would agree, however, that " He pushed the domain of poetry into a whole field of subjects hitherto unapproached by the poets; " that everywhere " he went straight to the inside of things," and that " this one characteristic set him in entire opposition to the art of the last century." [1]

We think of him chiefly as a poet of nature, but such also were Thomson and Cowper. With them, however, and with other poets before Wordsworth, Nature had no personality of her own. In her presence, the eye might be delighted, the mind terrified, or the spirit soothed, but she was always and only a material creation. Wordsworth saw much more in Nature. To him she was one of the manifestations of God, something endowed with a spirit of her own. Not only that, but different places showed special characteristics of this universal life that is in Nature. One spot may be laughing and gay; another, or the same under different influences, sober or stern. Furthermore, Nature enjoys this life that she has, and seeks to communicate her delight to man. She is ready, if man will put himself into the right frame of mind, to enter into his spirit. In other words, the two manifestations of God, in man and in nature, are always

---

[1] J. C. Shairp, " Studies in Poetry and Philosophy," pp 62 64.

seeking to be one, and the mind, if it accepts the union, can create something more lovely than either man could imagine or nature produce, without this marriage.

But the poet must not lose himself in idle revery, or give himself up to mere impulse as prompted by the contact with nature. He must strive consciously to put himself into the mood which harmonizes with the spirit pervading the scene before him. He must not allow himself to be intoxicated by the beauty or the grandeur, but must wait, drink in all the influences of the place, and sinking into the depths of his inner self, in quiet contemplation reproduce to the world the result of the insight into the heart of nature which his receptive mind has gained.

This was a sufficiently lofty ideal, and difficult to attain; but more than any poet except Milton, Wordsworth had a firm faith in his own dedication to poetry. His consecration of himself was the first and most important element of his existence. In his devotion to this mission, he lived the most abstemious of lives; his lofty egotism even demanded and accepted as right a continual service from others, as to a being set apart, whose calling was of more importance than that of mankind in general.

This self-consecration together with the habit of "sinking back upon himself," and his own conception of poetry that "it takes its origin from emotion recollected in tranquillity," etc., perhaps account for the sense of solitude in most of his poetry, that "pure, deep well of solitary joy." In reading it we do not think of the presence of others or of communication with others. We feel alone with nature.

Wordsworth is not only the interpreter of God in nature, but also of God in man; but in this character he is not pre-eminent. His spirit does not so unreservedly ally itself with the spirit without. He cannot enter so fully into the individual lives of men as into the special moods of Nature. When he does not use his men and women merely to bring out more sympathetically the character of the place, he still shows them too much as abstractions.

As for his theories about the soul and its past history, they have been erected into the Platonic system by Wordsworthians, and they have been called only " ideas of pre-existence and reminiscence which he liked and out of which he made his thought."[1] The " Ode on Intimations of Immortality " and some verses in "The Prelude " bring out the conception most definitely, but it pervades other poems. All of us have at times dim pictures and half-comprehended images in our minds, and Wordsworth, with whom these suggestions were peculiarly vivid, put them into poetic form. It is hardly necessary to maintain that he had formulated a definite system of philosophy on the subject.

In consequence of these characteristics of Wordsworth, we find that his work has a singular homogeneousness. As *Blackwood's Magazine* says, " A systematic correspondence pervades the whole, so that the perusal of one piece frequently leads the reader's own mind into a tract of thought which is afterwards found to be developed by the poet himself in some other performance." His life, passed almost wholly among the northern hills, his early formulation of a poetical creed, his never-weakening command over himself and his emotions, and his consequent ability to maintain the same spirit even in

---

[1] S. A. Brooke, " Theology in the English Poets," p. 22.

differing moods, account for this quality. He did not try experiments with his muse, but imposed upon her a consistent character.

For his style, the best description is that of R. H. Hutton: "The most characteristic earlier and the most characteristic later style are alike in the limpid coolness of their effect, the effect in the earlier style of bubbling water, in the later of morning dew." There is a buoyancy of restrained passion in some of his best known poems, and a chaste contemplativeness in part of his later work that soothes and calms the troubled spirit. This may be said of his good work. On the cumbrous heaviness of his preaching vein, when the sense of his mission got the better of his genuine emotions, it is needless to enlarge.

Coleridge was as unlike his friend as possible. With a much more deeply philosophical mind, with an infinitely greater power to suffer, and hence to echo the feelings of toiling, wronged humanity, with a sense of the unsubstantial, mysterious world hovering about us, and an imagination capable of portraying pictures which lie beyond reality, he tried various forms of expression, seemed to surpass in several, and then, before he had chosen the medium which best suited him, lost his hold upon himself and upon his creative power.

If he had found his theme, it would perhaps have been the relation of man to God and to mankind. As it is, his best poems vibrate with human emotion. There is a personal cry in them all; more than most poems they need to be read with the commentary of his daily life fresh in the mind. "The Ancient Mariner" is a masterpiece in the domain of romance, but at the end of its vivid imagery comes the little sermon, " He prayeth best who loveth best," as if Coleridge had suddenly forgotten his characters, and was speaking for himself. In " Christabel," also, there seems to be an undercurrent of feeling that pure, prayerful love will suffice to conquer the wiles of evil. As his mind was always seeking for psychological truth, so his heart yearned for affection. One might almost say that, like Shelley, he was in love with love; only that, unlike Shelley, his passion was not for transcendental, ideal love, but for plain, comforting, human love, and trust in God. In the poems which mention Sara and Little Hartley, Lamb and Wordsworth, there is always this tender love. In the " Ode on the Departing Year," the subject is the violation of the love of man to man, nation to nation.

With this simple faith in the power of love, with his far-reaching imagination and his eager inquiry into philosophic truth, he might in time have solved for us some of the problems of life, as Wordsworth has developed the teaching of nature, but he was a wrecked man before the time came. From his boyhood he had been subject to violent attacks of neuralgia, and he had not the resolute will necessary to endure pain. As early as 1792 he was familiar with the use of ether; by 1803 he was the prey of opium. It sapped his manhood, and wrung from him over and over again tears of blood, for he knew that without help he had not strength to free himself from his tormentor. In 1816, after years of fitful, homeless wandering, he put himself under the care of Mr. Gillman to be shielded from temptation.

His light of poetry was indeed gone out. Happy for

him that he could still recover his intellectual sway. In his later days he drew about him eager young men ready for the impress of high thoughts, and he lived to prove that always he was " one who loved the light and grew toward it."

Shelley was twenty years younger than Coleridge and grew to manhood when the influence of Wordsworth and Coleridge was already part of the literary environment. He came from a family of honorable antiquity, though apparently of no literary or special intellectual gifts. His father was a kindly, worldly, somewhat irascible gentleman of no imagination; his mother is described as beautiful and sensible.

The son Shelley would have been an ugly duckling in any family. Tall and slender, with an exceedingly small face and an abundance of wavy brown hair which he wore long in an age when fashion cropped the hair; so awkward that in later years he would upset the footman's gravity by tumbling over himself as he went upstairs, yet so agile that, as he walked through the streets of London, intent on a book, he would slip out of the press with unconscious ease when anyone in the crowd tried to jostle him; with a voice of singular depth and sweetness when reading calmly, but rising to a discordant screech if he was excited or incensed, he spent his life in a perpetual warfare between the deep love he bore mankind, and the hatred of the world which was outraged by his way of promulgating that love. If ever there was a boy who did not belong to the respectable, unimaginative, world-fearing—rather than God-fearing—family into which he was born, it was Shelley.

By the time he went to Oxford he was proud of the name of " Atheist," by which he meant that he did not believe in historical Christianity. In later years he had a profound reverence for the founder of Christianity, and a firm belief in the loving power which he conceived as ruling in the Universe; but he always felt a deep abhorrence for established orthodoxy.

In those days such sentiments were sufficiently startling; when they were accompanied by other beliefs which would destroy the morality as well as the religion of society, it is not surprising that he was branded as a demon. He was a disciple of William Godwin, whose " Inquiry concerning Political Justice " had given voice to some of the wildest ideas engendered by the French Revolution. Shelley honestly believed that marriage is wrong, and though he was twice married, he submitted against his own judgment to the prejudices of society. According to his standard, true love is the only force which should bind; if true love ceases the bond should be broken; if it holds there is no need of the marriage ceremony.

No wonder society stood aghast. Strangers could not know his deep love for his fellow-beings; his fixed belief that mankind left to itself is pure and good, and that sham government and sham religion have debased the world; his intense yearning for that perfect harmony between God and man and the universe which constitutes the true music of the spheres.

The hostility of the world had its effect on Shelley's poetry. When his father refused to receive him at Field

Place, when the cousin whom he loved drew away from him, when afterward all the world cried shame, and the Lord Chancellor refused him the custody of his own children, it is not strange that he was thrown back upon himself, or that his mood fluctuated between devotion to the cause of mankind and absorption in his own intellectual aspirations and personal affinities. His greatest work, " Prometheus Unbound," combines both elements; it is the poem of the conquest of the lover of mankind over the oppressor of mankind, cast in the highly spiritualized form which was congenial to himself. Most of his poems, however, show either one phase or the other of his genius; in his lyrics he forgets mankind to express his own illimitable thirst for ever-unattainable beauty, the beauty which is truth.

His " lyrical cry " is unlike the note of any other lyric poet. It has been said that he sings not what he feels, but what he wishes to feel, what is almost within his grasp, but always eluding him. He yearns with passionate intensity for intellectual beauty, but the passion is not of this world; his desires like his images are highly sublimated forms, always ideal beauty, ideal expression.

Though his mind in its reaching out did not understand all the mysteries which thrilled his being, at least he came near to a spiritual perception of nature and divinity, and his very song uplifts us. As a mere matter of harmonious melody the poem sings itself into our brains. If his words meant nothing we should still feel their charm. With him, however, the song is a subtle interweaving of thought with emotion. He has given expression to that bitter-sweet, half-comprehended longing for the unknown which pervades a large portion of society

in this nineteenth century. He has set his stamp upon
many a follower, and has influenced the thought of latter-
day poetry even more directly than Wordsworth himself.
Wordsworth has had a wider influence upon the thought
of the century, Shelley a more personal one upon individual characters.

The names of Shelley and Keats are often coupled,
partly, no doubt, because they were of nearly the same
age, partly also because Shelley in the " Adonais " so
passionately bewailed the younger poet's death; but during Keats's life-time the two men saw little of each other.
Apparently Keats half distrusted the brilliant, untam-
able iconoclast, who fought so desperate a fight with society, trying, it seemed, to batter down the good with the
bad, and believing in the perfectibility of man. Keats
himself knew nothing of such championship. The
strongest element of his early life was his love for his
own family, and as his affection was intense so it was
narrow. He had no natural interest in the problems of
humanity.

It is hardly easier in his case than in Shelley's to guess
the sources of his genius. Tradition says that his father,
a London stable-keeper, came from Devonshire. His
mother had a reputation for wit and talent. Certainly,
both his parents must have had more intelligence and
ambition than most people in their station, for the children were sent to a good school out in the country. Both
parents died, however, while Keats and his brothers were
still young.

At school, when Keats was not fighting the bigger boys,

he was dreaming away his time among books of Greek mythology. He knew them by heart. He read all the books on history, travel, and fiction that he could find; but he was not studious. It was not till after he had left school and was apprenticed to a surgeon that he felt a serious drawing toward literature. Then the reading of Spenser roused him. He "ramped" through "The Faery Queen" with delight, eagerly seizing upon any fine epithet or vivid bit of imagery, and soon began to imitate the stanza. Before his term of apprenticeship was over, he quarrelled with his master, and though he studied in the hospitals for two years, he finally gave himself unreservedly to poetry. His first volume of poems appeared in 1817, when he was twenty-two years old.

For the next two years his power steadily grew, till sorrow and trouble and sickness destroyed his energies. In 1818 he was nursing his brother Tom, who was dying of consumption. The next year he was himself attacked by the hereditary disease. In the meantime he was harassed by want of money, the ample portion left by his grandfather having been so badly managed and so poorly accounted for, that the children did not even know of the existence of part of it till after two of them had died.

In addition to these disturbances, he fell so passionately in love that his mind lost its vigor. To the lover of Keats the saddest thing about his life is, not that it was so short, but that love should have so unmanned him. Even if he had been well, it would have been difficult for him to wait and work till he could marry. His passion only hastened the end. He died at Rome in 1821, and was buried in the little Protestant cemetery by the pyramid of Cestius.

Keats has been called an Elizabethan because he so delighted in the physical beauty of outward nature; but his feeling was a sense of luxury in the voluptuousness and exuberance of nature, which is far from the active, keen enjoyment of the Elizabethans. Indeed, his early poems show so much sensuous weakness, that there is small wonder his work was not well received. " Endymion," his second volume, called forth a brutal review from the *Quarterly*, which was long popularly supposed to have caused his death; and another only less harsh, from *Blackwood*.

In reality Keats was far too manly to be seriously injured by the *Quarterly*. He acknowledged that " Endymion " was but the sloughing off of youthful feelings. He knew that he must get rid of these ideas in order to grow into something stronger. In the last three years of his life he gained that power to prune which he lacked in " Endymion." What he wrote showed reserve force as well as great beauty of imagery.

He did not write of the practical every-day matters which appealed to Wordsworth, nor did unfathomable intellectual beauty attract him as it did Shelley. His interest lay not in life around him, nor in things beyond him, but in classic legends,—stories which had already received a halo from past literatures.

In another direction, also, Keats was unlike the others. His theory was that a poet should have no personality of his own, but should absorb the moods of everyone around him; should give himself up wholly to influences outside of himself, because only thus can he feel the beauty and the truth of the world. This was very different from the aim of Wordsworth to put himself into the right mood, and then receive what nature had to tell, sinking deeper into contemplation in himself in order to interpret aright; or from the eager curiosity of Shelley consciously lifting the veil which covers the secrets of nature.

A third point of variance lay in his attitude toward his calling. Wordsworth wrote because he had something to teach; Shelley felt that the only way for him to lighten the burden of the world was by using his poetic gift; both wanted to help humanity. Keats adopted poetry because it was life to himself. He could not exist without it. The pleasure or profit of the world was of little importance to him, if he had once satisfied his nature by creating something beautiful.

Doubtless, had he lived, other motives would have developed in him. He began toward the end to appreciate the power for good which he might wield, and wrote of studies to be undertaken in order to fit himself for the mission of teaching mankind. That side of his character, however, had not time to mature. He died at the age of twenty-five, leaving behind him, besides his crude, early work, a few odes and poems which have never been surpassed for delicacy of touch and richness of imagery, and the mighty fragment of " Hyperion," begun on so lofty a scale that it could no more have been finished than Coleridge's " Christabel." The promise that the future would show wider sympathies with no less perfection of form was never fulfilled.

Of all the tragedies in the lives of the poets of Wordsworth's era, that of Byron seems both the most and the least pathetic; most pathetic because in his life of thirty-six years he had less real love and happiness than even the men who died younger; least so, because his genius seems to have been not so much in need of happiness to stimulate it to action. The best poetry of Wordsworth and Coleridge and Shelley and, to a certain extent, of Keats, was all written under the spell of domestic love; Byron wrote his best after he had been driven with reviling from England, when home-life was forever closed upon him, when he knew that his daughter was not even allowed to see his portrait. But the old Berserker blood flowed in his veins; perhaps he was more truly happy when fighting the world than when at peace with it.

His family had both good and evil elements in it. It was very old—he could trace it back to before the Conquest—and he was very proud of it; as for his parents—his father was a scamp who ran through the fortunes of two wives and deserted them; his mother was a vixen. For himself—a defect in the shape of one foot was the cause of much irritable sensitiveness, and he was as effectually spoiled, by the alternate petting and violence of his mother, as it was possible for a boy to be. All the good influences of Harrow and of Cambridge were not enough to tame a creature so erratic by inheritance and early treatment.

When he left the University and had taken his seat in the House of Lords, he travelled for two years through Spain, Greece, and Turkey, returning with the first two cantos of "Childe Harold" in his pocket. For the next four years he was the darling of London society. "Childe Harold," and the romantic tales which followed it, just suited the public taste; he had all the admiration his haughty soul demanded; he was a peer, the descendant of peers, and he was a poet.

During this time in London, he was advised to marry and settle down; and, having had his fling in the world, probably, also, hoping to retrieve his fortune, he proposed to Miss Milbank. Unfortunately he was accepted. He did not pretend to be deeply in love; perhaps the only real passion of his life was his youthful attachment to Mary Chaworth, the daughter of a neighbor and hereditary enemy. At all events her shadow rose before him at the altar. He seemed, however, to live happily enough with his wife for a year, and it was she who forced the separation between them. Soon after the birth of their daughter, she went home on a visit and from there informed him that she did not intend to return.

The reasons for her action may never be exactly known. Undoubtedly, Byron was of uneven temper, and had been disappointed in not coming into immediate possession of his wife's property. Perhaps Lady Byron was jealous. Be that as it may, the whole world rose against the man who during four years had been its idol. No invented story was too atrocious to be believed. His friends considered his very life in danger: he himself was anxious to leave a country where he was so detested, and a mode of life the hollowness of which had begun to tire him.

He spent the next seven years chiefly in Italy, at times leading a life unworthy of his better self, but profiting by the friendship of Shelley, and always displaying a keen interest in politics both at home and abroad. He even aided the movement toward liberty which swept over Italy in 1820-1821, although he saw clearly that the time for Italian unity had not yet come. When the Greeks broke out into rebellion, he was asked to see what his presence and negotiations might do. He went, but lived only long enough to win the confidence and affection of all parties by his diplomatic skill. He died of malarial fever, at Missolonghi, in 1824.

Pre-eminent among other poets of his time, Byron is the poet of the Revolution. The inherent conservatism of Wordsworth and Coleridge asserted itself soon after their first youthful outbreaks; they were frightened by the excesses of France into adherence to England, the product of evolution rather than of revolution. By the time Byron was old enough to understand something of politics, the reaction against Napoleon was at its height; on the other hand, the worst details of the years 1792-1794 had sunk into the background, so that Byron felt the grandeur of the ideal for which the French had striven, without its sickening horrors. Moreover, he was a hero-worshipper. Napoleon, the man of achievement, fired his soul. He burned with the zeal of self-assertion. He gloried in the joy of individual freedom.

This characteristic was not wholly the effect of the age in which he lived; it was the result of his strong personality. He was a man of exaggerated emotions. He judged everything in life as it affected himself. Every scene or incident was colored to his imagination by his own feelings, which were peculiarly vivid.

Another and less happy trait was a lack of reserve. The frankness which helped to ruin his own life, however, was of value to succeeding poets. He created a new style of poetry, which scattered broadcast a most intimate knowledge of his own personality; and, whatever its accompanying faults, the sincerity with which he struck this new note was true enough to make his name honored. Though he carried self-revelation to the point of weakness, his fearless expression of individuality was as important an element in the new era of poetry as Wordsworth's return to nature.

The force of Byron's sentiment and the boldness with which he revealed his personality captured the heart of society; but the rashness, the lack of self-control, the theatrical display of emotion which he exhibited in his earlier work have caused an eclipse of his popularity during the last forty years. Englishmen are only now beginning to appreciate his inherent strength, which foreigners perceived from the first; but even without an understanding of his merits, English poetry has shown the effect of his influence.

Another manifestation of the independence of Byron's nature lay in his strong historic sense. England had, it is true, a reverence for her own past, though little knowledge of the world's history; but men of the Revolutionary period had lived so entirely in the present, affairs of the moment were so overwhelmingly pressing, that continentals and English alike had lost all interest in the great names of former times. It is the distinguishing mark of Byron that, hand in hand with his capacity for hero-worship went a veneration for past achievement and forgotten splendors. Any evidences of man's activities, any battle-field or ruined castle, roused his emotional nature to reflection, and every place he visited in his varied travels gave rise to a picture or a monologue, which, in course of time, found its way into his poetry.

His method forbade any unity in most of his poems,

but it wakened in Englishmen a feeling for history, hitherto quite unknown. There is hardly a spot in Europe, ordinarily visited by travellers, which has not acquired an historic as well as a literary association because of his writing.

These two elements—the appeal to personal feeling and a sense of the historic past—are Byron's contribution to English poetry. Besides these qualities, his vivid description, his thrilling narrative, his caustic wit, the cleverness of his vocabulary, though they had their counterparts in earlier poetry, will be sufficient to preserve his fame, notwithstanding the roughness of his metre, the lack of harmony in his verse, the crudeness of many of his ideas. These blemishes are the marks of a strong but untrained nature, and are atoned for by the vigor and earnestness with which he wrote.

With the death of Byron, the poetic impulse for a time subsided; Tennyson and Browning came a generation later. Nevertheless, a lasting revolution had been effected and a new era begun. With all its varied growth, Nineteenth Century poetry still retains something of the spirit with which the century opened, and traces its development to the work of the five men represented in this volume.

TABLE OF DATES.

Contemporary History.	Wordsworth.	Coleridge.	Shelley.	Keats.	Byron.
1770.	April 7th. Birth at Cockermouth, Cumberland.				
1771. Death of Gray. Birth of Scott. Birth of Sydney Smith.					
1772.		October 21st. Birth at Ottery St. Mary, Devonshire.			
1773. Birth of Francis Jeffrey.					
1774. Death of Goldsmith. Birth of Southey.					
1775. Outbreak of American Revolution. Birth of Charles Lamb. Birth of Landor.					
1777. Birth of Campbell. Birth of Hallam.					
1778. Birth of Hazlitt.	Death of Mrs. Wordsworth. William sent to school at Hawkshead.				
1781.		Death of Rev. John Coleridge.			

Contemporary History.	Wordsworth.	Coleridge.	Shelley.	Keats.	Byron.
1783. End of American War.	Death of Mr. Wordsworth.	Presented at Christ's Hospital, London.			
1784. Death of Johnson. Birth of Leigh Hunt.					
1785. End of War in India.					
1787.	Matriculation at St. John's College, Cambridge.				
1788.					January 22d. Birth in London.
1789. Beginning of the French Revolution. Assembling of States-General.					
1790. Storming of the Bastille.					Removal to Aberdeen.
1791.	Degree at University. 1791–1793. Travels in France. "Evening Walk."	Entrance in residence at Jesus College, Cambridge.			
1792. War between France, and Austria, Prussia, etc. Jail deliveries in Paris. Abolition of Monarchy in France.			August 4th. Birth at Field Place, Horsham, Sussex.		Beginning of school life.

Contemporary History.	Wordsworth.	Coleridge.	Shelley.	Keats.	Byron.
1793. January 21st. Execution of Louis XVI. Declaration by England of War against France.	"Descriptive Sketches." **1793–1795.** Dejection over events in France, and despairing outlook upon life.	December 2d. Enlistment in Dragoons.			
1794. Reign of Terror. Fall of Robespierre.		April 4th. Discharge from the army. June. Introduction to Southey at Oxford. December. Final departure from Cambridge without a degree.			
1795. Birth of Carlyle.	**1795–1797.** Gradual recovery of peace of mind, through the companionship of Dorothy Wordsworth.	October 4th. Marriage to Sara Fricker at Bristol. Life at Clevedon.		October 31st. Birth in London (Finsbury Pavement).	
1796. Death of Burns. Napoleon's campaign in Italy.	Settlement at Racedown, Dorsetshire.	Publication of "Poems on Various Subjects." Project for *The Watchman.*			
1797.	July. Removal to Alfoxden.	Settlement at Nether Stowey. Composition of "The Ancient Mariner" and of "Christabel," Part I.			

Contemporary History.	Wordsworth.	Coleridge.	Shelley.	Keats.	Byron.
1798. Napoleon in Egypt. Battle of the Nile. Second Coalition against France.	Publication of "Lyrical Ballads." Winter in Goslar, Germany.	Annuity of £200 from the Wedgewoods. Winter in Ratzeburg, Germany.			Inheritance of title and of Newstead Abbey.
1799. Napoleon elected First Consul.	Settlement at Town-end, Grasmere.				School at Dulwich.
1800. Union of Great Britain and Ireland.		Settlement at Greta Hall, Keswick.			
1801. Napoleon takes possession of Holland, Switzerland, and Italy.					**1801-1803.** School at Harrow, under Dr. Drury.
1802. Peace of Amiens.	October 4th. Marriage to Mary Hutchinson.		School at Sion House.		
1803. Declaration of War with France.	Tour through Scotland with Dorothy Wordsworth. Friendship with Sir George Beaumont.			School at Enfield with the Clarks.	Passion for Mary Chaworth, daughter of an hereditary enemy.
1804. Napoleon declared Emperor.		**1804-1806.** Residence in Malta.		Death of Thomas Keats.	
1805. Third Coalition against France. Battle of Trafalgar. Death of Nelson.	Death of John Wordsworth, sailor brother of William. "Character of the Happy Warrior."		School at Eton.	Marriage of Mrs. Keats to William Rawlings.	Matriculation at Trinity College, Cambridge.

TABLE OF DATES—*Continued.*

CONTEMPORARY HISTORY.	WORDSWORTH.	COLERIDGE.	SHELLEY.	KEATS.	BYRON.
1806. Erection of dependent kingdoms by Napoleon. The Berlin Decree.					
1807. Treaty of Tilsit. Joseph Bonaparte made King of Spain. Napoleon's army invades Portugal.					March. Publication of "Hours of Idleness."
1808. Convention of Cintra.	Removal to Allan Bank, Grasmere.				March. *Edinburgh Review* on "Hours of Idleness." "English Bards and Scotch Reviewers."
1809. Battle of Corunna. Birth of Tennyson.		*The Friend.*			1809–1811. Travels in Portugal, Spain, Greece, Turkey, etc.
Birth of Gladstone. Birth of Darwin.					
1810.		Final departure from Greta Hall for London.	Entrance in residence at University College, Oxford.	Death of Mrs. Rawlings. Apprenticeship for five years to a surgeon at Edmonton.	

Contemporary History.	Wordsworth.	Coleridge.	Shelley.	Keats.	Byron.
1811. Insanity of George III. Regency Bill. Luddite Riots. Birth of Thackeray.		**1810 – 1816.** Lectures and wanderings.	February. "Necessity of Atheism." March 25th. Expulsion from the University. Life in London. Elopement with Harriet Westbrook and marriage in Edinburgh.		Death of Mrs. Byron. Return of Lord Byron to England. "Childe Harold," Cantos I. and II.
1812. Battle of Salamanca. Napoleon's campaign in Russia. Birth of Dickens. Birth of Browning.	Death of Catherine and Thomas Wordsworth, children of William.	"Remorse," a play, accepted at Drury Lane Theatre, through the influence of Lord Byron.	First letter to William Godwin. Expedition to Ireland.	Introduction to Spenser's poetry by Cowden Clarke.	**1812-1816.** Life in London. Literary activity. Metrical Romances. Friendship with Scott.
1813. Battle of Vittoria.	Settlement at Rydal Mount. Appointment as Distributor of Stamps for Westmoreland.		"Queen Mab." Intimacy with the Boinvilles and Godwins.		
1814. Abdication of Napoleon. Congress of Vienna.	**1795 – 1814.** "The Excursion." Tour in Scotland.		July 28th. Flight of Shelley with Mary Godwin to the Continent.	Quarrel with Hammond, the surgeon. Life in London.	
1815. Escape of Napoleon from Elba. Battle of Waterloo. Napoleon sent to St. Helena.			Death of Sir Bysshe Shelley, grandfather of Percy. "Alastor."		January 2d. Marriage to Anna Isabella Noel Milbank. December 10th. Birth of Augusta Ada.

TABLE OF DATES—*Continued.*

Contemporary History.	Wordsworth.	Coleridge.	Shelley.	Keats.	Byron.
1816. Riots among the laboring classes.		Settlement with Mr. Gillman at Highgate. Publication of "Christabel."	November 10th. Suicide by drowning of Harriet Shelley. December 30th. Marriage of Shelley and Mary Godwin.	Appointment at Guy's Hospital. Increasing love of literature and composition. Introduction to Leigh Hunt, Haydon, Reynolds, and others.	**January.** Visit of **Lady** Byron to her home, and refusal to return. April 25th. Departure of Lord Byron for the Continent. Summer in Switzerland. Friendship with Shelley.
1817. Repressive measures of the Government. Death of the Princess Charlotte, only child of the Prince Regent.		Publication of "Biographia Literaria" and of "Sibylline Leaves." Contributions to *The Courier.*	Chancery suit for possession of Harriet's children. August. Judgment of Lord Eldon against Shelley.	Decision to lead a literary life. March. First volume of poems. May. Beginning of "Endymion."	**1817–1820.** Life in Italy, chiefly in Venice. Literary activity. "Manfred," etc.
1818. Unpopularity of the Royal family.	"Evening Ode."	Lectures on Shakespeare.	January. "Laon and Cythna (Revolt of Islam)." March. Final departure from England for Italy. "Julian and Maddalo."	March. Publication of "Endymion." Marriage and emigration of George Keats, brother of John. July – August. Tour in Scotland. Undue exposure. *Blackwood* and *Quarterly* reviews on "Endymion." December. Death of Thomas Keats, brother of John. Love for Fanny Brawne and engagement.	Sale of Newstead Abbey to pay mortgages. Completion of First Canto of "Don Juan."

TABLE OF DATES—*Continued.*

Byron.	Keats.	Shelley.	Coleridge.	Wordsworth.	Contemporary History.
Meeting with Teresa Guiccioli. "Childe Harold." Cantos III. and IV.	"The Eve of St. Agnes," etc. Shanklin. Winchester. Wentworth Place with C. A. Browne.	Death of William Shelley, son of Percy. Rome. "Prometheus Unbound." Leghorn, "The Cenci." Florence, "The Mask of Anarchy."			1819. The Manchester Massacre. The Six Acts.
	February. Attack of illness, hemorrhage. Really. Publication of "Lamia" and other poems. September 18th. Departure for Italy with Joseph Severn.	Removal to Pisa. Companionship of Byron.		Tour through Switzerland and Italy. "Duddon Sonnets."	1820. Accession of George IV. Trial of the Queen and consequent alienation of the people. Insurrections in Spain, Portugal, and Naples.
1821-1823. Life chiefly in Florence and Pisa. Companionship of Teresa Guiccioli and her brothers.	February 23d. Death in Rome. Burial in the Protestant Cemetery.	"Adonais."		1821-1822. "Ecclesiastical Sonnets."	1821. Insurrection in Greece. French intervention in Spain against the people.
"The Vision of Judgment." Settlement of Leigh Hunt and his family in Byron's house in Pisa.		Companionship of Trelawney and the Williamses. April 26th. Removal to Lerici on the Gulf of Spezzia. July. Visit to Leghorn and Pisa to welcome Hunt. July 8th. Drowning on the way home from Leghorn. Burning of the body on the sands. Burial of the ashes in the Protestant Cemetery in Rome.			1822. Congress of Verona.

TABLE OF DATES—*Con*

Contemporary History.	Wordsworth.	Coleridge.	She
1823.			
1824.			
1828.	Tour on the Rhine.	Tour on the Rhine with Wordsworth.	
1829. Independence of Greece. Catholic Emancipation.		Second edition of Poetic and Dramatic Works.	
1830. Accession of William IV. Revolution in France.			
1832. Reform of the House of Commons.			
1834. Death of Charles Lamb.		July 25th. Death. Burial in Highgate Churchyard.	
1837. Accession of Queen Victoria.	Honorary degree of D.C.L., from Oxford.		
1842.	Annuity of £300 from the Government.		

TABLE OF DATES—*Continued.*

Contemporary History.	Wordsworth.	Coleridge.	Shelley.	Keats.	Byron.
1843. Death of Southey.	Acceptance of the title of Poet Laureate.				
1847.	Death of Dora Quillinan, daughter of Wordsworth.				
1850.	Death. Burial in Grasmere Churchyard.				

BIBLIOGRAPHY.

NOTE.—So far as feasible, the present publishers and the earliest date of publication are indicated.

WILLIAM WORDSWORTH.

EDITIONS RECOMMENDED.

Poems of Wordsworth. Selection by Matthew Arnold. [Golden Treasury Series, Macmillan.]

The Complete Poetical Works of William Wordsworth, with Introduction by John Morley. One volume. [Macmillan.] 1888.

The Poetical Works of William Wordsworth. Edited by William Knight. Eight volumes. Additional volumes with life and prose works. [Paterson.] 1882-86. (Revised edition published by Macmillan, 1897.)

BIOGRAPHICAL.

F. W. H. Myers, Wordsworth. [Harper's English Men of Letters Series.] 1880.

William Minto, Wordsworth. [Encyclopædia Britannica, Ninth Edition.] 1888.

William Knight, Life. Vols. IX, X, XI, of Knight's edition of Wordsworth's Works. [Paterson.] 1889.

CRITICAL.

R. H. Hutton, Essays, Theological and Literary. Vol. II. [Macmillan.] 1871.

S. A. Brooke, Theology in the English Poets. [H. S. King.] 1874.

Leslie Stephen, Hours in a Library. Third Series: Wordsworth's Ethics. [Smith & Elder.] 1879.

E. P. Whipple, Essays and Reviews, Vol. I. [Houghton, Mifflin & Co.] 1848.

Matthew Arnold, Essays in Criticism, Second Series. [Macmillan.] 1879. (The same essay is the Introduction to Arnold's Selections from Wordsworth.)

William Knight, editor, Wordsworthiana. [Macmillan.] 1889.

Walter Pater, Appreciations. [Macmillan.] 1874.

Walter Bagehot, Literary Studies, Vol. II: Wordsworth, Tennyson, and Browning. [Longmans.] 1879. (A cheap edition of Bagehot's works has been published by the Hartford Insurance Co.)

Aubrey de Vere, Essays chiefly on Poetry, Vol. I. [Macmillan.] 1887.

J. C. Shairp, 1. Studies in Poetry and Philosophy: Wordsworth, the Man and the Poet. [Douglas.] 1868. (Largely biographical.)
         2. Poetic Interpretation of Nature. [Douglas.] 1874.

S. T. Coleridge, Biographia Literaria. Chaps. IV, XIV, XVII, XVIII, XIX, XXII. [Bohn.] 1817.

J. R. Lowell, Among My Books, Vol. II. [Houghton, Mifflin & Co.] 1876. (Largely a discussion of Wordsworth's defects as a poet.)

Edmond Scherer, Essays in English Literature. Editor, Saintsbury. [Scribner.] 1891. (Foreigner's view.)

COLERIDGE.

Editions Recommended.

The Golden Book of Coleridge, edited with an introduction by Stopford A. Brooke. [J. M. Dent.] 1895.

The Poetical Works of Samuel Taylor Coleridge, edited with a biographical introduction by James Dykes Campbell. One volume. [Macmillan.] 1893.

The Poetical Works of Samuel Taylor Coleridge. Edited with introduction and notes by T. Ashe. Two volumes. [George Bell & Sons. Aldine Edition of the British Poets.]

Biographical.

H. D. Traill, Coleridge. [Harper's English Men of Letters Series.] 1884.

E. H. Coleridge, editor, Letters of S. T. Coleridge. [Heinemann.] 1895.

L. Stephen, Coleridge. [Dictionary of National Biography.]

Charles Lamb, 1. Letters. Edited by Alfred Ainger. Two volumes [Macmillan.] 1888.

      2. Essays of Elia: Christ's Hospital five and thirty years ago. [Armstrong.] 1823–33.

Critical.

E. P. Whipple, Essays and Reviews. Vol. I : Coleridge as a Poet and Critic. [Houghton, Mifflin & Co.] 1848.

S. A. Brooke, Theology in the English Poets. [Henry S. King.] 1874.

A. C. Swinburne, Essays and Studies. [Chatto & Windus.] 1888. (Praise of Coleridge's æsthetic qualities.)

Edward Dowden, New Studies in Literature. [Kegan Paul, Trench & Co.] 1895. (Points out the perfections of Coleridge's poetry and the frailties of his nature.)

Walter Pater, Appreciations. [Macmillan.] 1865–80. (Emphasizes the intellectual passion for absolute truth as shown in Coleridge's poetry.)

J. C. Shairp, Studies in Poetry and Philosophy : Coleridge, the Man and the Poet. [Douglas.] 1868. (Discussion of Coleridge's intellectual beliefs.)

SHELLEY.

Editions Recommended.

Poems from Shelley. Selected and arranged by Stopford A. Brooke.
[Golden Treasury Series, Macmillan]
The Poetical Works of Percy Bysshe Shelley. Edited by Edward
Dowden. One volume. [Macmillan.] 1890. (Notes, Life.)
The Poetical Works of Percy Bysshe Shelley. Edited by George E.
Woodberry. Four volumes. [Houghton, Mifflin & Co.] 1892.

Biographical.

J. A. Symonds, Shelley. [English Men of Letters Series.] 1879.
William Sharp. Life. [Great Writers Series, W. Scott.] 1887.
G. B. Smith, Shelley: A Critical Biography. [Douglas.] 1877.
Edward Dowden, Life of Shelley. Two volumes. [Kegan Paul,
Trench & Co.] 1886.

Critical.

R. H. Hutton, Essays, Theological and Literary, Vol. II: Shelley
and his Writings. [Macmillan.] Third edition, 1888. (Discus-
sion of Shelley's mysticism.)
E. P. Whipple, Essays and Reviews, Vol. I: Shelley. [Houghton,
Mifflin & Co.] 1848.
Walter Bagehot, Literary Studies, Vol. I. [Longmans.] 1879.
Edward Dowden, Transcripts and Studies: Last Words on Shelley.
[Kegan Paul, Trench & Co.] 1888.
J. C. Shairp, Aspects of Poetry: Shelley as a Lyric Poet. [Houghton,
Mifflin & Co.] 1882.
A. C. Swinburne, Essays and Studies: Notes on the Text of Shelley.
[Chatto & Windus.] 1876.
Matthew Arnold, Essays in Criticism, Second Series. [Macmillan.]
1879. (Criticism of Dowden's Life, Shelley's character as a man.)
Leslie Stephen, Hours in a Library, Third Series. [Smith & Elder.]
1879.
George E. Woodberry, Studies in Letters and Life: Remarks on
Shelley. [Houghton, Mifflin & Co.] 1890.

KEATS.

EDITIONS RECOMMENDED.

The Poetical Works of Keats, with notes by Francis T. Palgrave. [Golden Treasury Series.] (Containing, in convenient form, most of the important poems.)
Poetical Works of John Keats. Editor, William T. Arnold. [Kegan Paul, Trench & Co.] 1884-88.
The Poetical Works of John Keats. H. B. Forman. [Reeves & Turner.] Third edition, 1889. (Full notes and all the poems.)

BIOGRAPHICAL.

Sidney Colvin, Keats. [English Men of Letters Series.] 1887.
W. M. Rossetti, Life of Keats. [Great Writers Series, Scott.] 1887.
Sidney Colvin, Keats. [Dictionary of National Biography.]
A. C. Swinburne, Keats. [Encyclopædia Britannica, Ninth Edition.]
H. Buxton Forman, editor, The Letters of John Keats. [Reeves & Turner.] 1895.
Sidney Colvin, editor, Letters of John Keats. [Macmillan.] 1891.

CRITICAL.

Matthew Arnold, Essays in Criticism, Second Series. [Macmillan.] 1879.
J. R. Lowell, Among My Books, Vol. II. [Houghton, Mifflin & Co.] 1876. (Some statements shown to be false in the light of later investigations.)
A. C. Swinburne, Miscellanies. [Chatto & Windus.] 1886.
G. E. Woodberry, Studies in Letters and Life: On the Promise of Keats. [Houghton, Mifflin & Co.] 1890.
W. H. Hudson, Studies in Interpretation: Keats. [Putnam.] 1896. (Excellent presentation of Keats's attitude toward modern thought.)
David Masson, Wordsworth, Shelley, and Keats. [Macmillan.] 1856. (Purely intellectual treatment.)
Quarterly Review, April, 1818. Endymion: A Poetic Romance. (A savage criticism, supposed at one time to have caused the death of Keats.)

BYRON.

EDITIONS RECOMMENDED.

Childe Harold, edited with notes, by H. F. Tozer. [Clarendon Press Series.]
The Poetical Works of Lord Byron. One volume. [Murray.] 1873. (Notes by Scott, Moore, Lockhart, etc.)
Lord Byron's Works in Prose and Poetry. Edited by his grandson, the Earl of Lovelace. [Murray.] 1897. In preparation.

BIOGRAPHICAL.

Roden Noel, Byron. [Great Writers Series.] 1890.
John Nichol, Byron. [English Men of Letters Series.] 1890.
William Minto, Byron. [Encyclopædia Britannica, Ninth Edition.]
Leslie Stephen, Byron. [Dictionary of National Biography.]
The Works of Lord Byron. Edited by W. E. Henley. Volume I., Letters, 1804–1813. [Heinemann.] 1897. (To contain (1) Letters; (2) Journals and Memoranda; (3) Miscellanies.)

CRITICAL.

Matthew Arnold, Essays in Criticism, Second Series. [Macmillan.] 1879.
E. P. Whipple, Essays and Reviews, Vol. I. [Houghton, Mifflin & Co.] 1848.
John Morley, Critical Miscellanies, Vol. I. [Macmillan.] 1877.
H A. Taine, History of English Literature, Vol. IV. [Henry Holt & Co.] 1871.
A. C. Swinburne, 1. Essays and Studies. [Chatto & Windus.] 1876. 2. Miscellanies: Wordsworth and Byron. [Chatto & Windus.] 1886. (Violent attack upon Byron as a poet.)
Edinburgh Review, March. 1808. Review by Lord Brougham of Hours of Idleness. (Occasion of Byron's English Bards and Scotch Reviewers.)

BOOKS OF GENERAL REFERENCE.

Mrs. M. O. Oliphant, Literary History of England in the End of the Eighteenth and Beginning of the Nineteenth Century. Three volumes. [Macmillan.] 1882. (Easy reading.)

Edward Dowden. 1. Studies in Literature, 1789-1877. [Kegan Paul, Trench & Co.] Fifth edition, 1889.

                    2. The French Revolution and English Literature. [Scribner.] 1897.

T. Hall Caine, Cobwebs of Criticism. [Stock.] 1883. (A review of the first reviewers of Wordsworth, Coleridge, Shelley, Keats, Byron.)

G. Saintsbury, A History of Nineteenth Century Literature. [Macmillan.] 1896.

Thomas De Quincey, Literary Reminiscences and Biographical Essays, 1835-40. [Houghton, Mifflin & Co.] (Especially for Wordsworth and Coleridge.)

Charles Lamb, Letters. Edited by Alfred Ainger. [Macmillan.] 1888. (For Coleridge and Wordsworth.)

William Hazlitt. 1. The Spirit of the Age. [Bohn.]

                    2. Lectures on the English Poets. [Bohn.] 1818.

Leigh Hunt, Autobiography. Two volumes. [Harper.] 1850.

The Edinburgh and Quarterly Reviews and Blackwood's Magazine. (For contemporary criticism on the various poets. Most of the important essays may be found in Early Reviews of Great Writers, ed. Stevenson. Camelot Series, Scott.)

Thomas Carlyle, Reminiscences. Edited by C. E. Norton. [Macmillan.]

After Boxall 1831.

WILLIAM WORDSWORTH.

SELECTIONS FROM WORDSWORTH [1]

LINES

COMPOSED A FEW MILES ABOVE TINTERN ABBEY, ON RE-
VISITING THE BANKS OF THE WYE DURING A TOUR,
JULY 13, 1798.

Five years have past; five summers, with the length
Of five long winters! and again I hear
These waters, rolling from their mountain-springs
With a soft inland murmur.—Once again
Do I behold these steep and lofty cliffs,
That on a wild secluded scene impress
Thoughts of more deep seclusion; and connect
The landscape with the quiet of the sky.
The day is come when I again repose
Here, under this dark sycamore, and view   10
These plots of cottage-ground, these orchard-tufts,
Which at this season, with their unripe fruits,
Are clad in one green hue, and lose themselves
'Mid groves and copses. Once again I see
These hedge-rows, hardly hedge-rows, little lines
Of sportive wood run wild: these pastoral farms,
Green to the very door; and wreaths of smoke
Sent up, in silence, from among the trees!

---

[1] Original and early editions as well as late standard texts have been consulted for these selections, and in general, even at the risk of inconsistency, the early spelling, capitals, and punctuation have been retained. Such details help to re-create the atmosphere of the period to which they belong.

1

With some uncertain notice, as might seem
Of vagrant dwellers in the houseless woods,
Or of some Hermit's cave, where by his fire
The Hermit sits alone.

     These beauteous forms,
Through a long absence, have not been to me
As is a landscape to a blind man's eye:
But oft, in lonely rooms, and 'mid the din
Of towns and cities, I have owed to them,
In hours of weariness, sensations sweet,
Felt in the blood, and felt along the heart;
And passing even into my purer mind,
With tranquil restoration:—feelings too
Of unremembered pleasure: such, perhaps,
As have no slight or trivial influence
On that best portion of a good man's life,
His little, nameless, unremembered acts
Of kindness and of love. Nor less, I trust,
To them I may have owed another gift,
Of aspect more sublime; that blessed mood,
In which the burthen of the mystery,
In which the heavy and the weary weight
Of all this unintelligible world,
Is lightened:—that serene and blessed mood,
In which the affections gently lead us on,—
Until, the breath of this corporeal frame
And even the motion of our human blood
Almost suspended, we are laid asleep
In body, and become a living soul:
While with an eye made quiet by the power
Of harmony, and the deep power of joy,
We see into the life of things.

      If this
Be but a vain belief, yet, oh! how oft—
In darkness and amid the many shapes

Of joyless daylight; when the fretful stir
Unprofitable, and the fever of the world,
Have hung upon the beatings of my heart—
How oft, in spirit, have I turned to thee,
O sylvan Wye! thou wanderer thro' the woods,
How often has my spirit turned to thee!
    And now, with gleams of half-extinguished thought,
With many recognitions dim and faint,
And somewhat of a sad perplexity,   60
The picture of the mind revives again:
While here I stand, not only with the sense
Of present pleasure, but with pleasing thoughts
That in this moment there is life and food
For future years. And so I dare to hope,
Though changed, no doubt, from what I was when first
I came among these hills; when like a roe
I bounded o'er the mountains, by the sides
Of the deep rivers, and the lonely streams,
Wherever nature led: more like a man   70
Flying from something that he dreads, than one
Who sought the thing he loved. For nature then
(The coarser pleasures of my boyish days,
And their glad animal movements all gone by)
To me was all in all.—I cannot paint
What then I was. The sounding cataract
Haunted me like a passion: the tall rock,
The mountain, and the deep and gloomy wood,
Their colours and their forms, were then to me
An appetite; a feeling and a love,   80
That had no need of a remoter charm,
By thought supplied, nor any interest
Unborrowed from the eye.—That time is past,
And all its aching joys are now no more,
And all its dizzy raptures. Not for this
Faint I, nor mourn nor murmur: other gifts

Have followed; for such loss, I would believe,
Abundant recompence. For I have learned
To look on nature, not as in the hour
Of thoughtless youth; but hearing oftentimes   90
The still, sad music of humanity,
Nor harsh nor grating, though of ample power
To chasten and subdue. And I have felt
A presence that disturbs me with the joy
Of elevated thoughts; a sense sublime
Of something far more deeply interfused,
Whose dwelling is the light of setting suns,
And the round ocean and the living air,
And the blue sky, and in the mind of man;
A motion and a spirit, that impels   100
All thinking things, all objects of all thought,
And rolls through all things. Therefore am I still
A lover of the meadows and the woods,
And mountains; and of all that we behold
From this green earth; of all the mighty world
Of eye, and ear,—both what they half create,
And what perceive; well pleased to recognise
In nature and the language of the sense,
The anchor of my purest thoughts, the nurse,
The guide, the guardian of my heart, and soul   110
Of all my moral being.
                          Nor perchance,
If I were not thus taught, should I the more
Suffer my genial spirits to decay:
For thou art with me here upon the banks
Of this fair river; thou, my dearest Friend,
My dear, dear Friend; and in thy voice I catch
The language of my former heart, and read
My former pleasures in the shooting lights
Of thy wild eyes. Oh! yet a little while
May I behold in thee what I was once,   120

My dear, dear Sister! and this prayer I make,
Knowing that Nature never did betray
The heart that loved her; 'tis her privilege,
Through all the years of this our life, to lead
From joy to joy: for she can so inform
The mind that is within us, so impress
With quietness and beauty, and so feed
With lofty thoughts, that neither evil tongues,
Rash judgments, nor the sneers of selfish men,
Nor greetings where no kindness is, nor all   130
The dreary intercourse of daily life,
Shall e'er prevail against us, or disturb
Our cheerful faith, that all which we behold
Is full of blessings. Therefore let the moon
Shine on thee in thy solitary walk;
And let the misty mountain-winds be free
To blow against thee: and in after years,
When these wild ecstasies shall be matured
Into a sober pleasure; when thy mind
Shall be a mansion for all lovely forms,   140
Thy memory be as a dwelling-place
For all sweet sounds and harmonies: oh! then,
If solitude, or fear, or pain, or grief,
Should be thy portion, with what healing thoughts
Of tender joy wilt thou remember me,
And these my exhortations! Nor, perchance—
If I should be where I no more can hear
Thy voice, nor catch from thy wild eyes these gleams
Of past existence—wilt thou then forget
That on the banks of this delightful stream   150
We stood together; and that I, so long
A worshipper of Nature, hither came
Unwearied in that service: rather say
With warmer love—oh! with far deeper zeal
Of holier love. Nor will thou then forget,

That after many wanderings, many years
Of absence, these steep woods and lofty cliffs,
And this green pastoral landscape, were to me
More dear, both for themselves and for thy sake!

EXPOSTULATION AND REPLY.

" Why, William, on that old grey stone,
Thus for the length of half a day,
Why, William, sit you thus alone,
And dream your time away?

" Where are your books?—that light bequeathed
To Beings else forlorn and blind!
Up! up! and drink the spirit breathed
From dead men to their kind.

" You look round on your Mother Earth,
As if she for no purpose bore you;   10
As if you were her first-born birth,
And none had lived before you! "

One morning thus, by Esthwaite lake,
When life was sweet, I knew not why,
To me my good friend Matthew spake,
And thus I made reply.

" The eye—it cannot choose but see;
We cannot bid the ear be still;
Our bodies feel, where'er they be,
Against or with our will.

" Nor less I deem that there are Powers
Which of themselves our minds impress;
That we can feed this mind of ours
In a wise passiveness.

" Think you, 'mid all this mighty sum
Of things for ever speaking,
That nothing of itself will come,
But we must still be seeking?

" —Then ask not wherefore, here, alone,
Conversing as I may,
I sit upon this old grey stone,
And dream my time away."

                                                 30

Spring, 1798.]

THE TABLES TURNED.

AN EVENING SCENE ON THE SAME SUBJECT.

Up! up! my Friend, and quit your books:
Or surely you'll grow double:
Up! up! my Friend, and clear your looks;
Why all this toil and trouble?

The sun, above the mountain's head,
A freshening lustre mellow
Through all the long green fields has spread,
His first sweet evening yellow.

Books! 'tis a dull and endless strife:
Come, hear the woodland linnet,
How sweet his music! on my life,
There's more of wisdom in it.

                                                 10

And hark! how blithe the throstle sings!
He, too, is no mean preacher:
Come forth into the light of things,
Let Nature be your teacher.

She has a world of ready wealth,
Our minds and hearts to bless—
Spontaneous wisdom breathed by health,
Truth breathed by cheerfulness.   20

One impulse from a vernal wood
May teach you more of man,
Of moral evil and of good,
Than all the sages can.

Sweet is the lore which Nature brings;
Our meddling intellect
Mis-shapes the beauteous forms of things:—
We murder to dissect.

Enough of Science and of Art;
Close up those barren leaves: 30
Come forth, and bring with you a heart
That watches and receives.

1798.]

"SHE DWELT AMONG THE UNTRODDEN WAYS."

She dwelt among the untrodden ways
  Beside the springs of Dove,
A Maid whom there were none to praise
  And very few to love:

A violet by a mossy stone
  Half hidden from the eye!
—Fair as a star, when only one
  Is shining in the sky.

She lived unknown, and few could know
  When Lucy ceased to be;
But she is in her grave, and, oh,
  The difference to me!

199.]

"I TRAVELLED AMONG UNKNOWN MEN."

I travelled among unknown men,
  In lands beyond the sea;
Nor, England! did I know till then
  What love I bore to thee.

'Tis past, that melancholy dream!
  Nor will I quit thy shore
A second time; for still I seem
  To love thee more and more.

Among thy mountains did I feel
  The joy of my desire;
And she I cherished turned her wheel
  Beside an English fire.

Thy mornings showed, thy nights concealed
  The bowers where Lucy played;
And thine too is the last green field
  That Lucy's eyes surveyed.

1799.]

"THREE YEARS SHE GREW IN SUN AND SHOWER."

Three years she grew in sun and shower,
Then Nature said, " A lovelier flower
On earth was never sown;
This Child I to myself will take;
She shall be mine, and I will make
A Lady of my own.

" Myself will to my darling be
Both law and impulse: and with me
The Girl, in rock and plain,
In earth and heaven, in glade and bower,   10
Shall feel an overseeing power
To kindle or restrain.

" She shall be sportive as the fawn
That wild with glee across the lawn
Or up the mountain springs:
And hers shall be the breathing balm,
And hers the silence and the calm
Of mute insensate things.

" The floating clouds their state shall lend
To her: for her the willow bend;   20
Nor shall she fail to see
Even in the motions of the Storm
Grace that shall mould the Maiden's form
By silent sympathy.

"The stars of midnight shall be dear
To her; and she shall lean her ear
In many a secret place
Where rivulets dance their wayward round,
And beauty born of murmuring sound
Shall pass into her face.   35

" And vital feelings of delight
Shall rear her form to stately height,
Her virgin bosom swell:
Such thoughts to Lucy I will give
While she and I together live
Here in this happy dell."

Thus Nature spake—The work was done—
How soon my Lucy's race was run!
She died, and left to me
This heath, this calm, and quiet scene;   40
The memory of what has been,
And never more will be.

Hartz Forest, 1799.]

COMPOSED UPON WESTMINSTER BRIDGE, SEPTEMBER 3, 1802.

[Written on the roof of a coach, on my way to France.—W. W.]

Earth has not any thing to show more fair:
Dull would he be of soul who could pass by
A sight so touching in its majesty:
This City now doth, like a garment, wear
The beauty of the morning: silent, bare,
Ships, towers, domes, theatres, and temples lie

Open unto the fields, and to the sky;
All bright and glittering in the smokeless **air.**
Never did sun more beautifully steep,
In his first splendour, valley, rock, or hill;
Ne'er saw I, never felt, a calm so deep!
The river glideth at his own sweet will:
Dear God! the very houses seem asleep;
And all that mighty heart is lying still!

"IT IS A BEAUTEOUS EVENING, CALM AND FREE."

It is a beauteous evening, calm and free,
The holy time is quiet as a Nun
Breathless with adoration; the broad sun
Is sinking down in its tranquillity;
The gentleness of heaven is on the Sea:
Listen! the mighty Being is awake,
And doth with his eternal motion make
A sound like thunder—everlastingly.
Dear Child! dear Girl! that walkest with me here,
If thou appear'st untouched by solemn thought,
Thy nature is not therefore less divine:
Thou liest in Abraham's bosom all the year;
And worshipp'st at the Temple's inner shrine,
God being with thee when we know it not.

August, 1802.]

ON THE EXTINCTION OF THE VENETIAN REPUBLIC.

Once did She hold the gorgeous east in fee;
And was the safeguard of the west: the worth
Of Venice did not fall below her birth,
Venice, the eldest Child of Liberty.
She was a maiden City, bright and free;
No guile seduced, no force could violate;
And, when she took unto herself a Mate,
She must espouse the everlasting Sea.
And what if she had seen those glories fade,
Those titles vanish, and that strength decay;
Yet shall some tribute of regret be paid
When her long life hath reached its final day:
Men are we, and must grieve when even the Shade
Of that which once was great, is pass'd away.

August, 1802.]

SEPTEMBER, 1802. NEAR DOVER.

Inland, within a hollow vale, I stood:
And saw, while sea was calm and air was clear,
The coast of France—the coast of France how near!
Drawn almost into frightful neighbourhood.
I shrunk: for verily the barrier flood
Was like a lake, or river bright and fair,
A span of waters: yet what power is there!
What mightiness for evil and for good!
Even so doth God protect us if we be
Virtuous and wise. Winds blow, and waters roll,

Strength to the brave, and Power, and Deity;
Yet in themselves are nothing!   One decree
Spake laws to *them*, and said that by the soul
Only, the Nations shall be great and free.

LONDON, 1802.

Milton![1] thou should'st be living at this hour:
England hath need of thee: she is a fen
Of stagnant waters: altar, sword, and pen,
Fireside, the heroic wealth of hall and bower,
Have forfeited their ancient English dower
Of inward happiness. We are selfish men;
Oh! raise us up, return to us again;
And give us manners, virtue, freedom, power.
Thy soul was like a Star, and dwelt apart:
Thou hadst a voice whose sound was like the sea:
Pure as the naked heavens, majestic, free,
So didst thou travel on life's common way,
In cheerful godliness: and yet thy heart
The lowliest duties on herself did lay.

"GREAT MEN HAVE BEEN AMONG US; HANDS THAT PENNED."

Great men have been among us; hands that penned
And tongues that uttered wisdom—better none:
The later Sidney, Marvel, Harrington,
Young Vane, and others who called Milton friend.
These moralists could act and comprehend:

---

[1] Wordsworth imputed to Milton a union of tenderness and imagination far above other poets, and felt a greater kinship with him than with others.

They knew how genuine glory was put on;
Taught us how rightfully a nation shone
In splendour: what strength was, that would not bend
But in magnanimous meekness. France, 'tis strange,
Hath brought forth no such souls as we had then.
Perpetual emptiness! unceasing change!
No single volume paramount, no code,
No master spirit, no determined road;
But equally a want of books and men!

September, 1802.]

"IT IS NOT TO BE THOUGHT OF THAT THE FLOOD."

It is not to be thought of that the Flood
Of British freedom, which, to the open sea
Of the world's praise, from dark antiquity
Hath flowed, " with pomp of waters, unwithstood,"
Roused though it be full often to a mood
Which spurns the check of salutary bands,
That this most famous Stream in bogs and sands
Should perish; and to evil and to good
Be lost forever. In our halls is hung
Armoury of the invincible Knights of old:
We must be free or die, who speak the tongue
That Shakespeare spake: the faith and morals hold
Which Milton held.—In everything we are sprung
Of Earth's first blood, have titles manifold.

1802.]

STEPPING WESTWARD.

[While my Fellow-traveller and I were walking by the side of Loch Ketterine, one fine evening after sunset, in our road to a Hut where, in the course of our Tour, we had been hospitably entertained some weeks before, we met, in one of the loneliest parts of that solitary region, two well-dressed Women, one of whom said to us, by way of greeting, " What, you are stepping westward ? "]

" *What, you are stepping westward?* "—" *Yea.*"
—"Twould be a *wildish* destiny,
If we, who thus together roam
In a strange Land, and far from home,
Were in this place the guests of Chance:
Yet who would stop, or fear to advance,
Though home or shelter he had none,
With such a sky to lead him on?

The dewy ground was dark and cold;
Behind, all gloomy to behold: 10
And stepping westward seemed to be
A kind of *heavenly* destiny:
I liked the greeting: 'twas a sound
Of something without place or bound:
And seemed to give me spiritual right
To travel through that region bright.

The voice was soft, and she who spake
Was walking by her native lake:
The salutation had to me
The very sound of courtesy: 20
Its power was felt: and while my eye
Was fixed upon the glowing Sky,

The echo of the voice enwrought
A human sweetness with the thought
Of travelling through the world that lay
Before me in my endless way.

1803.]

THE SOLITARY REAPER.

Behold her, single in the field,
Yon solitary Highland Lass!
Reaping and singing by herself;
Stop here, or gently pass!
Alone she cuts and binds the grain,
And sings a melancholy strain;
O listen! for the Vale profound
Is overflowing with the sound.[1]

No Nightingale did ever chaunt
More welcome notes to weary bands   10
Of travellers in some shady haunt,
Among Arabian sands:
A voice so thrilling ne'er was heard
In spring-time from the Cuckoo-bird,
Breaking the silence of the seas
Among the farthest Hebrides.

Will no one tell me what she sings?—
Perhaps the plaintive numbers flow
For old, unhappy, far-off things,
And battles long ago: 20

[1] Wordsworth's ear was peculiarly alive to the sounds of nature. In this instance the spirit of the place expresses itself in the music.

2

Or is it some more humble lay,
Familiar matter of to-day?
Some natural sorrow, loss, or pain,
That has been, and may be again?

Whate'er the theme, the Maiden sang
As if her song could have no ending;
I saw her singing at her work,
And o'er the sickle bending;—
I listened, motionless and still;
And, as I mounted up the hill,   30
The music in my heart I bore,
Long after it was heard no more.

1803.]

YARROW UNVISITED.

[See the various Poems the scene of which is laid upon the banks of
the Yarrow; in particular, the exquisite Ballad of Hamilton, beginning

"Busk ye, busk ye, my bonny, bonny Bride,
Busk ye, busk ye, my winsome Marrow!"]

From Stirling castle we had seen
The mazy Forth unravelled:
Had trod the banks of Clyde, and Tay,
And with the Tweed had travelled;
And when we came to Clovenford,
Then said my "*winsome Marrow*,"
"Whate'er betide, we'll turn aside,
And see the Braes of Yarrow."

"Let Yarrow folk, *frae* Selkirk town,
Who have been buying, selling,   10
Go back to Yarrow, 'tis their own;
Each maiden to her dwelling!

On Yarrow's banks let herons feed,
Hares couch, and rabbits burrow!
But we will downward with the Tweed,
Nor turn aside to Yarrow.

" There's Galla Water, Leader Haughs,
Both lying right before us;
And Dryborough, where with chiming Tweed
The lintwhites sing in chorus;   20
There's pleasant Tiviot-dale, a land
Made blithe with plough and harrow:
Why throw away a needful day
To go in search of Yarrow?

" What's Yarrow but a river bare,
That glides the dark hills under?
There are a thousand such elsewhere
As worthy of your wonder."
—Strange words they seemed of slight and scorn;
My True-love sighed for sorrow: 30
And looked me in the face, to think
I thus could speak of Yarrow!

" Oh! green," said I, " are Yarrow's holms,
And sweet is Yarrow flowing!
Fair hangs the apple frae the rock,
But we will leave it growing.
O'er hilly path and open Strath,
We'll wander Scotland thorough;
But, though so near, we will not turn
Into the dale of Yarrow.   40

" Let beeves and home-bred kine partake
The sweets of Burn-mill meadow;

The swan on still St. Mary's Lake
Float double, swan and shadow!
We will not see them; will not go,
To-day, nor yet to-morrow;
Enough if in our hearts we know
There's such a place as Yarrow.

" Be Yarrow stream unseen, unknown! [1]
It must, or we shall rue it: 50
We have a vision of our own;
Ah! why should we undo it?
The treasured dreams of times long past,
We'll keep them, winsome Marrow!
For when we're there, although 'tis fair,
'Twill be another Yarrow!

" If Care with freezing years should come,
And wandering seem but folly,—
Should we be loth to stir from home,
And yet be melancholy;   60
Should life be dull, and spirits low,
'Twill soothe us in our sorrow,
That earth has something yet to show,
The bonny holms of Yarrow! "

1803.]

---

[1] In the reserve of his nature, Wordsworth always held himself back from a pleasure, in order to enjoy it in moderation.

"ENGLAND! THE TIME IS COME WHEN THOU SHOULD'ST WEAN."

England! The time is come when thou should'st wean
Thy heart from its emasculating food;
The truth should now be better understood;
Old things have been unsettled; we have seen
Fair seed-time, better harvest might have been
But for thy trespasses; and, at this day,
If for Greece, Egypt, India, Africa,
Aught good were destined, thou would'st step between.
England! all nations in this charge agree:
But worse, more ignorant in love and hate,
Far—far more abject, is thine Enemy:
Therefore the wise pray for thee, though the freight
Of thy offences be a heavy weight:
Oh grief that Earth's best hopes rest all with Thee!

1803.'

"THERE IS A BONDAGE WORSE, FAR WORSE, TO BEAR."

There is a bondage worse, far worse, to bear
Than his who breathes, by roof, and floor, and wall,
Pent in, a Tyrant's solitary Thrall:
'Tis his who walks about in the open air,
One of a Nation who, henceforth, must wear
Their fetters in their souls. For who could be,
Who, even the best, in such condition, free
From self-reproach, reproach that he must share

With Human-nature? Never be it ours
To see the sun how brightly it will shine,
And know that noble feelings, manly powers,
Instead of gathering strength, must droop and pine;
And earth with all her pleasant fruits and flowers
Fade, and participate in man's decline.

1803.]

TO THE CUCKOO.

O blithe New-comer! I have heard,
  I hear thee and rejoice.
O Cuckoo! shall I call thee Bird,
  Or but a wandering Voice?

While I am lying on the grass
  Thy twofold shout I hear,
From hill to hill it seems to pass,
  At once far off, and near.

Though babbling only to the Vale
  Of sunshine and of flowers,
Thou bringest unto me a tale
  Of visionary hours.

Thrice welcome, darling of the Spring!
  Even yet thou art to me
No bird, but an invisible thing,
  A voice, a mystery:

The same whom in my school-boy days
  I listened to; that Cry
Which made me look a thousand ways
  In bush, and tree, and sky.

To seek thee did I often rove
Through woods and on the green;
And thou wert still a hope, a love;
Still longed for, never seen.

And I can listen to thee yet;
Can lie upon the plain
And listen, till I do beget
That golden time again.

O blessed Bird! the earth we pace
Again appears to be
An unsubstantial, fairy place,
That is fit home for Thee!

1804.]

"SHE WAS A PHANTOM OF DELIGHT."

[Written at Town-end, Grasmere. The germ of this poem was four lines composed as a part of the verses on the Highland Girl. Though beginning in this way, it was written from my heart, as is sufficiently obvious.—W. W.]

She was a Phantom of delight
When first she gleamed upon my sight;
A lovely Apparition, sent
To be a moment's ornament:
Her eyes as stars of Twilight fair;
Like Twilight's, too, her dusky hair:
But all things else about her drawn
From May-time and the cheerful Dawn;
A dancing Shape, an Image gay.
To haunt, to startle, and way-lay.   10

I saw her upon nearer view,
A Spirit, yet a Woman too!
Her household motions light and free,
And steps of virgin-liberty;
A countenance in which did meet
Sweet records, promises as sweet;
A Creature not too bright or good
For human nature's daily food;
For transient sorrows, simple wiles,
Praise, blame, love, kisses, tears, and smiles.   20

And now I see with eye serene
The very pulse of the machine; [1]
A Being breathing thoughtful breath,
A traveller between life and death;
The reason firm, the temperate will,
Endurance, foresight, strength, and skill;
A perfect Woman, nobly planned
To warn, to comfort, and command;
And yet a Spirit still, and bright
With something of angelic light.   30

1804.]

---

[1] Machine : compare "The Waggoner," Canto IV., line 803.

Forgive me, then ; for I had been
On friendly terms with this Machine.

The progress of mechanical industry in Britain since the beginning of the present century has given a more limited, and purely technical, meaning to the word, than it bore when Wordsworth used it in these two instances.   WM. KNIGHT.

THE DAFFODILS.

I wandered lonely as a cloud
That floats on high o'er vales and hills,
When all at once I saw a crowd,
A host, of golden daffodils;
Beside the lake, beneath the trees,
Fluttering and dancing in the breeze.

Continuous as the stars that shine
And twinkle on the milky way,
They stretched in never-ending line
Along the margin of a bay: 10
Ten thousand saw I at a glance,
Tossing their heads in sprightly dance.

The waves beside them danced: but they
Out-did the sparkling waves in glee:
A poet could not but be gay,
In such a jocund company:
I gazed—and gazed—but little thought
What wealth the show to me had brought:

For oft, when on my couch I lie
In vacant or in pensive mood,   20
They flash upon that inward eye
Which is the bliss of solitude:[1]
And then my heart with pleasure fills,
And dances with the daffodils.

1804.]

---

[1] These two lines were composed by Mrs. Wordsworth.

ODE TO DUTY.

"Jam non consilio bonus, sed more eò perductus, ut non tantum
rectè facere possim, sed nisi rectè facere non possim."

[This Ode is on the model of Gray's Ode to Adversity, which is copied
from Horace's Ode to Fortune.—WORDSWORTH.]

Stern Daughter of the Voice of God!
O Duty! if that name thou love
Who art a light to guide, a rod
To check the erring, and reprove;
Thou, who art victory and law
When empty terrors overawe;
From vain temptations dost set free;
And calm'st the weary strife of frail humanity!

There are who ask not if thine eye
Be on them: who, in love and truth,   10
Where no misgiving is, rely
Upon the genial sense of youth:
Glad Hearts! without reproach or blot;
Who do thy work, and know it not:
Oh! if through confidence misplaced
They fail, thy saving arms, dread Power! around them cast.

Serene will be our days and bright,
And happy will our nature be,
When love is an unerring light,
And joy its own security.   20
And they a blissful course may hold
Even now, who, not unwisely bold,
Live in the spirit of this creed:
Yet seek thy firm support, according to their need.

I, loving freedom, and untried;
No sport of every random gust,
Yet being to myself a guide,
Too blindly have reposed my trust:
And oft, when in my heart was heard
Thy timely mandate, I deferred   30
The task, in smoother walks to stray;
But thee I now would serve more strictly, if I may.

Through no disturbance of my soul,
Or strong compunction in me wrought,
I supplicate for thy control;
But in the quietness of thought:
Me this unchartered freedom tires;
I feel the weight of chance-desires:
My hopes no more must change their name,
I long for a repose that ever is the same.   40

Stern Lawgiver! yet thou dost wear
The Godhead's most benignant grace;
Nor know we any thing so fair
As is the smile upon thy face:
Flowers laugh before thee on their beds
And fragrance in thy footing treads;
Thou dost preserve the stars from wrong;
And the most ancient heavens, through Thee, are fresh and
   strong.

To humbler functions, awful Power!
I call thee: I myself commend   50
Unto thy guidance from this hour;
Oh, let my weakness have an end!
Give unto me, made lowly wise,
The spirit of self-sacrifice:
The confidence of reason give;
And in the light of truth thy Bondman let me live!
1805.]

CHARACTER OF THE HAPPY WARRIOR.[1]

—Who is the happy Warrior? Who is he
That every man in arms should wish to be?
—It is the generous Spirit, who, when brought
Among the tasks of real life, hath wrought
Upon the plan that pleased his childish thought:
Whose high endeavours are an inward light
That makes the path before him always bright:
Who, with a natural instinct to discern
What knowledge can perform, is diligent to learn;
Abides by this resolve, and stops not there,   10
But makes his moral being his prime care;
Who, doomed to go in company with Pain,
And Fear, and Bloodshed, miserable train!
Turns his necessity to glorious gain;
In face of these doth exercise a power
Which is our human nature's highest dower;
Controls them and subdues, transmutes, bereaves
Of their bad influence, and their good receives:
By objects, which might force the soul to abate
Her feeling, rendered more compassionate;   20
Is placable—because occasions rise
So often that demand such sacrifice;
More skilful in self-knowledge, even more pure,
As tempted more; more able to endure,
As more exposed to suffering and distress;
Thence, also, more alive to tenderness.
—'Tis he whose law is reason: who depends
Upon that law as on the best of friends;

---

[1] Written after the death of Nelson, whose name, except for one supposed blot, Wordsworth would have wished to connect with the poem ; some elements are borrowed from the character of Wordsworth's sailor brother, John, who had been drowned but a short time before.

Whence, in a state where men are tempted still
To evil for a guard against worse ill,   30
And what in quality or act is best
Doth seldom on a right foundation rest,
He labours good on good to fix, and owes
To virtue every triumph that he knows:
—Who, if he rise to station of command,
Rises by open means; and there will stand
On honourable terms, or else retire,
And in himself possess his own desire;
Who comprehends his trust, and to the same
Keeps faithful with a singleness of aim;   40
And therefore does not stoop, nor lie in wait
For wealth, or honours, or for worldly state;
Whom they must follow; on whose head must fall,
Like showers of manna, if they come at all:
Whose powers shed round him in the common strife,
Or mild concerns of ordinary life,
A constant influence, a peculiar grace:
But who, if he be called upon to face
Some awful moment to which Heaven has joined
Great issues, good or bad for human kind,   50
Is happy as a Lover; and attired
With sudden brightness, like a Man inspired;
And, through the heat of conflict, keeps the law
In calmness made, and sees what he foresaw;
Or if an unexpected call succeed,
Come when it will, is equal to the need:
—He who, though thus endued as with a sense
And faculty for storm and turbulence,
Is yet a Soul whose master-bias leans
To homefelt pleasures and to gentle scenes;   60
Sweet images! which, wheresoe'er he be,
Are at his heart; and such fidelity
It is his darling passion to approve;

More brave for this, that he hath much to love:—
'Tis, finally, the Man, who, lifted high,
Conspicuous object in a Nation's eye,
Or left unthought-of in obscurity,—
Who, with a toward or untoward lot,
Prosperous or adverse, to his wish or not —
Plays, in the many games of life, that one   70
Where what he most doth value must be won:
Whom neither shape of danger can dismay,
Nor thought of tender happiness betray;
Who, not content that former worth stand fast,
Looks forward, persevering to the last,
From well to better, daily self-surpast:
Who, whether praise of him must walk the earth
For ever, and to noble deeds give birth,
Or he must fall, to sleep without his fame,
And leave a dead unprofitable name—   80
Finds comfort in himself and in his cause;
And, while the mortal mist is gathering, draws
His breath in confidence of Heaven's applause:
This is the happy **Warrior; this is He**
That every Man in arms should wish to be.

1806.]

"WITH HOW SAD STEPS, O MOON, THOU CLIMB'ST THE SKY."

With how sad steps, O Moon, thou climb'st the sky,
How silently, and with how wan a face! [1]
Where art thou? thou so often seen on high
Running among the clouds a Wood-nymph's race!
Unhappy Nuns, whose common breath's a sigh
Which they would stifle, move at such a pace!

[1] From a sonnet of Sir Philip Sydney. No. XXXI. of "Astrophel and Stella."

The northern Wind, to call thee to the chase,
Must blow to-night his bugle horn.   Had I
    The power of Merlin, Goddess!   this should be:
    And all the stars, fast as the clouds were riven,
    Should sally forth, to keep thee company,
    Hurrying and sparkling through the clear blue heaven;
    But, Cynthia! should to thee the palm be given,
    Queen both for beauty and for majesty.

1806.]

"THE WORLD IS TOO MUCH WITH US: LATE AND SOON."

    The world is too much with us: late and soon,
    Getting and spending, we lay waste our powers:
    Little we see in Nature that is ours;
    We have given our hearts away, a sordid boon!
    This Sea that bares her bosom to the moon;
    The winds that will be howling at all hours,
    And are up-gathered now like sleeping flowers;
    For this, for every thing, we are out of tune;
    It moves us not.—Great God! I'd rather be
    A Pagan suckled in a creed outworn;
    So might I, standing on this pleasant lea,
    Have glimpses that would make me less forlorn;
    Have sight of Proteus rising from the sea;
    Or hear old Triton blow his wreathed horn.

1806.]

"A FLOCK OF SHEEP THAT LEISURELY PASS BY."

A flock of sheep that leisurely pass by,
One after one; the sound of rain, and bees
Murmuring; the fall of rivers, winds and seas,
Smooth fields, white sheets of water, and pure sky;
I have thought of all by turns, and yet do lie
Sleepless! and soon the small birds' melodies
Must hear, first uttered from my orchard trees;
And the first cuckoo's melancholy cry.
Even thus last night, and two nights more, I lay,
And could not win thee, Sleep! by any stealth:
So do not let me wear to-night away:
Without Thee what is all the morning's wealth?
Come, blessed barrier between day and day,
Dear mother of fresh thoughts and joyous health!

1806.]

"WHERE LIES THE LAND TO WHICH YON SHIP MUST GO?"

Where lies the Land to which yon Ship must go?
Fresh as a lark mounting at break of day,
Festively she puts forth in trim array;
Is she for tropic suns, or polar snow?
What boots the inquiry?—Neither friend nor foe
She cares for; let her travel where she may,
She finds familiar names, a beaten way
Ever before her, and a wind to blow.
Yet still I ask, what haven is her mark?
And, almost as it was when ships were rare,

(From time to time, like Pilgrims, here and there
Crossing the waters) doubt, and something dark,
Of the old Sea some reverential fear,
Is with me at thy farewell, joyous Bark.

1806.]

ODE.

INTIMATIONS OF IMMORTALITY FROM RECOLLECTIONS OF EARLY CHILDHOOD.

The Child is father of the Man;
And I could wish my days to be
Bound each to each by natural piety.

I.

There was a time when meadow, grove, and stream,
The earth, and every common sight,
To me did seem
Apparelled in celestial light,
The glory and the freshness of a dream.
It is not now as it hath been of yore:—
Turn whereso'er I may,
By night or day,
The things which I have seen I now can see no more.

II.

The Rainbow comes and goes,
And lovely is the Rose;
The Moon doth with delight
Look round her when the heavens are bare,
Waters on a starry night
Are beautiful and fair;
The sunshine is a glorious birth;
But yet I know, where'er I go,
That there hath passed away a glory from the earth.

III.

Now, while the birds thus sing a joyous song,
    And while the young lambs bound   20
      As to the tabor's sound,
To me alone there came a thought of grief:
A timely utterance gave that thought relief,
    And I again am strong:
The cataracts blow their trumpets from the steep;
No more shall grief of mine the season wrong;
I hear the Echoes through the mountains throng,
The Winds come to me from the fields of sleep,
    And all the earth is gay;
      Land and sea   30
   Give themselves up to jollity,
    And with the heart of May
Doth every Beast keep holiday;—
    Thou Child of Joy,
Shout round me, let me hear thy shouts, thou happy
   Shepherd boy!

IV.

Ye blessed Creatures, I have heard the call
    Ye to each other make: I see
The heavens laugh with you in your jubilee;
    My heart is at your festival,
    My head hath its coronal,   40
The fulness of your bliss, I feel—I feel it all.
    Oh evil day! if I were sullen
    While the Earth herself is adorning,
      This sweet May-morning,
    And the Children are culling
      On every side,
    In a thousand valleys far and wide,
    Fresh flowers; while the sun shines warm,
And the Babe leaps up on his Mother's arm:—

I hear, I hear, with joy I hear! 50
    —But there's a Tree, of many, one,
A single Field which I have looked upon,
Both of them speak of something that is gone:
    The Pansy at my feet
    Doth the same tale repeat:
Whither is fled the visionary gleam?
Where is it now, the glory and the dream?

V.

Our birth is but a sleep and a forgetting:
The Soul that rises with us, our life's Star,
    Hath had elsewhere its setting, 60
      And cometh from afar:
    Not in entire forgetfulness,
    And not in utter nakedness,
But trailing clouds of glory do we come
    From God, who is our home:
Heaven lies about us in our infancy!
Shades of the prison-house begin to close
    Upon the growing Boy,
But He beholds the light, and whence it flows,
    He sees it in his joy; 70
The Youth, who daily farther from the east
    Must travel, still is Nature's Priest,
      And by the vision splendid
      Is on his way attended;
At length the Man perceives it die away,
And fade into the light of common day.

VI.

Earth fills her lap with pleasures of her own:
Yearnings she hath in her own natural kind,
And, even with something of a Mother's mind,
    And no unworthy aim, 80

The homely Nurse doth all she can
To make her Foster-child, her Inmate Man,
 Forget the glories he hath known,
And that imperial palace whence he came.

VII.

Behold the Child among his new-born blisses,
A six-years' Darling of a pigmy size!
See, where 'mid work of his own hand he lies,
Fretted by sallies of his mother's kisses,
With light upon him from his father's eyes!
See, at his feet, some little plan or chart,   90
Some fragment from his dream of human life,
Shaped by himself with newly-learned art;
  A wedding or a festival,
  A mourning or a funeral;
   And this hath now his heart,
  And unto this he frames his song:
   Then will he fit his tongue
To dialogues of business, love, or strife;
  But it will not be long
  Ere this be thrown aside,   100
  And with new joy and pride
The little Actor cons another part;
Filling from time to time his ' humorous stage '
With all the Persons, down to palsied Age,
That Life brings with her in her equipage;
  As if his whole vocation
  Were endless imitation.

VIII.

Thou, whose exterior semblance doth belie
  Thy Soul's immensity;
Thou best Philosopher, who yet dost keep   110
Thy heritage, thou Eye among the blind,

That, deaf and silent, read'st the eternal deep,
Haunted for ever by the eternal mind,—
  Mighty Prophet! Seer blest!
  On whom those truths do rest,
Which we are toiling all our lives to find,
In darkness lost, the darkness of the grave;
Thou, over whom thy Immortality
Broods like the Day, a Master o'er a Slave,
A Presence which is not to be put by;   120
Thou little Child, yet glorious in the might
Of heaven-born freedom on thy being's height,
Why with such earnest pains dost thou provoke
The years to bring the inevitable yoke.
Thus blindly with thy blessedness at strife?
Full soon thy Soul shall have her earthly freight,
And custom lie upon thee with a weight,
Heavy as frost, and deep almost as life!

      IX.

  O joy! that in our embers
  Is something that doth live,   130
  That nature yet remembers
  What was so fugitive!
The thought of our past years in me doth breed
Perpetual benediction: not indeed
For that which is most worthy to be blest;
Delight and liberty, the simple creed
Of Childhood, whether busy or at rest,
With new-fledged hope still fluttering in his breast:—
  Not for these I raise
  The song of thanks and praise: 140
  But for those obstinate questionings
  Of sense and outward things,
  Fallings from us, vanishings;
  Blank misgivings of a Creature

Moving about in worlds not realised,
High instincts before which our mortal Nature
Did tremble like a guilty Thing surprised:
    But for those first affections,
    Those shadowy recollections,
  Which, be they what they may,   150
Are yet the fountain light of all our day,
Are yet a master-light of all our seeing;
  Uphold us, cherish, and have power to make
Our noisy years seem moments in the being
Of the eternal Silence: truths that wake,
    To perish never;
Which neither listlessness, nor mad endeavour,
    Nor Man nor Boy,
  Nor all that is at enmity with joy,
  Can utterly abolish or destroy!   160
    Hence, in a season of calm weather,
    Though inland far we be,
Our Souls have sight of that immortal sea
    Which brought us hither,
  Can in a moment travel thither,
And see the Children sport upon the shore,
And hear the mighty waters rolling evermore.

X.

Then sing, ye Birds, sing, sing a joyous song!
    And let the young Lambs bound
    As to the tabor's sound!   170
We in thought will join your throng,
    Ye that pipe and ye that play,
    Ye that through your hearts to-day
    Feel the gladness of the May!
What though the radiance which was once so bright
Be now for ever taken from my sight,

Though nothing can bring back the hour
Of splendour in the grass, of glory in the flower;
    We will grieve not, rather find
    Strength in what remains behind;   180
    In the primal sympathy
    Which having been must ever be;
    In the soothing thoughts that spring
    Out of human suffering;
    In the faith that looks through death,
In years that bring the philosophic mind.

XI.

And O, ye Fountains, Meadows, Hills, and Groves,
Forebode not any severing of our loves!
Yet in my heart of hearts I feel your might;
I only have relinquished one delight   190
To live beneath your more habitual sway.
I love the Brooks which down their channels fret,
Even more than when I tripped lightly as they;
The innocent brightness of a new-born Day
    Is lovely yet;
The Clouds that gather round the setting sun
Do take a sober colouring from an eye
That hath kept watch o'er man's mortality;
Another race hath been, and other palms are won.
Thanks to the human heart by which we live,   200
Thanks to its tenderness, its joys, and fears,
To me the meanest flower that blows can give
Thoughts that do often lie too deep for tears.[1]

1803–1806.]

------

[1] Wordsworth protests that he does not mean to inculcate a belief in previous existence, though there is nothing in revelation to contradict it.

THOUGHT OF A BRITON ON THE SUBJUGATION OF SWITZERLAND.

Two Voices are there; one is of the sea,
One of the mountains; each a mighty Voice:
In both from age to age thou didst rejoice,
They were thy chosen music, Liberty!
There came a Tyrant, and with holy glee
Thou fought'st against him; but hast vainly striven:
Thou from thy Alpine holds at length art driven,
Where not a torrent murmurs heard by thee.
Of one deep bliss thine ear hath been bereft:
Then cleave, O cleave to that which still is left;
For, high-souled Maid, what sorrow would it be
That Mountain floods should thunder as before,
And Ocean bellow from his rocky shore,
And neither awful Voice be heard by thee!

1807.]

SONG AT THE FEAST OF BROUGHAM CASTLE,

UPON THE RESTORATION OF LORD CLIFFORD, THE SHEPHERD, TO THE ESTATES AND HONOURS OF HIS ANCESTORS.[1]

High in the breathless Hall the Minstrel sate,
And Emont's murmur mingled with the Song.—
The words of ancient time I thus translate,
A festal strain that hath been silent long:—

------

[1] During the Wars of the Roses, the Cliffords had drawn upon themselves the hatred of the House of York ; in particular John Lord Clifford, father of Henry, the subject of this poem, had murdered the young son of the Duke of York, after the battle of

" From town to town, from tower to tower,
The red rose is a gladsome flower.
Her thirty years of winter past,
The red rose is revived at last;
She lifts her head for endless spring,
For everlasting blossoming:	10
Both roses flourish, red and white:
In love and sisterly delight
The two that were at strife are blended,
And all old troubles now are ended.—
Joy! joy to both! but most to her
Who is the flower of Lancaster!
Behold her how She smiles to-day
On this great throng, this bright array!
Fair greeting doth she send to all
From every corner of the hall;	20
But chiefly from above the board
Where sits in state our rightful Lord,
A Clifford to his own restored!

" They came with banner, spear, and shield;
And it was proved in Bosworth-field.
Not long the Avenger was withstood—
Earth helped him with the cry of blood:
St. George was for us, and the might
Of blessed Angels crowned the right.
Loud voice the Land has uttered forth,	30
We loudest in the faithful north:
Our fields rejoice, our mountains ring,
Our streams proclaim a welcoming;
Our strong-abodes and castles see
The glory of their loyalty.

Towton. For this, his lands were confiscated ; and Henry was brought up in con-
cealment. He was restored to his rights after twenty-four years, in the reign of
Henry VII., who by his marriage with Elizabeth of York, united the factions of the
Red and the White Roses.

"How glad is Skipton at this hour—
Though lonely, a deserted Tower;
Knight, squire, and yeoman, page and groom:
We have them at the feast of Brough'm.[1]
How glad Pendragon[1]—though the sleep   40
Of years be on her!—She shall reap
A taste of this great pleasure, viewing
As in a dream her own renewing.
Rejoiced is Brough,[1] right glad I deem
Beside her little humble stream;
And she that keepeth watch and ward
Her statelier Eden's course to guard;
They both are happy at this hour,
Though each is but a lonely Tower:—
But here is perfect joy and pride   50
For one fair House by Emont's side,
This day, distinguished without peer
To see her Master and to cheer—
Him, and his Lady-mother dear!

"Oh! it was a time forlorn
When the fatherless was born—
Give her wings that she may fly,
Or she sees her infant die!
Swords that are with slaughter wild
Hunt the Mother and the Child.   60
Who will take them from the light?
—Yonder is a man in sight—
Yonder is a house—but where?
No, they must not enter there.
To the caves, and to the brooks,
To the clouds of heaven she looks;

[1] These "Castles" or towers of defence, relics of feudal times, have been alternately repaired and demolished by the Cliffords and their enemies. They were a source of special pride in the family.

She is speechless, but her eyes
Pray in ghostly agonies.
Blissful Mary, Mother mild,
Maid and Mother undefiled,   70
Save a Mother and her Child!

" Now Who is he that bounds with joy
On Carrock's side, a Shepherd-boy?
No thoughts hath he but thoughts that pass
Light as the wind along the grass.
Can this be He who hither came
In secret, like a smothered flame?
O'er whom such thankful tears were shed
For shelter, and a poor man's bread!
God loves the Child; and God hath willed 80
That those dear words should be fulfilled,
The Lady's words, when forced away,
The last she to her Babe did say:
' My own, my own, thy Fellow-guest
I may not be: but rest thee, rest,
For lowly shepherd's life is best!'

" Alas! when evil men are strong
No life is good, no pleasure long.
The Boy must part from Mosedale's groves,
And leave Blencathara's rugged coves, 90
And quit the flowers that summer brings
To Glenderamakin's lofty springs:
Must vanish, and his careless cheer
Be turned to heaviness and fear.
—Give Sir Lancelot Threlkeld praise!
Hear it, good man, old in days!
Thou tree of covert and of rest
For this young Bird that is distrest;
Among thy branches safe he lay,

And he was free to sport and play,   100
When falcons were abroad for prey.

" A recreant harp, that sings of fear
And heaviness in Clifford's ear!
I said, when evil men are strong,
No life is good, no pleasure long,
A weak and cowardly untruth!
Our Clifford was a happy Youth,
And thankful through a weary time,
That brought him up to manhood's prime.
—Again he wanders forth at will,   110
And tends a flock from hill to hill:
His garb is humble: ne'er was seen
Such garb with such a noble mien;
Among the shepherd grooms no mate
Hath he, a Child of strength and state!
Yet lacks not friends for simple glee,
Nor yet for higher sympathy.
To his side the fallow-deer
Came, and rested without fear;
The eagle, lord of land and sea,   120
Stooped down to pay him fealty;
And both the undying fish that swim [1]
Through Bowscale-tarn did wait on him;
The pair were servants of his eye
In their immortality;
And glancing, gleaming, dark or bright,
Moved to and fro, for his delight.
He knew the rocks which Angels haunt
Upon the mountains visitant;
He hath kenned them taking wing;   130
And into caves where Fairies sing

---

[1] It is imagined by the people of the country, that there are two immortal Fish, inhabitants of this Tarn, which lies in the mountains not far from Threlkeld.—W. W.

He hath entered; and been told
By Voices how men lived of old.
Among the heavens his eye can see
The face of thing that is to be;
And, if that men report him right,
His tongue could whisper words of might.
—Now another day is come,
Fitter hope, and nobler doom;
He hath thrown aside his crook,   140
And hath buried deep his book;
Armour rusting in his halls
On the blood of Clifford calls;—
' Quell the Scot,' exclaims the Lance—
Bear me to the heart of France,
Is the longing of the Shield—
Tell thy name, thou trembling Field;
Field of death, where'er thou be,
Groan thou with our victory!
Happy day, and mighty hour,   150
When our Shepherd, in his power,
Mailed and horsed, with lance and sword,
To his ancestors restored
Like a re-appearing Star,
Like a glory from afar,
First shall head the flock of war! "

Alas! the impassioned minstrel did not know
How, by Heaven's grace, this Clifford's heart was framed,
How he, long forced in humble walks to go,
Was softened into feeling, soothed, and tamed.   160

Love had he found in huts where poor men lie:
His daily teachers had been woods and rills,
The silence that is in the starry sky,
The sleep that is among the lonely hills.

In him the savage virtue of the Race,
Revenge, and all ferocious thoughts were dead:
Nor did he change; but kept in lofty place
The wisdom which adversity had bred.

Glad were the vales, and every cottage hearth;
The Shepherd-lord was honoured more and more;   170
And, ages after he was laid in earth,
" The good Lord Clifford " was the name he bore.

1807.]

LAODAMIA.

" With sacrifice before the rising morn
Vows have I made by fruitless hope inspired;
And from the infernal Gods, 'mid shades forlorn
Of night, my slaughtered Lord have I required:
Celestial pity I again implore:—
Restore him to my sight—great Jove, restore! "

So speaking, and by fervent love endowed
With faith, the Suppliant heavenward lifts her hands;
While, like the sun emerging from a cloud,
Her countenance brightens—and her eye expands;   10
Her bosom heaves and spreads, her stature grows;
And she expects the issue in repose.

O terror! what hath she perceived?—O joy!
What doth she look on?—whom doth she behold?
Her Hero slain upon the beach of Troy?
His vital presence? his corporeal mould?
It is—if sense deceive her not—'tis He!
And a God leads him—winged Mercury!

Mild Hermes spake—and touched her with his wand
That calms all fear; " Such grace hath crowned thy prayer,
Laodamía! that at Jove's command   21
Thy Husband walks the paths of upper air:
He comes to tarry with thee three hours' space;
Accept the gift, behold him face to face! "

Forth sprang the impassioned Queen her Lord to clasp;
Again that consummation she essayed;
But unsubstantial Form eludes her grasp
As often as that eager grasp was made.
The Phantom parts—but parts to re-unite,
And re-assume his place before her sight.   30

" Protesiláus, lo! thy guide is gone!
Confirm, I pray, the Vision with thy voice:
This is our palace,—yonder is thy throne;
Speak, and the floor thou tread'st on will rejoice.
Not to appal me have the Gods bestowed
This precious boon; and blest a sad abode."

" Great Jove, Laodamía! doth not leave
His gifts imperfect:—Spectre though I be,
I am not sent to scare thee or deceive:
But in reward of thy fidelity,   40
And something also did my worth obtain:
For fearless virtue bringeth boundless gain.

" Thou knowest, the Delphic oracle foretold
That the first Greek who touched the Trojan strand
Should die; but me the threat could not withhold:
A generous cause a victim did demand;
And forth I leapt upon the sandy plain;
A self-devoted chief—by Hector slain."

" Supreme of Heroes—bravest, noblest, best!
Thy matchless courage I bewail no more,
Which then, when tens of thousands were deprest
By doubt, propelled thee to the fatal shore;
Thou found'st—and I forgive thee—here thou art—
A nobler counsellor than my poor heart.

" But thou, though capable of sternest deed,
Wert kind as resolute, and good as brave;
And he, whose power restores thee, hath decreed
Thou should'st elude the malice of the grave:
Redundant are thy locks, thy lips as fair
As when their breath enriched Thessalian air.

" No Spectre greets me,—no vain Shadow this:
Come, blooming Hero, place thee by my side!
Give, on this well-known couch, one nuptial kiss
To me, this day, a second time thy bride! "
Jove frowned in heaven: the conscious Parcæ threw
Upon those roseate lips a Stygian hue.

" This visage tells thee that my doom is past:
Nor should the change be mourned, even if the joys
Of sense were able to return as fast
And surely as they vanish.   Earth destroys
Those raptures duly—Erebus disdains:
Calm pleasures there abide—majestic pains.

" Be taught, O faithful Consort, to controul
Rebellious passion: for the Gods approve
The depth, and not the tumult, of the soul;
A fervent, not ungovernable, love.
Thy transports moderate; and meekly mourn
When I depart, for brief is my sojourn—"

" Ah, wherefore?—Did not Hercules by force
Wrest from the guardian Monster of the tomb 80
Alcestis, a reanimated corse,
Given back to dwell on earth in vernal bloom?
Medea's spells dispersed the weight of years,
And Æson stood a youth 'mid youthful peers.

" The Gods to us are merciful—and they
Yet further may relent: for mightier far
Than strength of nerve and sinew, or the sway
Of magic potent over sun and star,
Is love, though oft to agony distrest,
And though his favorite seat be feeble woman's breast. 90

" But if thou goest, I follow—" " Peace! " he said,—
She looked upon him and was calmed and cheered;
The ghastly colour from his lips had fled;
In his deportment, shape, and mien, appeared
Elysian beauty, melancholy grace,
Brought from a pensive though a happy place.

He spake of love, such love as Spirits feel
In worlds whose course is equable and pure;
No fears to beat away—no strife to heal—
The past unsighed for, and the future sure; 100
Spake of heroic arts in graver mood
Revived, with finer harmony pursued;

Of all that is most beauteous—imaged there
In happier beauty; more pellucid streams,
An ampler ether, a diviner air,
And fields invested with purpureal gleams;
Climes which the sun, who sheds the brightest day
Earth knows, is all unworthy to survey.

Yet there the Soul shall enter which hath earned
That privilege by virtue.—" Ill," said he,   110
" The end of man's existence I discerned,
Who from ignoble games and revelry
Could draw, when we had parted, vain delight,
While tears were thy best pastime, day and night;

" And while my youthful peers, before my eyes
(Each hero following his peculiar bent)
Prepared themselves for glorious enterprise
By martial sports,—or, seated in the tent,
Chieftains and kings in council were detained;
What time the fleet at Aulis lay enchained.   120

" The wished-for wind was given:—I then revolved
The oracle, upon the silent sea;
And, if no worthier led the way, resolved
That, of a thousand vessels, mine should be
The foremost prow in pressing to the strand,—
Mine the first blood that tinged the Trojan sand.

" Yet bitter, oft-times bitter, was the pang
When of thy loss I thought, beloved Wife!
On thee too fondly did my memory hang,
And on the joys we shared in mortal life,—   130
The paths which we had trod—these fountains, flowers;
My new-planned cities, and unfinished towers.

" But should suspense permit the Foe to cry,
' Behold they tremble!—haughty their array,
Yet of their number no one dares to die '?
In soul I swept the indignity away:
Old frailties then recurred:—but lofty thought,
In act embodied, my deliverance wrought.

" And Thou, though strong in love, art all too weak
In reason, in self-government too slow;   140
I counsel thee by fortitude to seek
Our blest re-union in the shades below.
The invisible world with thee hath sympathised;
Be thy affections raised and solemnised.

" Learn, by a mortal yearning, to ascend—
Seeking a higher object. Love was given,
Encouraged, sanctioned, chiefly for that end;
For this the passion to excess was driven—
That self might be annulled; her bondage prove
The fetters of a dream, opposed to love."——   150

Aloud she shrieked; for Hermes re-appears!
Round the dear Shade she would have clung—'tis vain:
The hours are past—too brief had they been years;
And him no mortal effort can detain:
Swift, toward the realms that know not earthly day,
He through the portal takes his silent way,
And on the palace floor a lifeless corse She lay.

Thus, all in vain exhorted and reproved,
She perished; and, as for a wilful crime,
By the just Gods whom no weak pity moved,   160
Was doomed to wear out her appointed time,
Apart from happy Ghosts, that gather flowers
Of blissful quiet 'mid unfading bowers.

—Yet tears to human suffering are due:
And mortal hopes defeated and o'erthrown
Are mourned by man, and not by man alone,
As fondly he believes.—Upon the side
Of Hellespont (such faith was entertained)
A knot of spiry trees for ages grew

From out of the tomb of him for whom she died;　170
And ever, when such stature they had gained
That Ilium's walls were subject to their view,
The trees' tall summits withered at the sight:
A constant interchange of growth and blight! [1]

1814.]

YARROW VISITED,

SEPTEMBER, 1814.

And is this—Yarrow?—*This* the Stream
Of which my fancy cherished,
So faithfully, a waking dream?
An image that hath perished!
O that some Minstrel's harp were near,
To utter notes of gladness,
And chase this silence from the air,
That fills my heart with sadness!

Yet why?—a silvery current flows
With uncontrolled meanderings;　10
Nor have these eyes by greener hills
Been soothed, in all my wanderings.
And, through her depths, Saint Mary's Lake
Is visibly delighted:
For not a feature of those hills
Is in the mirror slighted.

A blue sky bends o'er Yarrow vale,
Save where that pearly whiteness

---

[1] For other endings of " Laodamia " consult Knight's Wordsworth.

Is round the rising sun diffused,
A tender hazy brightness; 20
Mild dawn of promise! that excludes
All profitless dejection;
Though not unwilling here to admit
A pensive recollection.

Where was it that the famous Flower
Of Yarrow Vale lay bleeding?
His bed perchance was yon smooth mound
On which the herd is feeding:
And haply from this crystal pool,
Now peaceful as the morning, 30
The Water-wraith ascended thrice—
And gave his doleful warning.

Delicious is the Lay that sings
The haunts of happy Lovers,
The path that leads them to the grove,
The leafy grove that covers:
And Pity sanctifies the Verse
That paints, by strength of sorrow,
The unconquerable strength of love;
Bear witness, rueful Yarrow! 40

But thou, that didst appear so fair
To fond imagination,
Dost rival in the light of day
Her delicate creation:
Meek loveliness is round thee spread,
A softness still and holy;
The grace of forest charms decayed,
And pastoral melancholy.

That region left, the vale unfolds
Rich groves of lofty stature,   50
With Yarrow winding through the pomp
Of cultivated nature;
And, rising from those lofty groves,
Behold a Ruin hoary!
The shattered front of Newark's Towers,
Renowned in Border story.

Fair scenes for childhood's opening bloom,
For sportive youth to stray in;
For manhood to enjoy his strength;
And age to wear away in!   60
Yon cottage seems a bower of bliss,
A covert for protection
Of tender thoughts, that nestle there—
The brood of chaste affection.

How sweet, on this autumnal day,
The wild-wood fruits to gather,
And on my True-love's forehead plant
A crest of blooming heather!
And what if I enwreathed my own!
'Twere no offence to reason;   70
The sober Hills thus deck their brows
To meet the wintry season.

I see—but not by sight alone,
Loved Yarrow, have I won thee;
A ray of fancy still survives—
Her sunshine plays upon thee!
Thy ever-youthful waters keep
A course of lively pleasure;
And gladsome notes my lips can breathe,
Accordant to the measure.   80

The vapours linger round the Heights,
They melt, and soon must vanish;
One hour is theirs, no more is mine—
Sad thought, which I would banish,
But that I know, where'er I go,
Thy genuine image, Yarrow!
Will dwell with me—to heighten joy,
And cheer my mind in sorrow.

TO A SKYLARK.

Ethereal minstrel! pilgrim of the sky!
Dost thou despise the earth where cares abound?
Or, while the wings aspire, are heart and eye
Both with thy nest upon the dewy ground?
Thy nest which thou canst drop into at will,
Those quivering wings composed, that music still!

To the last point of vision, and beyond,
Mount, daring warbler! that love-prompted strain
('Twixt thee and thine a never-failing bond)
Thrills not the less the bosom of the plain:
Yet might'st thou seem, proud privilege! to sing
All independent of the leafy spring.[1]

Leave to the nightingale her shady wood;
A privacy of glorious light is thine;
Whence thou dost pour upon the world a flood
Of harmony, with instinct more divine;
Type of the wise who soar, but never roam;
True to the kindred points of Heaven and Home!

1825.]

---

[1] This stanza appeared only in the editions of 1827–43.   In 1845 it was transferred
to "A Morning Exercise."

S. T. COLERIDGE.

Into the Depth of Clouds, that Veil thy breast—
Thou too once more, stupendous Mountain! thou,
That as I raise my Head, awhile bow'd low
In adoration, upward from thy Base
Slow - travelling, with dim eyes, suffused with - Tears,
Solemnly seemest, like a Vapoury Cloud,
To rise before me - Rise, o ever Rise, &
Rise, like a Cloud of Incense, from the Earth!

Thou Kingly Spirit throned among the Hills,
Thou dread Ambassador from Earth to Heaven,
Great Hierarch! tell thou the silent Sky,
And tell the Stars, and tell yon rising Sun,
Earth with her thousand Voices praises God.

S. T. Coleridge

SAMUEL TAYLOR COLERIDGE.

Fac-simile of one stanza of "Hymn before Sunrise in the Vale of Chamounix," copied by Coleridge in a letter to Mrs. Brabant, 1815.

SELECTIONS FROM COLERIDGE

THE EOLIAN HARP.

COMPOSED AT CLEVEDON, SOMERSETSHIRE.

My pensive Sara! thy soft cheek reclined
Thus on mine arm, most soothing sweet it is
To sit beside our cot, our cot o'ergrown
With white-flowered Jasmin and the broad-leaved Myrtle
(Meet emblems they of Innocence and Love!),
And watch the clouds, that late were rich with light,
Slow saddening round, and mark the star of eve
Serenely brilliant (such should wisdom be)
Shine opposite! How exquisite the scents
Snatched from yon bean-field! and the world so hushed!   10
The stilly murmur of the distant Sea
Tells us of Silence.
              And that simplest Lute,
Placed lengthways in the clasping casement, hark!
How by the desultory breeze caressed,
Like some coy maid half yielding to her lover,
It pours such sweet upbraiding, as must needs
Tempt to repeat the wrong! And now, its strings
Boldlier swept, the long sequacious notes
Over delicious surges sink and rise,
Such a soft floating witchery of sound   20
As twilight Elfins make, when they at eve
Voyage on gentle gales from Fairy-Land,
Where Melodies round honey-dropping flowers,

Footless and wild, like birds of Paradise,
Nor pause, nor perch, hovering on untamed wing!
O the one life within us and abroad,
Which meets all motion and becomes its soul,
A light in sound, a sound-like power in light,
Rhythm in all thought, and joyance everywhere—
Methinks, it should have been impossible   30
Not to love all things in a world so filled;
Where the breeze warbles, and the mute still air
Is Music slumbering on her instrument.

And thus, my love! as on the midway slope
Of yonder hill I stretch my limbs at noon,
Whilst through my half-closed eyelids I behold
The sunbeams dance, like diamonds, on the main,
And tranquil muse upon tranquillity;
Full many a thought uncalled and undetained,
And many idle flitting phantasies,   40
Traverse my indolent and passive brain,
As wild and various as the random gales
That swell and flutter on this subject lute!

And what if all of animated nature
Be but organic harps diversely framed,
That tremble into thought, as o'er them sweeps,
Plastic and vast, one intellectual breeze,
At once the Soul of each, and God of All?

But thy more serious eye a mild reproof
Darts, O beloved woman! nor such thoughts   50
Dim and unhallowed dost thou not reject,
And biddest me walk humbly with my God.
Meek daughter in the family of Christ!
Well hast thou said and holily dispraised
These shapings of the unregenerate mind;

Bubbles that glitter as they rise and break
On vain Philosophy's aye-babbling spring.
For never guiltless may I speak of him,
The Incomprehensible! save when with awe
I praise him, and with Faith that inly feels;   60
Who with his saving mercies healed me,
A sinful and most miserable Man,
Wildered and dark, and gave me to possess
Peace, and this Cot, and thee, dear honoured Maid!

August 20, 1795.]

SONNET.

TO A FRIEND WHO ASKED, HOW I FELT WHEN THE NURSE FIRST PRESENTED MY INFANT TO ME.

Charles! my slow heart was only sad, when first
I scanned that face of feeble infancy:
For dimly on my thoughtful spirit burst
All I had been, and all my child might be!
But when I saw it on its Mother's arm,
And hanging at her bosom (she the while
Bent o'er its features with a tearful smile),
Then I was thrilled and melted, and most warm
Impressed a Father's kiss: and all beguiled
Of dark remembrance and presageful fear.
I seemed to see an angel-form appear—
'Twas even thine, beloved woman mild!
So for the Mother's sake the Child was dear,
And dearer was the Mother for the Child.

1796.]

THE RIME OF THE ANCIENT MARINER.[1]

IN SEVEN PARTS.

Facile credo, plures esse Naturas invisibiles quam visibiles in rerum universitate. Sed horum omnium familiam quis nobis enarrabit, et gradus et cognationes et discrimina et singulorum munera? Quid agunt? quæ loca habitant? Harum rerum notitiam semper ambivit ingenium humanum, nunquam attigit. Juvat, interea, non diffiteor, quandoque in animo, tanquam in tabulâ, majoris et melioris mundi imaginem contemplari : ne mens assuefacta hodiernæ vitæ minutiis se contrahat nimis, et tota subsidat in pusillas cogitationes. Sed veritati interea invigilandum est, modusque servandus, ut certa ab incertis, diem a nocte, distinguamus.

T. BURNET : "Archæol. Phil.," p. 68.

Argument.

How a Ship having passed the Line was driven by storms to the cold Country toward the South Pole; and how from thence she made her course to the tropical Latitude of the Great Pacific Ocean; and of the strange things that befell; and in what manner the Ancyent Marinere came back to his own Country.   [1798.]

PART I.

<table>
<tr><td>An ancient Mariner meeteth three Gallants bidden to a wedding-feast, and detaineth one.</td><td>

It is an ancient Mariner,
And he stoppeth one of three.
' By thy long grey beard and glittering eye,
Now wherefore stopp'st thou me?

The Bridegroom's doors are opened wide,
And I am next of kin;
The guests are met, the feast is set:
May'st hear the merry din.'

</td></tr>
</table>

---

[1] This poem formed the beginning of " Lyrical Ballads " as first printed.   For its genesis see " Biographia Literaria," Chap. XIV., and the notes of Campbell's edition of " Coleridge's Poetical Works." [Macmillan.] The text here given is approximately that of the " Lyrical Ballads," edition of 1800. For the original version, 1798, with archaic spelling and many variations in the text, see Appendix E of Campbell's Coleridge.

The marginal glosses were added in " Sibylline Leaves," 1817.

He holds him with his skinny hand,
'There was a ship,' quoth he.   10
'Hold off! unhand me, grey-beard loon!'
Eftsoons his hand dropt he.

<table>
<tr><td>

The Wedding-
Guest is spell-
bound by the
eye of the old
seafaring
man, and con-
strained to
hear his tale.

</td><td>

He holds him with his glittering eye—
The Wedding-Guest stood still,
And listens like a three years' child:
The Mariner hath his will.

</td></tr>
</table>

The Wedding-Guest sat on a stone:
He cannot choose but hear;
And thus spake on that ancient man,
The bright-eyed Mariner.   20

' The ship was cheered, the harbour cleared,
Merrily did we drop
Below the kirk, below the hill,
Below the lighthouse top.

The Mariner
tells how the
ship sailed
southward
with a good
wind and fair
weather, till
it reached the
Line.

The sun came up upon the left,
Out of the sea came he!
And he shone bright, and on the right
Went down into the sea.

Higher and higher every day,
Till over the mast at noon—'   30
The Wedding-Guest here beat his breast,
For he heard the loud bassoon.

The Wedding-
Guest heareth
the bridal
music ; but
the Mariner
continueth his
tale.

The bride hath paced into the hall,
Red as a rose is she;
Nodding their heads before her goes
The merry minstrelsy.

The Wedding-Guest he beat his breast,
Yet he cannot choose but hear:

And thus spake on that ancient man,
The bright-eyed Mariner.   40

The ship
drawn by a
storm toward
the south pole.

'And now the Storm-Blast came, and he
Was tyrannous and strong:
He struck with his o'ertaking wings,
And chased us south along.

With sloping masts and dipping prow,
As who pursued with yell and blow
Still treads the shadow of his foe,
And forward bends his head,
The ship drove fast, loud roared the blast,
And southward aye we fled.   50

And now there came both mist and snow,
And it grew wondrous cold:
And ice, mast-high, came floating by,
As green as emerald.

The land of
ice, and of
fearful
sounds, where
no living
thing was to be
seen.

And through the drifts the snowy clifts
Did send a dismal sheen:
Nor shapes of men nor beasts we ken—
The ice was all between.

The ice was here, the ice was there,
The ice was all around: 60
It cracked and growled, and roared and howled,
Like noises in a swound!

Till a great
sea-bird,
called the
Albatross,
came through
the snow-fog,
and was re-
ceived with
great joy and
hospitality.

At length did cross an Albatross,
Thorough the fog it came:
As if it had been a Christian soul,
We hailed it in God's name.

It ate the food it ne'er had eat,
And round and round it flew.

The ice did split with a thunder-fit;
The helmsman steered us through! 70

And lo! the Albatross proveth a bird of good omen, and followeth the ship as it returned northward, through fog and floating ice.

And a good south wind sprung up behind;
The Albatross did follow,
And every day, for food or play,
Came to the mariner's hollo!

In mist or cloud, on mast or shroud,
It perched for vespers nine;
Whiles all the night, through fog-smoke white,
Glimmered the white moon-shine.'

The ancient Mariner inhospitably killeth the pious bird of good omen.

' God save thee, ancient Mariner!
From the fiends, that plague thee thus!— 80
Why look'st thou so? '—With my cross-bow
I shot the Albatross.

Part II.

The sun now rose upon the right:
Out of the sea came he,
Still hid in mist, and on the left
Went down into the sea.

And the good south wind still blew behind,
But no sweet bird did follow,
Nor any day for food or play
Came to the mariner's hollo! 90

His shipmates cry out against the ancient Mariner, for killing the bird of good luck.

And I had done a hellish thing,
And it would work 'em woe:
For all averred, I had killed the bird
That made the breeze to blow.
Ah wretch! said they, the bird to slay,
That made the breeze to blow!

But when the
fog cleared
off, they jus-
tify the same,
and thus make
themselves
accomplices
in the crime.

Nor dim nor red, like God's own head,
The glorious Sun uprist:
Then all averred, I had killed the bird
That brought the fog and mist.   100
'Twas right, said they, such birds to slay,
That bring the fog and mist.

The fair breeze
continues ; the
ship enters the
Pacific Ocean,
and sails north-
ward, even till
it reaches the
Line.

The fair breeze blew, the white foam flew,
The furrow followed free: [1]
We were the first that ever burst
Into that silent sea.

The ship hath
been suddenly
becalmed.

Down dropt the breeze, the sails dropt down,
'Twas sad as sad could be;
And we did speak only to break
The silence of the sea!   110

All in a hot and copper sky,
The bloody Sun, at noon,
Right up above the mast did stand,
No bigger than the Moon.

Day after day, day after day,
We stuck, nor breath nor motion;
As idle as a painted ship
Upon a painted ocean.

And the Al-
batross begins
to be avenged.

Water, water, every where,
And all the boards did shrink;   120
Water, water, every where,
Nor any drop to drink.

---

[1] This is the original reading. In "Sibylline Leaves," Coleridge having observed
that this was the appearance as seen by a spectator from the shore or from another
vessel, changed the line to:

The furrow stream'd off free.

In 1828 he replaced the more euphonious, if less correct form.

The very deep did rot: O Christ!
That ever this should be!
Yea, slimy things did crawl with legs
Upon the slimy sea.

About, about, in reel and rout
The death-fires danced at night;
The water, like a witch's oils,
Burnt green, and blue and white.   130

And some in dreams assured were
Of the Spirit that plagued us so:
Nine fathom deep he had followed us
From the land of mist and snow.

And every tongue, through utter drought,
Was withered at the root;
We could not speak, no more than if
We had been choked with soot.

Ah! well-a-day! what evil looks
Had I from old and young!   140
Instead of the cross, the Albatross
About my neck was hung.

PART III.

There passed a weary time.   Each throat
Was parched, and glazed each eye.
A weary time! a weary time!
How glazed each weary eye!
When looking westward, I beheld
A something in the sky.

At first it seemed a little speck,
And then it seemed a mist:

It moved and moved, and took at last
A certain shape, I wist.

A speck, a mist, a shape, I wist!
And still it neared and neared:
As if it dodged a water-sprite,
It plunged and tacked and veered.

With throats unslaked, with black lips baked,
We could nor laugh nor wail;
Through utter drought all dumb we stood!
I bit my arm, I sucked the blood,   160
And cried, A sail! a sail!

With throats unslaked, with black lips baked,
Agape they heard me call:
Gramercy! they for joy did grin,
And all at once their breath drew in,
As they were drinking all.

See! see! (I cried) she tacks no more!
Hither to work us weal;
Without a breeze, without a tide,
She steadies with upright keel!   170

The western wave was all a-flame,
The day was well nigh done!
Almost upon the western wave
Rested the broad bright Sun:
When that strange shape drove suddenly
Betwixt us and the Sun.

And straight the Sun was flecked with bars,
(Heaven's Mother send us grace!)
As if through a dungeon-grate he peered,
With broad and burning face.   180

Gloss (left margin):

At its nearer approach, it seemeth him to be a ship; and at a dear ransom he freeth his speech from the bonds of thirst.

A flash of joy;

And horror follows. For can it be a ship that comes onward without wind or tide?

It seemeth him but the skeleton of a ship.

Alas! (thought I, and my heart beat loud)
How fast she nears and nears!
Are those her sails that glance in the Sun,
Like restless gossameres?

And its ribs are seen as bars on the face of the setting Sun.
The Spectre-Woman and her Death-mate, and no other on board the skeleton-ship.

Are those her ribs through which the Sun
Did peer, as through a grate?
And is that Woman all her crew?
Is that a Death? and are there two?
Is Death that Woman's mate? [1]

Like vessel, like crew!

Her lips were red, her looks were free,   190
Her locks were yellow as gold:
Her skin was as white as leprosy,
The Night-mare Life-in-Death was she,
Who thicks man's blood with cold.

Death and Life-in-Death have diced for the ship's crew, and she (the latter) winneth the ancient Mariner.

The naked hulk alongside came,
And the twain were casting dice:
' The game is done! I've won, I've won!'
Quoth she, and whistles thrice.

No twilight within the courts of the Sun.

The Sun's rim dips: the stars rush out:
At one stride comes the dark;   200
With far-heard whisper, o'er the sea,
Off shot the spectre-bark.

At the rising of the Moon,

We listened and looked sideways up!
Fear at my heart, as at a cup,
My life-blood seemed to sip!
The stars were dim, and thick the night,
The steersman's face by his lamp gleamed white;

---

[1] In the edition of 1798, the account of Death and the Woman was much more horrible, as was the case also in the first draft of the description of Geraldine in " Christabel"; later, Coleridge with his fine perceptions saw that it would be more effective not to present too distinct a visual image, but to leave more to the imagination.

From the sails the dew did drip—
Till clomb above the eastern bar
The horned Moon, with one bright star   210
Within the nether tip.[1]

One after
another,

One after one, by the star-dogged Moon,
Too quick for groan or sigh,
Each turned his face with a ghastly pang,
And cursed me with his eye.

His shipmates
drop down
dead.

Four times fifty living men,
(And I heard nor sigh nor groan)
With heavy thump, a lifeless lump,
They dropped down one by one.

But Life-in-
Death be-
gins her work
on the ancient
Mariner.

The souls did from their bodies fly,—   220
They fled to bliss or woe!
And every soul, it passed me by,
Like the whizz of my cross-bow!

PART IV.

The Wedding-
Guest feareth
that a Spirit is
talking to him;

'I fear thee, ancient Mariner!
I fear thy skinny hand!
And thou art long, and lank, and brown,
As is the ribbed sea-sand.[2]

I fear thee and thy glittering eye,
And thy skinny hand, so brown.'—

[1] Coleridge had heard of a "superstition among sailors that something evil is about to happen whenever a star dogs the moon." Perhaps it is hardly necessary to call attention to the fact that a star can never be seen between the horns of the crescent moon.

[2] For the last two lines of this stanza I am indebted to Mr. Wordsworth. —S. T. C.

Fear not, fear not, thou Wedding-Guest! 230
This body dropt not down.

Alone, alone, all, all alone,
Alone on a wide wide sea!
And never a saint took pity on
My soul in agony.

The many men, so beautiful!
And they all dead did lie:
And a thousand thousand slimy things
Lived on; and so did I.

I looked upon the rotting sea, 240
And drew my eyes away;
I looked upon the rotting deck,
And there the dead men lay.

I looked to heaven, and tried to pray;
But or ever a prayer had gusht,
A wicked whisper came, and made
My heart as dry as dust.

I closed my lids, and kept them close,
And the balls like pulses beat;
For the sky and the sea, and the sea and the
    sky 250
Lay like a load on my weary eye,
And the dead were at my feet.

The cold sweat melted from their limbs,
Nor rot nor reek did they:
The look with which they looked on me
Had never passed away.

An orphan's curse would drag to hell
A spirit from on high;

But oh! more horrible than that
Is a curse in a dead man's eye! 260
Seven days, seven nights, I saw that curse,
And yet I could not die.

The moving Moon went up the sky,
And no where did abide:
Softly she was going up,
And a star or two beside—

Her beams bemocked the sultry main,
Like April hoar-frost spread:
But where the ship's huge shadow lay,
The charmed water burnt alway 270
A still and awful red.

Beyond the shadow of the ship,
I watched the water-snakes:
They moved in tracks of shining white,
And when they reared, the elfish light
Fell off in hoary flakes.

Within the shadow of the ship
I watched their rich attire:
Blue, glossy green, and velvet black,
They coiled and swam; and every track 280
Was a flash of golden fire.

O happy living things! no tongue
Their beauty might declare:
A spring of love gushed from my heart,
And I blessed them unaware:

Sure my kind saint took pity on me,
And I blessed them unaware!

The spell be-
gins to break.

The selfsame moment I could pray;
And from my neck so free
The Albatross fell off, and sank   290
Like lead into the sea.

Part V.

Oh sleep! it is a gentle thing,
Beloved from pole to pole!
To Mary Queen the praise be given!
She sent the gentle sleep from Heaven,
That slid into my soul.

By grace of
the holy
Mother, the
ancient Mari-
ner is refreshed
with rain.

The silly buckets on the deck,
That had so long remained.
I dreamt that they were filled with dew;
And when I awoke, it rained.   300

My lips were wet, my throat was cold,
My garments all were dank;
Sure I had drunken in my dreams,
And still my body drank.

I moved, and could not feel my limbs:
I was so light—almost
I thought that I had died in sleep,
And was a blessed ghost.

He heareth
sounds, and
seeth strange
sights and
commotions in
the sky and
the element.

And soon I heard a roaring wind:
It did not come anear: 310
But with its sound it shook the sails,
That were so thin and sere.

The upper air burst into life!
And a hundred fire-flags sheen,

To and fro they were hurried about!
And to and fro, and in and out,
The wan stars danced between.

And the coming wind did roar more loud,
And the sails did sigh like sedge;
And the rain poured down from one black cloud;
The Moon was at its edge.   321

The thick black cloud was cleft, and still
The Moon was at its side:
Like waters shot from some high crag,
The lightning fell with never a jag,
A river steep and wide.

The loud wind never reached the ship,
Yet now the ship moved on!
Beneath the lightning and the Moon
The dead men gave a groan.   330

They groaned, they stirred, they all uprose,
Nor spake, nor moved their eyes:
It had been strange, even in a dream,
To have seen those dead men rise.

The helmsman steered, the ship moved on;
Yet never a breeze up-blew;
The mariners all 'gan work the ropes,
Where they were wont to do:
They raised their limbs like lifeless tools—
We were a ghastly crew.   340

The body of my brother's son
Stood by me, knee to knee:
The body and I pulled at one rope,
But he said nought to me.

'I fear thee, ancient Mariner!'
Be calm, thou Wedding-Guest!
'Twas not those souls that fled in pain,
Which to their corses came again,
But a troop of spirits blest:

For when it dawned—they dropped their arms,
And clustered round the mast;　351
Sweet sounds rose slowly through their mouths,
And from their bodies passed.

Around, around, flew each sweet sound,
Then darted to the Sun;
Slowly the sounds came back again,
Now mixed, now one by one.

Sometimes a-dropping from the sky
I heard the sky-lark sing;
Sometimes all little birds that are,　360
How they seemed to fill the sea and air
With their sweet jargoning!

And now 'twas like all instruments,
Now like a lonely flute;
And now it is an angel's song,
That makes the heavens be mute.

It ceased; yet still the sails made on
A pleasant noise till noon,
A noise like of a hidden brook
In the leafy month of June,　370
That to the sleeping woods all night
Singeth a quiet tune.

Till noon we quietly sailed on,
Yet never a breeze did breathe:

Slowly and smoothly went the ship,
Moved onward from beneath.

The lonesome
Spirit from the
south-pole
carries on the
ship as far as
the Line, in
obedience to
the angelic
troop, but
still requireth
vengeance.

Under the keel nine fathom deep,
From the land of mist and snow,
The spirit slid: and it was he
That made the ship to go.   380
The sails at noon left off their tune
And the ship stood still also.

The Sun, right up above the mast,
Had fixed her to the ocean:
But in a minute she 'gan stir,
With a short uneasy motion—
Backwards and forwards half her length
With a short uneasy motion.

Then like a pawing horse let go,
She made a sudden bound: 390
It flung the blood into my head,
And I fell down in a swound.

The Polar
Spirit's fel-
low-dæmons,
the invisible
inhabitants of
the element,
take part in
his wrong;
and two of
them relate,
one to the
other, that
penance long
and heavy for
the ancient
Mariner hath
been accorded
to the Polar
Spirit, who
returneth
southward.

How long in that same fit I lay,
I have not to declare;
But ere my living life returned,
I heard and in my soul discerned
Two voices in the air.

'Is it he?' quoth one, 'Is this the man?
By him who died on cross,
With his cruel bow he laid full low,   400
The harmless Albatross.

The spirit who bideth by himself
In the land of mist and snow.
He loved the bird that loved the man
Who shot him with his bow.'

The other was a softer voice,
As soft as honey-dew:
Quoth he, 'The man hath penance done,
And penance more will do.'

Part VI.

FIRST VOICE.

'But tell me, tell me! speak again, 410
Thy soft response renewing—
What makes that ship drive on so fast?
What is the ocean doing?'

SECOND VOICE.

'Still as a slave before his lord,
The Ocean hath no blast;
His great bright eye most silently
Up to the Moon is cast—

If he may know which way to go:
For she guides him smooth or grim.
See, brother, see! how graciously 420
She looketh down on him.'

FIRST VOICE.

'But why drives on that ship so fast,
Without or wave or wind?'

SECOND VOICE.

'The air is cut away before,
And closes from behind.

The Mariner hath been cast into a trance; for the angelic power causeth the vessel to drive northward faster than human life could endure.

Fly, brother, fly! more high, more high!
Or we shall be belated:
For slow and slow that ship will go,
When the Mariner's trance is abated.'

The supernatural motion is retarded; the Mariner awakes, and his penance begins anew.

I woke, and we were sailing on   430
As in a gentle weather:
'Twas night, calm night, the Moon was high;
The dead men stood together.

All stood together on the deck,
For a charnel-dungeon fitter:
All fixed on me their stony eyes
That in the Moon did glitter.

The pang, the curse, with which they died,
Had never passed away:
I could not draw my eyes from theirs,   440
Nor turn them up to pray.

The curse is finally expiated.

And now this spell was snapt: once more
I viewed the ocean green,
And looked far forth, yet little saw
Of what had else been seen—

Like one that on a lonesome road
Doth walk in fear and dread,
And having once turned round walks on,
And turns no more his head:
Because he knows, a frightful fiend   450
Doth close behind him tread.

But soon there breathed a wind on me,
Nor sound nor motion made:
Its path was not upon the sea,
In ripple or in shade.

It raised my hair, it fanned my cheek
Like a meadow-gale of spring—
It mingled strangely with my fears,
Yet it felt like a welcoming.

Swiftly, swiftly flew the ship, 460
Yet she sailed softly too:
Sweetly, sweetly blew the breeze—
On me alone it blew.

And the ancient Mariner beholdeth his native country.

Oh! dream of joy! is this indeed
The light-house top I see?
Is this the hill? is this the kirk?
Is this mine own countree?

We drifted o'er the harbour-bar,
And I with sobs did pray—
O let me be awake, my God! 470
Or let me sleep alway.

The harbour-bay was clear as glass,
So smoothly it was strewn!
And on the bay the moonlight lay,
And the shadow of the Moon.

The rock shone bright, the kirk no less,
That stands above the rock:
The moonlight steeped in silentness
The steady weathercock.

And the bay was white with silent light, 480
Till rising from the same,

The angelic spirits leave the dead bodies,

Full many shapes, that shadows were,
In crimson colors came.

And appear in their own forms of light.

A little distance from the prow
Those crimson shadows were:

I turned my eyes upon the deck—
Oh, Christ! what saw I there!

Each corse lay flat, lifeless and flat,
And, by the holy rood!
A man all light, a seraph-man   490
On every corse there stood.

This seraph-band, each waved his hand:
It was a heavenly sight!
They stood as signals to the land,
Each one a lovely light:

This seraph-band, each waved his hand,
No voice did they impart—
No voice; but oh! the silence sank
Like music on my heart.

But soon I heard the dash of oars,   500
I heard the Pilot's cheer;
My head was turned perforce away,
And I saw a boat appear.

The Pilot, and the Pilot's boy,
I heard them coming fast:
Dear Lord in Heaven! it was a joy
The dead men could not blast.

I saw a third—I heard his voice:
It is the Hermit good!
He singeth loud his godly hymns   510
That he makes in the wood.
He'll shrieve my soul, he'll wash away
The Albatross's blood.

Part VII.

The Hermit of the wood,

This Hermit good lives in that wood
Which slopes down to the sea.
How loudly his sweet voice he rears!
He loves to talk with marineres
That come from a far countree.

He kneels at morn, and noon, and eve—
He hath a cushion plump: 520
It is the moss that wholly hides
The rotted old oak-stump.

The skiff-boat neared: I heard them talk,
'Why, this is strange, I trow!
Where are those lights so many and fair,
That signal made but now?'

Approacheth the ship with wonder.

'Strange, by my faith!' the Hermit said—
'And they answered not our cheer!
The planks look warped! and see those sails,
How thin they are and sere! 530
I never saw aught like to them,
Unless perchance it were

Brown skeletons of leaves that lag
My forest-brook along;
When the ivy-tod is heavy with snow,
And the owlet whoops to the wolf below,
That eats the she-wolf's young.'

'Dear Lord! it hath a fiendish look—
(The Pilot made reply)
I am a-feared '—' Push on, push on! ' 540
Said the Hermit cheerily.

The boat came closer to the ship,
But I nor spake nor stirred;
The boat came close beneath the ship,
And straight a sound was heard.

The ship sud-
denly sinketh.

Under the water it rumbled on,
Still louder and more dread:
It reached the ship, it split the bay;
The ship went down like lead.

The ancient
Mariner is
saved in the
Pilot's boat.

Stunned by that loud and dreadful sound,   550
Which sky and ocean smote,
Like one that hath been seven days drowned
My body lay afloat;
But swift as dreams, myself I found
Within the Pilot's boat.

Upon the whirl, where sank the ship,
The boat spun round and round:
And all was still, save that the hill
Was telling of the sound.

I moved my lips—the Pilot shrieked   560
And fell down in a fit:
The Holy Hermit raised his eyes
And prayed where he did sit.

I took the oars: the Pilot's boy,
Who now doth crazy go,
Laughed loud and long, and all the while
His eyes went to and fro.
'Ha! ha!' quoth he, 'full plain I see,
The Devil knows how to row.'

And now, all in my own countree,   570
I stood on the firm land!

The Hermit stepped forth from the boat,
And scarcely he could stand.

'O shrieve me, shrieve me, holy man!'
The Hermit crossed his brow.
'Say quick,' quoth he, 'I bid thee say—
What manner of man art thou?'

Forthwith this frame of mine was wrenched
With a woful agony,
Which forced me to begin my tale;   580
And then it left me free.

Since then, at an uncertain hour,
That agony returns;
And till my ghastly tale is told,
This heart within me burns.

I pass, like night, from land to land;
I have strange power of speech:
That moment that his face I see,
I know the man that must hear me:
To him my tale I teach.   590

What loud uproar bursts from that door!
The wedding-guests are there:
But in the garden-bower the bride
And bride-maids singing are:
And hark the little vesper bell,
Which biddeth me to prayer!

O Wedding-Guest! this soul hath been
Alone on a wide wide sea:
So lonely 'twas, that God himself
Scarce seemed there to be.   600

O sweeter than the marriage-feast,
'Tis sweeter far to me,
To walk together to the kirk
With a goodly company!—

To walk together to the kirk,
And all together pray,
While each to his great Father bends,
Old men, and babes, and loving friends,
And youths and maidens gay!

And to teach,
by his own
example,
love and
reverence to
all things that
God made and
loveth.

Farewell, farewell! but this I tell   610
To thee, thou Wedding-Guest!
He prayeth well, who loveth well
Both man and bird and beast.

He prayeth best, who loveth best
All things both great and small;
For the dear God who loveth us,
He made and loveth all.

The Mariner, whose eye is bright,
Whose beard with age is hoar,
Is gone: and now the Wedding-Guest   620
Turned from the bridegroom's door.

He went like one that hath been stunned,
And is of sense forlorn:
A sadder and a wiser man,
He rose the morrow morn.

1797—1798]

KUBLA KHAN.[1]

In Xanadu did Kubla Khan
  A stately pleasure-dome decree:
Where Alph, the sacred river, ran
Through caverns measureless to man
  Down to a sunless sea.
So twice five miles of fertile ground
With walls and towers were girdled round:
And here were gardens bright with sinuous rills,
Where blossomed many an incense-bearing tree;
And here were forests ancient as the hills,   10
Enfolding sunny spots of greenery.

But, oh that deep romantic chasm which slanted
Down the green hill athwart a cedarn cover!
A savage place! as holy and enchanted
As e'er beneath a waning moon was haunted
By woman wailing for her demon-lover!
And from this chasm, with ceaseless turmoil seething,
As if this earth in fast thick pants were breathing,
A mighty fountain momently was forced:
Amid whose swift, half-intermitted burst   20
Huge fragments vaulted like rebounding hail.

---

[1] In 1798, not the summer of 1797 (" Letters of S. T. Coleridge," ed'ted by E H. Coleridge, p. 245), Coleridge, having quarrelled with his friend Lloyd who l'ved with him, and feeling otherwise depressed, retired to a lonely farm-house where he first resorted to the use of opium. He had been reading, according to his account in *Purchas's* " Pilgrimage," the sentence, " Here the Khan Kubla commanded a pa'ace to be built, and a stately garden thereunto. And thus ten miles of fertile ground were inclosed with a wall," when he fell asleep, and dreamed, as he says, from two to three hundred lines of poetry. On waking he wrote down what we have of " Kubla Khan "; but being called away on business and returning an hour later, he found that all the rest, except a few confused images, had faded from his mind In later years he talked of completing it, but it remains to us only as a bit of the most sumptuous music in our poetry, expressive of " heaven and elysian bowers."

Or chaffy grain beneath the thresher's flail:
And 'mid these dancing rocks at once and ever
It flung up momently the sacred river.
Five miles meandering with a mazy motion
Through wood and dale the sacred river ran,
Then reached the caverns measureless to man,
And sank in tumult to a lifeless ocean:
And 'mid this tumult Kubla heard from far
Ancestral voices prophesying war!

    The shadow of the dome of pleasure
    Floated midway on the waves;
    Where was heard the mingled measure
    From the fountain and the caves.
It was a miracle of rare device,
A sunny pleasure-dome with caves of ice!

    A damsel with a dulcimer
    In a vision once I saw:
    It was an Abyssinian maid,
    And on her dulcimer she played,
    Singing of Mount Abora.
    Could I revive within me
    Her symphony and song.
    To such a deep delight 'twould win me,
That with music loud and long,
I would build that dome in air,
That sunny dome! those caves of ice!
And all who heard should see them there,
And all should cry, Beware! Beware!
His flashing eyes, his floating hair!
Weave a circle round him thrice,
And close your eyes with holy dread,
For he on honey-dew hath fed,
And drunk the milk of Paradise.

CHRISTABEL.[1]

PART I.

'Tis the middle of night by the castle clock,
And the owls have awakened the crowing cock;
Tu — whit! —— Tu — whoo!
And hark, again! the crowing cock,
How drowsily it crew.

Sir Leoline, the Baron rich,
Hath a toothless mastiff, which
From her kennel beneath the rock
Maketh answer to the clock.
Four for the quarters, and twelve for the hour;   10
Ever and aye, by shine and shower,
Sixteen short howls, not over loud;
Some say, she sees my lady's shroud.

---

[1] Coleridge was preparing "Christabel" for the second volume of "Lyrical Ballads," but during the printing other poems were inserted. Part I. was written in 1798, Part II., in Keswick, in 1800, when Coleridge was already beginning to feel the depression which ultimately overmastered him. Though he often talked of finishing it and dec'ared that he had the whole story planned, it is certain that he never could have carr'ed it on in the spirit with which it was begun.

It is written, as Coleridge says, upon a new principle (borrowed from Chatterton): that of counting in each line the accents not the syllables—always four accents, though the number of syllables is irregular. Pauses, even including an accent, are sometimes introduced in a manner quite new in literary poetry, though familiar to any child who knows Mother Goose, cf.:

| Is | John Smith with | in! |

| Ay, that he | is. |

Borrowed from Lanier's "Science of English Verse," p. 188.

Is the night chilly and dark?
The night is chilly, but not dark.
The thin grey cloud is spread on high,
It covers but not hides the sky.
The moon is behind, and at the full;
And yet she looks both small and dull.
The night is chill, the cloud is grey: 20
'Tis a month before the month of May,
And the Spring comes slowly up this way.

The lovely lady, Christabel,
Whom her father loves so well,
What makes her in the wood so late,
A furlong from the castle gate?
She had dreams all yesternight
Of her own betrothed knight:
And she in the midnight wood will pray
For the weal of her lover that's far away.   30

She stole along, she nothing spoke,
The sighs she heaved were soft and low,
And nought was green upon the oak
But moss and rarest mistletoe:
She kneels beneath the huge oak-tree,
And in silence prayeth she.

The lady sprang up suddenly,
The lovely lady, Christabel!
It moaned as near, as near can be,
But what it is she cannot tell.—   40
On the other side it seems to be,
Of the huge, broad-breasted, old oak-tree.

The night is chill; the forest bare;
Is it the wind that moaneth bleak?

There is not wind enough in the air
To move away the ringlet curl
From the lovely lady's cheek—
There is not wind enough to twirl
The one red leaf, the last of its clan,
That dances as often as dance it can, 50
Hanging so light, and hanging so high,
On the topmost twig that looks up at the sky.

Hush, beating heart of Christabel!
Jesu, Maria, shield her well!
She folded her arms beneath her cloak,
And stole to the other side of the oak.
      What sees she there?

There she sees a damsel bright,
Drest in a silken robe of white,
That shadowy in the moonlight shone: 60
The neck that made that white robe wan,
Her stately neck, and arms were bare;
Her blue-veined feet unsandal'd were,
And wildly glittered here and there
The gems entangled in her hair.
I guess, 'twas frightful there to see
A lady so richly clad as she—
Beautiful exceedingly!

Mary mother, save me now!
(Said Christabel,) And who art thou? 70

The lady strange made answer meet,
And her voice was faint and sweet:—
Have pity on my sore distress,
I scarce can speak for weariness:
Stretch forth thy hand, and have no fear!
Said Christabel, How camest thou here?

And the lady, whose voice was faint and sweet,
Did thus pursue her answer meet:—

My sire is of a noble line,
And my name is Geraldine: 80
Five warriors seized me yestermorn,
Me, even me, a maid forlorn:
They choked my cries with force and fright,
And tied me on a palfrey white.
The palfrey was as fleet as wind,
And they rode furiously behind.
They spurred amain, their steeds were white;
And once we crossed the shade of night.
As sure as Heaven shall rescue me,
I have no thought what men they be; 90
Nor do I know how long it is
(For I have lain entranced I wis)
Since one, the tallest of the five,
Took me from the palfrey's back,
A weary woman, scarce alive.
Some muttered words his comrades spoke:
He placed me underneath this oak,
He swore they would return with haste;
Whither they went I cannot tell—
I thought I heard, some minutes past, 100
Sounds as of a castle bell.
Stretch forth thy hand (thus ended she),
And help a wretched maid to flee.

Then Christabel stretched forth her hand
And comforted fair Geraldine:
O well, bright dame! may you command
The service of Sir Leoline;
And gladly our stout chivalry
Will he send forth and friends withal

To guide and guard you safe and free 110
Home to your noble father's hall.

She rose: and forth with steps they passed
That strove to be, and were not, fast.
Her gracious stars the lady blest,
And thus spake on sweet Christabel:
All our household are at rest,
The hall as silent as the cell;
Sir Leoline is weak in health
And may not well awakened be,
But we will move as if in stealth, 120
And I beseech your courtesy,
This night, to share your couch with me.

They crossed the moat, and Christabel
Took the key that fitted well:
A little door she opened straight,
All in the middle of the gate:
The gate that was ironed within and without,
Where an army in battle array had marched out.
The lady sank, belike through pain,
And Christabel with might and main 130
Lifted her up, a weary weight,
Over the threshold of the gate:
Then the lady rose again,
And moved, as she were not in pain.

So free from danger, free from fear,
They crossed the court: right glad they were.
And Christabel devoutly cried
To the lady by her side,
Praise we the Virgin all divine
Who hath rescued thee from thy distress! 140
Alas, alas! said Geraldine,
I cannot speak for weariness.

So free from danger, free from fear,
They crossed the court: right glad they were.

Outside her kennel, the mastiff old
Lay fast asleep, in moonshine cold.
The mastiff old did not awake,
Yet she an angry moan did make!
And what can ail the mastiff bitch?
Never till now she uttered yell   150
Beneath the eye of Christabel.
Perhaps it is the owlet's scritch:
For what can ail the mastiff bitch?

They passed the hall, that echoes still,
Pass as lightly as you will!
The brands were flat, the brands were dying,
Amid their own white ashes lying;
But when the lady passed, there came
A tongue of light, a fit of flame;
And Christabel saw the lady's eye,   160
And nothing else saw she thereby,
Save the boss of the shield of Sir Leoline tall,
Which hung in a murky old niche in the wall.
O softly tread, said Christabel,
My father seldom sleepeth well.

Sweet Christabel her feet doth bare,
And, jealous of the listening air,
They steal their way from stair to stair,
Now in glimmer, and now in gloom,
And now they pass the Baron's room,   170
As still as death, with stifled breath!
And now have reached her chamber door;
And now doth Geraldine press down
The rushes of the chamber floor.

The moon shines dim in the open air,
And not a moonbeam enters here.
But they without its light can see
The chamber carved so curiously,
Carved with figures strange and sweet,
All made out of the carver's brain, 180
For a lady's chamber meet:
The lamp with twofold silver chain
Is fastened to an angel's feet.

The silver lamp burns dead and dim;
But Christabel the lamp will trim.
She trimmed the lamp, and made it bright,
And left it swinging to and fro,
While Geraldine, in wretched plight,
Sank down upon the floor below.

O weary lady, Geraldine, 190
I pray you, drink this cordial wine!
It is a wine of virtuous powers;
My mother made it of wild flowers.

And will your mother pity me,
Who am a maiden most forlorn?
Christabel answered—Woe is me!
She died the hour that I was born.
I have heard the grey-haired friar tell
How on her death-bed she did say,
That she should hear the castle bell 200
Strike twelve upon my wedding-day.
O mother dear! that thou wert here!
I would, said Geraldine, she were!

But soon with altered voice, said she—
' Off, wandering mother! Peak and pine!
I have power to bid thee flee.'

Alas! what ails poor Geraldine?
Why stares she with unsettled eye?
Can she the bodiless dead espy?
And why with hollow voice cries she, 210
'Off, woman, off! this hour is mine—
Though thou her guardian spirit be,
Off, woman, off! 'tis given to me.'

Then Christabel knelt by the lady's side,
And raised to heaven her eyes so blue—
Alas! said she, this ghastly ride—
Dear lady! it hath wildered you!
The lady wiped her moist cold brow,
And faintly said, ' 'Tis over now!'

Again the wild-flower wine she drank: 220
Her fair large eyes 'gan glitter bright,
And from the floor whereon she sank,
The lofty lady stood upright:
She was most beautiful to see,
Like a lady of a far countrée.

And thus the lofty lady spake—
' All they who live in the upper sky,
Do love you, holy Christabel!
And you love them, and for their sake
And for the good which me befel, 230
Even I in my degree will try,
Fair maiden, to requite you well.
But now unrobe yourself; for I
Must pray, ere yet in bed I lie.'

Quoth Christabel, so let it be!
And as the lady bade, did she.
Her gentle limbs did she undress,
And lay down in her loveliness.

But through her brain of weal and woe
So many thoughts moved to and fro, 240
That vain it were her lids to close;
So half-way from the bed she rose,
And on her elbow did recline
To look at the lady Geraldine.

Beneath the lamp the lady bowed,
And slowly rolled her eyes around;
Then drawing in her breath aloud,
Like one that shuddered, she unbound
The cincture from beneath her breast:
Her silken robe, and inner vest, 250
Dropt to her feet, and full in view,
Behold! her bosom and half her side—
A sight to dream of, not to tell!
O shield her! shield sweet Christabel!

Yet Geraldine nor speaks nor stirs:
Ah! what a stricken look was hers!
Deep from within she seems half-way
To lift some weight with sick assay.
And eyes the maid and seeks delay:
Then suddenly, as one defied, 260
Collects herself in scorn and pride,
And lay down by the Maiden's side!—
And in her arms the maid she took,
        Ah well-a-day!
And with low voice and doleful look
These words did say:
' In the touch of this bosom there worketh a spell,
Which is lord of thy utterance, Christabel!
Thou knowest to-night, and wilt know to-morrow
This mark of my shame, this seal of my sorrow: 270
    But vainly thou warrest,
        For this is alone in

Thy power to declare,
   That in the dim forest
Thou heard'st a low moaning,
And found'st a bright lady, surpassingly fair:
And didst bring her home with thee in love
    and in charity,
To shield her and shelter her from the damp air.'

THE CONCLUSION TO PART THE FIRST.

It was a lovely sight to see
The lady Christabel, when she   280
Was praying at the old oak-tree.
    Amid the jagged shadows
    Of mossy leafless boughs,
    Kneeling in the moonlight,
    To make her gentle vows;
Her slender palms together prest,
Heaving sometimes on her breast;
Her face resigned to bliss or bale—
Her face, oh call it fair not pale,
And both blue eyes more bright than clear,   290
Each about to have a tear.

With open eyes (ah woe is me!)
Asleep, and dreaming fearfully,
Fearfully dreaming, yet, I wis,
Dreaming that alone, which is—
O sorrow and shame! Can this be she,
The lady, who knelt at the old oak-tree?
And lo! the worker of these harms,
That holds the maiden in her arms,
Seems to slumber still and mild,   300
As a mother with her child.

A star hath set, a star hath risen,
O Geraldine! since arms of thine
Have been the lovely lady's prison.
O Geraldine! one hour was thine—
Thou'st had thy will! By tairn and rill,
The night-birds all that hour were still.
But now they are jubilant anew,
From cliff and tower, tu — whoo! tu — whoo!
Tu—whoo! tu—whoo! from wood and fell!	310

And see! the lady Christabel
Gathers herself from out her trance;
Her limbs relax, her countenance
Grows sad and soft; the smooth thin lids
Close o'er her eyes: and tears she sheds—
Large tears that leave the lashes bright!   ·
And oft the while she seems to smile
As infants at a sudden light!

Yea, she doth smile, and she doth weep,
Like a youthful hermitess.	320
Beauteous in a wilderness,
Who, praying always, prays in sleep.
And, if she move unquietly,
Perchance, 'tis but the blood so free,
Comes back and tingles in her feet.
No doubt, she hath a vision sweet.
What if her guardian spirit 'twere,
What if she knew her mother near?
But this she knows, in joys and woes,
That saints will aid if men will call:	330
For the blue sky bends over all!

FRANCE: AN ODE.

I.

Ye Clouds! that far above me float and pause,[1]
  Whose pathless march no mortal may controul!
  Ye Ocean-Waves! that, wheresoe'er ye roll,
Yield homage only to eternal laws!
Ye Woods! that listen to the night-birds' singing,
  Midway the smooth and perilous slope reclined,
Save when your own imperious branches swinging,
  Have made a solemn music of the wind!
Where, liked a man beloved of God,
Through glooms, which never woodman trod,   10
    How oft, pursuing fancies holy,
My moonlight way o'er flowering weeds I wound,
    Inspired, beyond the guess of folly,
By each rude shape and wild unconquerable sound!
O ye loud Waves! and O ye Forests high!
  And O ye Clouds that far above me soared!
Thou rising Sun! thou blue rejoicing Sky!
  Yea, every thing that is and will be free!
  Bear witness for me, wheresoe'er ye be,
With what deep worship I have still adored   20
    The spirit of divinest Liberty.

II.

When France in wrath her giant-limbs upreared,
  And with that oath, which smote air, earth, and sea,

---

[1] The more billowy the metrical waves the better suited they are to render the emotions expressed by the ode, as the reader will see by referring to Coleridge's "Ode to France," and giving special attention to the first stanza; to the way in which the first metrical wave, after it had gently fallen at the end of the first quatrain, leaps up again on the double rhymes (which are expressly introduced for this effect) and goes bounding on, billow after billow, to the end of the stanza. T. WATTS, "Encyclopedia Britannica," Vol. XIX., p. 272.

Stamped her strong foot and said she would be free,
Bear witness for me, how I hoped and feared!
With what a joy my lofty gratulation
    Unawed I sang, amid a slavish band:
And when to whelm the disenchanted nation,
    Like fiends embattled by a wizard's wand,
        The Monarchs marched in evil day,.   30
        And Britain joined the dire array:
    Though dear her shores and circling ocean,
Though many friendships, many youthful loves
    Had swoln the patriot emotion
And flung a magic light o'er all her hills and groves;
Yet still my voice, unaltered, sang defeat
    To all that braved the tyrant-quelling lance,
And shame too long delayed and vain retreat!
For ne'er, O Liberty! with partial aim
I dimmed thy light or damped thy holy flame;   40
    But blessed the pæans of delivered France,
And hung my head and wept at Britain's name.[1]

III.

' And what,' I said, ' though Blasphemy's loud scream
    With that sweet music of deliverance strove!
    Though all the fierce and drunken passions wove
A dance more wild than e'er was maniac's dream!
    Ye storms, that round the dawning east assembled,
The Sun was rising, though ye hid his light! '
    And when, to soothe my soul, that hoped and trembled,
The dissonance ceased, and all seemed calm and bright;   50
    When France her front deep-scarred and gory
    Concealed with clustering wreaths of glory;
        When, insupportably advancing,

Her arm made mockery of the warrior's ramp;
  While timid looks of fury glancing,
Domestic treason, crushed beneath her fatal stamp,
Writhed like a wounded dragon in his gore;
  Then I reproached my fears that would not flee;
'And soon,' I said, ' shall Wisdom teach her lore
In the low huts of them that toil and groan!   60
And, conquering by her happiness alone,
  Shall France compel the nations to be free,
Till Love and Joy look round, and call the Earth their own.'

IV.

Forgive me, Freedom! O forgive those dreams!
  I hear thy voice, I hear thy loud lament,
  From bleak Helvetia's icy caverns sent—[1] ,
I hear thy groans upon her blood-stained streams!
  Heroes, that for your peaceful country perished,
And ye that, fleeing, spot your mountain-snows
  With bleeding wounds; forgive me, that I cherished   70
One thought that ever blessed your cruel foes!
  To scatter rage, and traitorous guilt.
  Where Peace her jealous home had built;
    A patriot-race to disinherit
Of all that made their stormy wilds so dear;
    And with inexpiable spirit
To taint the bloodless freedom of the mountaineer—
O France, that mockest Heaven, adulterous, blind,
  And patriot only in pernicious toils!
Are these thy boasts, Champion of human kind?   80
  To mix with Kings in the low lust of sway,
Yell in the hunt, and share the murderous prey;
To insult the shrine of Liberty with spoils
  From freemen torn; to tempt and to betray?

---

[1] This ode was inspired by the French invasion of Switzerland.

V.

The Sensual and the Dark rebel in vain,
 Slaves by their own compulsion! In mad game
 They burst their manacles and wear the name
  Of Freedom, graven on a heavier chain!
 O Liberty! with profitless endeavour
Have I pursued thee, many a weary hour;   90
 But thou nor swell'st the victor's strain, nor ever
Didst breathe thy soul in forms of human power.
 Alike from all, howe'er they praise thee,
  (Nor prayer nor boastful name delays thee)
   Alike from Priestcraft's harpy minions,
 And factious Blasphemy's obscener slaves,
  Thou speedest on thy subtle pinions,
The guide of homeless winds, and playmate of the waves!
And there I felt thee!—on that sea-cliff's verge,
 Whose pines, scarce travelled by the breeze above,   100
Had made one murmur with the distant surge!
Yes, while I stood and gazed, my temples bare,
And shot my being through earth, sea, and air,
 Possessing all things with intensest love,
  O Liberty! my spirit felt thee there.

February, 1798.]

FROST AT MIDNIGHT.

The Frost performs its secret ministry,
Unhelped by any wind. The owlet's cry
Came loud—and hark, again! loud as before.
The inmates of my cottage, all at rest,
Have left me to that solitude, which suits
Abstruser musings: save that at my side

My cradled infant slumbers peacefully.
'Tis calm indeed! so calm, that it disturbs
And vexes meditation with its strange
And extreme silentness. Sea, hill, and wood,   10
This populous village! Sea, and hill, and wood,
With all the numberless goings-on of life,
Inaudible as dreams! the thin blue flame
Lies on my low burnt fire, and quivers not;
Only that film, which fluttered on the grate,
Still flutters there, the sole unquiet thing.
Methinks, its motion in this hush of nature
Gives it dim sympathies with me who live,
Making it a companionable form,
Whose puny flaps and freaks the idling Spirit   20
By its own moods interprets, every where
Echo or mirror seeking of itself
And makes a toy of Thought.

                    But, O! how oft,
How oft, at school, with most believing mind,
Presageful, have I gazed upon the bars,
To watch that fluttering *stranger!* and as oft
With unclosed lids, already had I dreamt
Of my sweet birth-place, and the old church-tower,
Whose bells, the poor man's only music, rang
From morn to evening, all the hot Fair-day,   30
So sweetly, that they stirred and haunted me
With a wild pleasure, falling on mine ear
Most like articulate sounds of things to come!
So gazed I, till the soothing things, I dreamt,
Lulled me to sleep, and sleep prolonged my dreams!
And so I brooded all the following morn.
Awed by the stern preceptor's face, mine eye
Fixed with mock study on my swimming book:
Save if the door half opened, and I snatched

A hasty glance, and still my heart leaped up,   40
For still I hoped to see the *stranger's* face,
Townsman, or aunt, or sister more beloved,
My play-mate when we both were clothed alike!

  Dear Babe, that sleepest cradled by my side,
Whose gentle breathings, heard in this deep calm,
Fill up the interspersed vacancies
And momentary pauses of the thought!
My babe so beautiful! it thrills my heart
With tender gladness, thus to look at thee,
And think that thou shalt learn far other lore,   50
And in far other scenes! For I was reared
In the great city, pent 'mid cloisters dim,
And saw nought lovely but the sky and stars.
But *thou*, my babe! shalt wander like a breeze
By lakes and sandy shores, beneath the crags
Of ancient mountain, and beneath the clouds,
Which image in their bulk both lakes and shores
And mountain crags: so shalt thou see and hear
The lovely shapes and sounds intelligible
Of that eternal language, which thy God   60
Utters, who from eternity doth teach
Himself in all, and all things in himself.
Great universal Teacher! he shall mould
Thy spirit, and by giving make it ask.

  Therefore all seasons shall be sweet to thee,
Whether the summer clothe the general earth
With greenness, or the redbreast sit and sing
Betwixt the tufts of snow on the bare branch
Of mossy apple-tree, while the nigh thatch
Smokes in the sun-thaw: whether the eave-drops fall   70
Heard only in the trances of the blast,

Or if the secret ministry of frost
Shall hang them up in silent icicles,
Quietly shining in the quiet Moon.

February, 1798.]

LOVE.

All thoughts, all passions, all delights,
Whatever stirs this mortal frame,
All are but ministers of Love,
 And feed his sacred flame.

Oft in my waking dreams do I
Live o'er again that happy hour,
When midway on the mount I lay,
 Beside the ruined tower.

The Moonshine, stealing o'er the scene,
Had blended with the lights of eve;   10
And she was there, my hope, my joy,
 My own dear Genevieve!

She leant against the armed man,
The statue of the armed knight;
She stood and listened to my lay,
 Amid the lingering light.

Few sorrows hath she of her own,
My hope! my joy! my Genevieve!
She loves me best, whene'er I sing
 The songs that make her grieve.   20

I played a soft and doleful air,
I sang an old and moving story—
An old rude song, that suited well
 That ruin wild and hoary.

She listened with a flitting blush,
With downcast eyes and modest grace;
For well she knew I could not choose
    But gaze upon her face.

I told her of the Knight that wore
Upon his shield a burning brand;   30
And that for ten long years he wooed
    The Lady of the Land.

I told her how he pined: and, ah!
The deep, the low, the pleading tone
With which I sang another's love
    Interpreted my own.

She listened with a flitting blush,
With downcast eyes, and modest grace;
And she forgave me, that I gazed
    Too fondly on her face!   40

But when I told the cruel scorn
That crazed that bold and lovely Knight,
And that he crossed the mountain-woods,
    Nor rested day nor night;

That sometimes from the savage den,
And sometimes from the darksome shade,
And sometimes starting up at once
    In green and sunny glade,

There came and looked him in the face
An angel beautiful and bright;   50
And that he knew it was a Fiend,
    This miserable Knight!

And that unknowing what he did,
He leaped amid a murderous band,

And saved from outrage worse than death
    The Lady of the Land!

And how she wept, and clasped his knees;
And how she tended him in vain—
And ever strove to expiate
    The scorn that crazed his brain;—   60

And that she nursed him in a cave;
And how his madness went away,
When on the yellow forest-leaves
    A dying man he lay.

His dying words—But when I reached
That tenderest strain of all the ditty,
My faltering voice and pausing harp
    Disturbed her soul with pity!

All impulses of soul and sense
Had thrilled my guileless Genevieve;   70
The music and the doleful tale,
    The rich and balmy eve;

And hopes, and fears that kindle hope,
An undistinguishable throng,
And gentle wishes long subdued,
    Subdued and cherished long!

She wept with pity and delight,
She blushed with love, and virgin-shame;
And like the murmur of a dream,
    I heard her breathe my name.   80

Her bosom heaved—she stepped aside,
As conscious of my look she stepped—
Then suddenly, with timorous eye
    She fled to me and wept.

She half enclosed me with her arms,
She pressed me with a meek embrace;
And bending back her head, looked up,
　　And gazed upon my face.

'Twas partly Love, and partly Fear,
And partly 'twas a bashful art,   90
That I might rather feel, than see,
　　The swelling of her heart.

I calmed her fears, and she was calm,
And told her love with virgin pride;
And so I won my Genevieve,
　　My bright and beauteous Bride.

1798–1799.]

DEJECTION: AN ODE.[1]

WRITTEN APRIL 4, 1802.

Late, late yestreen I saw the new Moon,
With the old Moon in her arms;
And I fear, I fear, my Master dear!
We shall have a deadly storm.
　　　　　" Ballad of Sir Patrick Spence."

I.

Well! If the Bard was weather-wise, who made
　The grand old ballad of Sir Patrick Spence,
　　This night, so tranquil now, will not go hence
Unroused by winds, that ply a busier trade

---

[1] Originally dedicated to Wordsworth, but afterward altered to efface any marks of a personal character. When first published " William " was changed to " Edmund," and before 1817, when it was printed in " Sibylline Leaves," an estrangement between the two friends caused still further changes, besides the insertion of " Lady " in place of " Edmund."

Than those which mould yon cloud in lazy flakes,
Or the dull sobbing draft, that moans and rakes
    Upon the strings of this Æolian lute,
    Which better far were mute.
  For lo! the New-moon winter-bright!
  And overspread with phantom light,   10
  (With swimming phantom light o'erspread
  But rimmed and circled by a silver thread)
I see the old Moon in her lap, foretelling
  The coming on of rain and squally blast.
And oh! that even now the gust were swelling,
  And the slant night-shower driving loud and fast!
Those sounds which oft have raised me, whilst they awed,
    And sent my soul abroad,
Might now perhaps their wonted impulse give,
Might startle this dull pain, and make it move and live!   20

II.

A grief without a pang, void, dark, and drear,
  A stifled, drowsy, unimpassioned grief,
  Which finds no natural outlet, no relief,
    In word, or sigh, or tear—
O Lady! in this wan and heartless mood,
To other thoughts by yonder throstle woo'd,
  All this long eve, so balmy and serene,
Have I been gazing on the western sky,
  And its peculiar tint of yellow green:
And still I gaze—and with how blank an eye!   30
And those thin clouds above, in flakes and bars,
That give away their motion to the stars:
Those stars, that glide behind them or between,
Now sparkling, now bedimmed, but always seen:
Yon crescent Moon, as fixed as if it grew
In its own cloudless, starless lake of blue;

I see them all so excellently fair,
I see, not feel how beautiful they are!

III.

    My genial spirits fail;
    And what can these avail   40
To lift the smothering weight from off my breast?
    It were a vain endeavour,
    Though I should gaze for ever
On that green light that lingers in the west:
I may not hope from outward forms to win
The passion and the life, whose fountains are within.

IV.

O Lady! we receive but what we give,
And in our life alone does nature live:
Ours is her wedding-garment, ours her shroud!
    And would we aught behold, of higher worth,   50
Than that inanimate cold world allowed
To the poor loveless ever-anxious crowd,
    Ah! from the soul itself must issue forth,
A light, a glory, a fair luminous cloud
    Enveloping the Earth—
And from the soul itself must there be sent
    A sweet and potent voice, of its own birth,
Of all sweet sounds the life and element!

V.

O pure of heart! thou need'st not ask of me
What this strong music in the soul may be!   60
What, and wherein it doth exist,
This light, this glory, this fair luminous mist,

This beautiful and beauty-making power.
　　Joy, virtuous Lady! Joy that ne'er was given,
Save to the pure, and in their purest hour,
Life, and Life's effluence, cloud at once and shower,
Joy, Lady! is the spirit and the power,
Which wedding Nature to us gives in dower,
　　A new Earth and new Heaven,
Undreamt of by the sensual and the proud—
Joy is the sweet voice, Joy the luminous cloud—
　　　We in ourselves rejoice!
And thence flows all that charms or ear or sight,
　　All melodies the echoes of that voice,
All colours a suffusion from that light.

VI.

There was a time when, though my path was rough,
　　This joy within me dallied with distress,
And all misfortunes were but as the stuff
　　Whence Fancy made me dreams of happiness:
For hope grew round me, like the twining vine,
And fruits, and foliage, not my own, seemed mine.
But now afflictions bow me down to earth:
Nor care I that they rob me of my mirth;
　　　But oh! each visitation
Suspends what nature gave me at my birth,
　　My shaping spirit of Imagination.
For not to think of what I needs must feel,
　　But to be still and patient, all I can:
And haply by abstruse research to steal
　　From my own nature all the natural man—
　　This was my sole resource, my only plan:
Till that which suits a part infects the whole,
And now is almost grown the habit of my soul.

VII.

Hence, viper thoughts, that coil around my mind,
    Reality's dark dream!
I turn from you, and listen to the wind,
Which long has raved unnoticed. What a scream
Of agony by torture lengthened out
That lute sent forth! Thou Wind, that rav'st without,
    Bare crag, or mountain-tairn, or blasted tree,   100
Or pine-grove whither woodman never clomb,
Or lonely house, long held the witches' home,
    Methinks were fitter instruments for thee,
Mad Lutanist! who in this month of showers,
Of dark brown gardens, and of peeping flowers,
Mak'st Devils' yule, with worse than wintry song,
The blossoms, buds, and timorous leaves among.
    Thou Actor, perfect in all tragic sounds!
Thou mighty Poet, e'en to frenzy bold!
      What tell'st thou now about?   110
      'Tis of the rushing of a host in rout,
With groans of trampled men, with smarting wounds—
At once they groan with pain, and shudder with the cold!
But, hush! there is a pause of deepest silence!
    And all that noise, as of a rushing crowd,
With groans, and tremulous shudderings—all is over—
    It tells another tale, with sounds less deep and loud!
      A tale of less affright,
      And tempered with delight.
As Otway's self had framed the tender lay,   120
      'Tis of a little child
      Upon a lonesome wild,[1]

---

[1] Otway, of course, is only a change from Wordsworth. "Lucy Gray" had just
been printed when Coleridge wrote almost these same words in a letter to Poole.
See Campbell's edition of Coleridge, p. 628.

Not far from home, but she hath lost her way:
And now moans low in bitter grief and fear,
And now screams loud, and hopes to make her mother hear.

VIII.

'Tis midnight, but small thoughts have I of sleep:
Full seldom may my friend such vigils keep!
Visit her, gentle Sleep! with wings of healing,
    And may this storm be but a mountain-birth,
May all the stars hang bright above her dwelling,   130
    Silent as though they watched the sleeping Earth!
        With light heart may she rise,
        Gay fancy, cheerful eyes,
    Joy lift her spirit, joy attune her voice;
To her may all things live, from pole to pole,
Their life the eddying of her living soul!
    O simple spirit, guided from above,
Dear Lady! friend devoutest of my choice,
Thus mayest thou ever, evermore rejoice!

SHELLEY AS A CHILD.

(00)

To a Sky-Lark

Hail to thee blithe Spirit!
    Bird thou never wert,
That from Heaven, or near it,
    Pourest thy full heart
In profuse strains of unpremeditated art.
                    — meet

PERCY BYSSHE SHELLEY.

Fac-simile of part of "The Skylark."   By permission of the Library of Harvard University, from their reproduction of the Shelley manuscript in their possession.

SELECTIONS FROM SHELLEY

HYMN TO INTELLECTUAL BEAUTY.

I.

The awful shadow of some unseen Power
  Floats tho' unseen among us,—visiting
  This various world with as inconstant wing
As summer winds that creep from flower to flower.—
Like moonbeams that behind some piny mountain shower,
    It visits with inconstant glance
    Each human heart and countenance;
Like hues and harmonies of evening,—
    Like clouds in starlight widely spread,—
    Like memory of music fled,—
    Like aught that for its grace may be
Dear, and yet dearer for its mystery.

II.

Spirit of Beauty, that dost consecrate
  With thine own hues all thou dost shine upon
  Of human thought or form,—where art thou gone?
Why dost thou pass away, and leave our state,
This dim vast vale of tears, vacant and desolate?
    Ask why the sunlight not for ever
    Weaves rainbows o'er yon mountain river,
Why aught should fail and fade that once is shown,

Why fear and dream and death and birth
Cast on the daylight of this earth
Such gloom,—why man has such a scope
For love and hate, despondency and hope?

III.

No voice from some sublimer world hath ever
  To sage or poet these responses given—
  Therefore the names of Demon, Ghost, and Heaven,
Remain the records of their vain endeavour,
Frail spells—whose uttered charm might not avail to sever,
    From all we hear and all we see,
    Doubt, chance and mutability.
Thy light alone—like mist o'er mountains driven,
    Or music by the night wind sent,
    Thro' strings of some still instrument,
    Or moonlight on a midnight stream,
Gives grace and truth to life's unquiet dream.

IV.

Love, Hope, and Self-esteem, like clouds depart
  And come, for some uncertain moments lent.
  Man were immortal, and omnipotent,
Didst thou, unknown and awful as thou art,
Keep with thy glorious train firm state within his heart.
    Thou messenger of sympathies,
    That wax and wane in lovers' eyes—
Thou—that to human thought art nourishment,
    Like darkness to a dying flame!
    Depart not as thy shadow came,
    Depart not—lest the grave should be,
Like life and fear, a dark reality.

V.

While yet a boy I sought for ghosts, and sped
  Thro' many a listening chamber, cave and ruin,
  And starlight wood, with fearful steps pursuing
Hopes of high talk with the departed dead.
I called on poisonous names with which our youth is fed,
    I was not heard—I saw them not—
    When musing deeply on the lot
Of life, at that sweet time when winds are wooing
    All vital things that wake to bring
    News of birds and blossoming,—
    Sudden, thy shadow fell on me;
I shrieked, and clasped my hands in ecstasy!

VI.

I vowed that I would dedicate my powers
  To thee and thine—have I not kept the vow?
  With beating heart and streaming eyes, even now
I call the phantoms of a thousand hours
Each from his voiceless grave: they have in visioned bowers
    Of studious zeal or love's delight
    Outwatched with me the envious night—
They know that never joy illumed my brow
    Unlinked with hope that thou wouldst free
    This world from its dark slavery,
    That thou—O awful LOVELINESS,
Wouldst give whate'er these words cannot express.

VII.

The day becomes more solemn and serene
  When noon is past—there is a harmony
  In autumn, and a lustre in its sky,
Which thro' the summer is not heard or seen,

As if it could not be, as if it had not been!
   Thus let thy power, which like the truth
   Of nature on my passive youth
Descended, to my onward life supply
   Its calm—to one who worships thee,
   And every form containing thee,
   Whom, SPIRIT fair, thy spells did bind
To fear himself, and love all human kind.

1816.]

STANZAS.

WRITTEN IN DEJECTION, NEAR NAPLES.

I.

The sun is warm, the sky is clear,
   The waves are dancing fast and bright,
Blue isles and snowy mountains wear
   The purple moon's transparent might,
   The breath of the moist earth is light,
Around its unexpanded buds:
   Like many a voice of one delight,
The winds, the birds, the ocean floods,
The City's voice itself is soft like Solitude's.

II.

I see the Deep's untrampled floor
   With green and purple seaweeds strown;
I see the waves upon the shore,
   Like light dissolved in star-showers, thrown:
   I sit upon the sands alone,
The lightning of the noon-tide ocean
   Is flashing round me, and a tone
Arises from its measured motion.
How sweet! did any heart now share in my emotion.

III.

Alas! I have nor hope nor health,
   Nor peace within nor calm around,
Nor that content surpassing wealth
   The sage in meditation found,
   And walked with inward glory crowned—
Nor fame, nor power, nor love, nor leisure.
   Others I see whom these surround—
Smiling they live, and call life pleasure;—
To me that cup has been dealt in another measure.

IV.

Yet now despair itself is mild,
   Even as the winds and waters are;
I could lie down like a tired child,
   And weep away the life of care
   Which I have borne and yet must bear,
Till death like sleep might steal on me,
   And I might feel in the warm air
My cheek grow cold, and hear the sea
Breathe o'er my dying brain its last monotony.

V.

Some might lament that I were cold,
   As I, when this sweet day is gone,
Which my lost heart, too soon grown old,
   Insults with this untimely moan;
   They might lament—for I am one
Whom men love not,—and yet regret,
   Unlike this day, which, when the sun
Shall on its stainless glory set,
Will linger, though enjoyed, like joy in memory yet.

1818.]

ENGLAND IN 1819.

An old, mad, blind, despised, and dying king,—
Princes, the dregs of their dull race, who flow
Through public scorn,—mud from a muddy spring,—
Rulers who neither see, nor feel, nor know,
But leech-like to their fainting country cling,
Till they drop, blind in blood, without a blow,—
A people starved and stabbed in the untilled field,—
An army, which liberticide and prey
Makes as a two-edged sword to all who wield
Golden and sanguine laws which tempt and slay;
Religion Christless, Godless—a book sealed;
A Senate,—Time's worst statute unrepealed,—
Are graves, from which a glorious Phantom may
Burst, to illumine our tempestuous day.[1]

ODE TO THE WEST WIND.[2]

I.

O, wild West Wind, thou breath of Autumn's being,
Thou, from whose unseen presence the leaves dead
Are driven, like ghosts from an enchanter fleeing,

Yellow, and black, and pale, and hectic red,
Pestilence-stricken multitudes: O, thou,
Who chariotest to their dark wintry bed

---

[1] That this fierce scourging does not represent a passing mood or merely personal feeling, is evidenced by such poems as "The Mask of Anarchy," "Swellfoot the Tyrant," Byron's "Irish Avatar," and many passages in Byron's longer poems.

[2] Composed in the wood near Florence, after a tempestuous day in the autumn.

The wingèd seeds, where they lie cold and low,
Each like a corpse within its grave, until
Thine azure sister of the spring shall blow

Her clarion o'er the dreaming earth, and fill
(Driving sweet buds like flocks to feed in air)
With living hues and odours plain and hill:

Wild Spirit, which art moving every where;
Destroyer and preserver; hear, O, hear!

II.

Thou on whose stream, 'mid the steep sky's commotion,
Loose clouds like earth's decaying leaves are shed,
Shook from the tangled boughs of Heaven and Ocean,

Angels of rain and lightning: there are spread
On the blue surface of thine airy surge,
Like the bright hair uplifted from the head

Of some fierce Mænad, even from the dim verge
Of the horizon to the zenith's height,
The locks of the approaching storm. Thou dirge

Of the dying year, to which this closing night
Will be the dome of a vast sepulchre,
Vaulted with all thy congregated might

Of vapours, from whose solid atmosphere
Black rain, and fire, and hail will burst: O, hear!

III.

Thou who didst waken from his summer dreams
The blue Mediterranean, where he lay,
Lulled by the coil of his crystalline streams,

Beside a pumice isle in Baiæ's bay,
And saw in sleep old palaces and towers
Quivering within the wave's intenser day,

All overgrown with azure moss and flowers
So sweet, the sense faints picturing them!   Thou
For whose path the Atlantic's level powers

Cleave themselves into chasms, while far below
The sea-blooms and the oozy woods which wear
The sapless foliage of the ocean, know

Thy voice, and suddenly grow grey with fear,
And tremble and despoil themselves: O, hear!

IV.

If I were a dead leaf thou mightest bear:
If I were a swift cloud to fly with thee;
A wave to pant beneath thy power, and share

The impulse of thy strength, only less free
Than thou, O, uncontrollable!   If even
I were as in my boyhood, and could be

The comrade of thy wanderings over heaven,
As then, when to outstrip thy skiey speed
Scarce seemed a vision; I would ne'er have striven

As thus with thee in prayer in my sore need.
Oh! lift me as a wave, a leaf, a cloud!
I fall upon the thorns of life!   I bleed!

A heavy weight of hours has chained and bowed
One too like thee: tameless, and swift, and proud.

V.

Make me thy lyre, even as the forest is:
What if my leaves are falling like its own!
The tumult of thy mighty harmonies

Will take from both a deep, autumnal tone,
Sweet though in sadness.   Be thou, spirit fierce,
My spirit! Be thou me, impetuous one!

Drive my dead thoughts over the universe
Like withered leaves to quicken a new birth!
And, by the incantation of this verse,

Scatter, as from an unextinguished hearth
Ashes and sparks, my words among mankind!
Be through my lips to unawakened earth

The trumpet of a prophecy! O, wind,
If Winter comes, can Spring be far behind?

1819.]

LYRICS FROM PROMETHEUS UNBOUND.

SONG OF SPIRITS.

To the deep, to the deep,
    Down, down!
Through the shade of sleep,
Through the cloudy strife
Of Death and of Life:
Through the veil and the bar
Of things which seem and are,
Even to the steps of the remotest throne,
    Down, down!

While the sound whirls around,
    Down, down!
As the fawn draws the hound,
As the lightning the vapour,
As a weak moth the taper;
Death, despair; love, sorrow;
Time, both; to-day, to-morrow;
As steel obeys the spirit of the stone,
    Down, down!

Through the grey, void abysm,
    Down, down!
Where the air is no prism,
And the moon and stars are not,
And the cavern-crags wear not
The radiance of Heaven,
Nor the gloom to Earth given.
Where there is one pervading, one alone,
    Down, down!

In the depth of the deep
    Down, down!
Like veiled lightning asleep.
Like the spark nursed in embers,
The last look Love remembers.
Like a diamond, which shines
On the dark wealth of mines,
A spell is treasured but for thee alone,
    Down, down!

We have bound thee, we guide thee;
    Down, down!
With the bright form beside thee;
Resist not the weakness,
Such strength is in meekness

That the Eternal, the Immortal,
Must unloose through life's portal
The snake-like Doom coiled underneath his throne
          By that alone.

II iii. 54—98.

SPIRIT.

My coursers are fed with the lightning,
    They drink of the whirlwind's stream,
And when the red morning is bright'ning
    They bathe in the fresh sunbeam;
    They have strength for their swiftness I deem,
Then ascend with me, daughter of Ocean.

I desire: and their speed makes night kindle;
    I fear: they outstrip the Typhoon:
Ere the cloud piled on Atlas can dwindle
    We encircle the earth and the moon: 10
    We shall rest from long labours at noon:
Then ascend with me, daughter of Ocean.

On the brink of the night and the morning
    My coursers are wont to respire:
But the Earth has just whispered a warning
    That their flight must be swifter than fire:
    They shall drink the hot speed of desire!

II. iv. 163—179.

HYMN TO ASIA.

Life of Life! thy lips enkindle
    With their love the breath between them:
And thy smiles before they dwindle
    Make the cold air fire: then screen them
In those looks, where whoso gazes
Faints, entangled in their mazes.

Child of Light! thy limbs are burning
   Thro' the vest which seems to hide them;
As the radiant lines of morning
   Thro' the clouds ere they divide them;   10
And this atmosphere divinest
Shrouds thee wheresoe'er thou shinest.

Fair are others; none beholds thee,
   But thy voice sounds low and tender
Like the fairest, for it folds thee
   From the sight, that liquid splendour,
And all feel, yet see thee never,
As I feel now, lost for ever!

Lamp of Earth! where'er thou movest
   Its dim shapes are clad with brightness,   20
And the souls of whom thou lovest
   Walk upon the winds with lightness,
Till they fail, as I am failing,
Dizzy, lost, yet unbewailing!

II. v. 50—73.

1819.]

THE CLOUD.

I bring fresh showers for the thirsting flowers,
   From the seas and the streams;
I bear light shade for the leaves when laid
   In their noon-day dreams.
From my wings are shaken the dews that waken
   The sweet buds every one,
When rocked to rest on their mother's breast,
   As she dances about the sun.

I wield the flail of the lashing hail,
    And whiten the green plains under, 10
And then again I dissolve it in rain,
    And laugh as I pass in thunder.

I sift the snow on the mountains below,
    And their great pines groan aghast;
And all the night 'tis my pillow white,
    While I sleep in the arms of the blast.
Sublime on the towers of my skiey bowers,
    Lightning my pilot sits,
In a cavern under is fettered the thunder,
    It struggles and howls at fits; 20
Over earth and ocean with gentle motion,
    This pilot is guiding me,
Lured by the love of the genii that move
    In the depths of the purple sea;
Over the rills, and the crags, and the hills,
    Over the lakes and the plains.
Wherever he dream, under mountain or stream,
    The Spirit he loves remains;
And I all the while bask in heaven's blue smile,
    Whilst he is dissolving in rains. 30

The sanguine sunrise, with its meteor eyes,
    And his burning plumes outspread,
Leaps on the back of my sailing rack,
    When the morning star shines dead,
As on the jag of a mountain crag,
    Which an earthquake rocks and swings
An eagle alit one moment may sit
    In the light of its golden wings.
And when sunset may breathe, from the lit sea beneath,
    Its ardours of rest and of love, 40

And the crimson pall of eve may fall
    From the depth of heaven above,
With wings folded I rest, on mine airy nest,
    As still as a brooding dove.

That orbèd maiden, with white fire laden,
    Whom mortals call the moon,
Glides glimmering o'er my fleece-like floor,
    By the midnight breezes strewn;
And wherever the beat of her unseen feet,
    Which only the angels hear,   50
May have broken the woof of my tent's thin roof,
    The stars peep behind her and peer;
And I laugh to see them whirl and flee,
    Like a swarm of golden bees,
When I widen the rent in my wind-built tent,
    Till the calm rivers, lakes, and seas,
Like strips of the sky fallen through me on high,
    Are each paved with the moon and these.

I bind the sun's throne with a burning zone,
    And the moon's with a girdle of pearl;   60
The volcanoes are dim, and the stars reel and swim,
    When the whirlwinds my banner unfurl.
From cape to cape, with a bridge-like shape,
    Over a torrent sea,
Sunbeam-proof, I hang like a roof,
    The mountains its columns be.
The triumphal arch through which I march
    With hurricane, fire, and snow,
When the powers of the air are chained to my chair,
    Is the million-coloured bow;   70
The sphere-fire above its soft colours wove,
    While the moist earth was laughing below.

I am the daughter of earth and water,
    And the nursling of the sky;
I pass through the pores of the ocean and shores;
    I change, but I cannot die.
For after the rain, when with never a stain,
    The pavilion of heaven is bare,
And the winds and sunbeams with their convex gleams,
    Build up the blue dome of air,   80
I silently laugh at my own cenotaph,
    And out of the caverns of rain,
Like a child from the womb, like a ghost from the tomb,
    I arise and unbuild it again.

1820.]

TO A SKYLARK.

    Hail to thee, blithe spirit!
      Bird thou never wert,
    That from heaven, or near it,
      Pourest thy full heart
In profuse strains of unpremeditated art.

    Higher still and higher
      From the earth thou springest
    Like a cloud of fire:
      The blue deep thou wingest.
And singing still dost soar, and soaring ever singest.   10

    In the golden lightning
      Of the sunken sun,
    O'er which clouds are bright'ning,
      Thou dost float and run:
Like an unbodied joy whose race is just begun.

The pale purple even
   Melts around thy flight;
Like a star of heaven,
   In the broad day-light
Thou art unseen, but yet I hear thy shrill delight,   20

Keen as are the arrows
   Of that silver sphere,
Whose intense lamp narrows
   In the white dawn clear,
Until we hardly see, we feel that it is there.

All the earth and air
   With thy voice is loud,
As, when night is bare,
   From one lonely cloud
The moon rains out her beams, and heaven is overflowed.   30

What thou art we know not;
   What is most like thee?
From rainbow clouds there flow not
   Drops so bright to see,
As from thy presence showers a rain of melody.

Like a poet hidden
   In the light of thought,
Singing hymns unbidden,
   Till the world is wrought
To sympathy with hopes and fears it heeded not: 40

Like a high-born maiden
   In a palace tower,
Soothing her love-laden
   Soul in secret hour
With music sweet as love, which overflows her bower:

Like a glow-worm golden
   In a dell of dew,
Scattering unbeholden
   Its aërial hue   [50
Among the flowers and grass, which screen it from the view:

Like a rose embowered
   In its own green leaves,
By warm winds deflowered,
   Till the scent it gives
Makes faint with too much sweet those heavy-wingèd
      thieves:

Sound of vernal showers
   On the twinkling grass,
Rain-awakened flowers,
   All that ever was
Joyous, and clear, and fresh, thy music doth surpass.   60

Teach us, sprite or bird,
   What sweet thoughts are thine:
I have never heard
   Praise of love or wine
That panted forth a flood of rapture so divine.

Chorus Hymæneal,
   Or triumphal chaunt,
Matched with thine would be all
   But an empty vaunt,
A thing wherein we feel there is some hidden want.   70

What objects are the fountains
   Of thy happy strain?
What fields, or waves, or mountains?
   What shapes of sky or plain?
What love of thine own kind? what ignorance of pain?

With thy clear keen joyance
  Languor cannot be:
Shadow of annoyance
  Never came near thee:
Thou lovest; but ne'er knew love's sad satiety.   80

Waking or asleep,
  Thou of death must deem
Things more true and deep
  Than we mortals dream,
Or how could thy notes flow in such a crystal stream?

We look before and after,
  And pine for what is not:
Our sincerest laughter
  With some pain is fraught;
Our sweetest songs are those that tell of saddest thought. 90

Yet if we could scorn
  Hate, and pride, and fear;
If we were things born
  Not to shed a tear,
I know not how thy joy we ever should come near.

Better than all measures
  Of delightful sound,
Better than all treasures
  That in books are found,
Thy skill to poet were, thou scorner of the ground!   100

Teach me half the gladness
  That thy brain must know,
Such harmonious madness
  From my lips would flow,
The world should listen then, as I am listening now.

Leghorn. 1820.]

ODE TO LIBERTY.

Yet, Freedom, yet thy banner torn but flying,
Streams like a thunder-storm against the wind.

BYRON.

I.

A glorious people vibrated again
  The lightning of the nations: Liberty
From heart to heart, from tower to tower, o'er Spain,
  Scattering contagious fire into the sky,
Gleamed. My soul spurned the chains of its dismay,
      And, in the rapid plumes of song,
      Clothed itself, sublime and strong;
As a young eagle soars the morning clouds among,
  Hovering in verse o'er its accustomed prey;
    Till from its station in the heaven of fame
  The Spirit's whirlwind rapt it, and the ray
    Of the remotest sphere of living flame
Which paves the void was from behind it flung,
  As foam from a ship's swiftness, when there came
  A voice out of the deep: I will record the same.

II.

The Sun and the serenest Moon sprang forth:
  The burning stars of the abyss were hurled
Into the depths of heaven. The dædal earth,
  That island in the ocean of the world,
Hung in its cloud of all-sustaining air:
      But this divinest universe
      Was yet a chaos and a curse,
For thou wert not: but power from worst producing worse,
  The spirit of the beasts was kindled there,

9

And of the birds, and of the watery forms,
  And there was war among them, and despair
  Within them, raging without truce or terms:
The bosom of their violated nurse
    Groaned, for beasts warred on beasts, and worms on
        worms,
  And men on men; each heart was as a hell of storms.

III.

Man, the imperial shape, then multiplied
  His generations under the pavilion
Of the Sun's throne: palace and pyramid,
  Temple and prison, to many a swarming million,
Were, as to mountain wolves their ragged caves.
    This human living multitude
      Was savage, cunning, blind, and rude,
For thou wert not; but o'er the populous solitude,
  Like one fierce cloud over a waste of waves
    Hung Tyranny; beneath, sate deified
  The sister-pest, congregator of slaves;
    Into the shadow of her pinions wide
Anarchs and priests who feed on gold and blood,
  Till with the stain their inmost souls are dyed,
  Drove the astonished herds of men from every side.

IV.

The nodding promontories, and blue isles,
  And cloud-like mountains, and dividuous waves
Of Greece, basked glorious in the open smiles
  Of favouring heaven: from their enchanted caves
Prophetic echoes flung dim melody.
    On the unapprehensive wild
      The vine, the corn, the olive mild,

Grew savage yet, to human use unreconciled;
  And, like the unfolded flowers beneath the sea,
    Like the man's thought dark in the infant's brain,
  Like aught that is which wraps what is to be,
    Art's deathless dreams lay veiled by many a vein
Of Parian stone; and yet a speechless child,
  Verse murmured, and Philosophy did strain
  Her lidless eyes for thee; when o'er the Ægean main

V.

Athens arose: a city such as vision
  Builds from the purple crags and silver towers
Of battlemented cloud, as in derision
  Of kingliest masonry: the ocean floors
Pave it; the evening sky pavilions it;
        Its portals are inhabited
        By thunder-zonèd winds, each head
Within its cloudy wings with sun fire garlanded,
  A divine work! Athens diviner yet
    Gleamed with its crest of columns, on the will
  Of man, as on a mount of diamond, set;
    For thou wert, and thine all-creative skill
Peopled with forms that mock the eternal dead
  In marble immortality, that hill
  Which was thine earliest throne and latest oracle.

VI.

Within the surface of Time's fleeting river
  Its wrinkled image lies, as then it lay
Immovably unquiet, and for ever
  It trembles, but it cannot pass away!
The voices of thy bards and sages thunder
        With an earth-awakening blast
        Through the caverns of the past;

Religion veils her eyes; Oppression shrinks aghast:
  A wingèd sound of joy, and love, and wonder,
    Which soars where Expectation never flew,
    Rending the veil of space and time asunder!
      One ocean feeds the clouds, and streams, and dew;
One sun illumines heaven; one spirit vast
  With life and love makes chaos ever new,
  As Athens doth the world with thy delight renew.

VII.

Then Rome was, and from thy deep bosom fairest,
  Like a wolf-cub from a Cadmæan Mænad,[1]
She drew the milk of greatness, though thy dearest
  From that Elysian food was yet unweanèd;
And many a deed of terrible uprightness
    By thy sweet love was sanctified;
    And in thy smile, and by thy side,
Saintly Camillus lived, and firm Atilius died.
  But when tears stained thy robe of vestal whiteness,
    And gold profaned thy capitolian throne,
  Thou didst desert, with spirit-wingèd lightness,
    The senate of the tyrants: they sunk prone
Slaves of one tyrant: Palatinus sighed
  Faint echoes of Ionian song: that tone
  Thou didst delay to hear, lamenting to disown.

VIII.

From what Hyrcanian glen or frozen hill,
  Or piny promontory of the Arctic main,
Or utmost islet inaccessible,
  Didst thou lament the ruin of thy reign,

---

[1] Unless one is familiar with classical mythology and history, one should read
Shelley with a classical dictionary at his elbow.

Teaching the woods and waves, and desert rocks,
    And every Naiad's ice-cold urn,
    To talk in echoes sad and stern,
Of that sublimest lore which man had dared unlearn?
  For neither didst thou watch the wizard flocks
    Of the Scald's dreams, nor haunt the Druid's sleep.
  What if the tears rained through thy shattered locks
    Were quickly dried? for thou didst groan, not weep,
When from its sea of death to kill and burn,
  The Galilean serpent forth did creep,
  And made thy world an undistinguishable heap.

IX.

A thousand years the Earth cried, Where art thou?
  And then the shadow of thy coming fell
On Saxon Alfred's olive-cinctured brow:
  And many a warrior-peopled citadel,
Like rocks which fire lifts out of the flat deep,
    Arose in sacred Italy,
    Frowning o'er the tempestuous sea
Of kings, and priests, and slaves, in tower-crowned majesty:
  That multitudinous anarchy did sweep,
    And burst around their walls, like idle foam.
  Whilst from the human spirit's deepest deep
    Strange melody with love and awe struck dumb
Dissonant arms; and Art, which cannot die,
  With divine wand traced on our earthly home
  Fit imagery to pave heaven's everlasting dome.

X.

Thou huntress swifter than the Moon! thou terror
  Of the world's wolves! thou bearer of the quiver,
Whose sun-like shafts pierce tempest-wingèd Error,
  As light may pierce the clouds when they dissever

In the calm regions of the orient day!
        Luther caught thy wakening glance,
        Like lightning, from his leaden lance
Reflected, it dissolved the visions of the trance
    In which, as in a tomb, the nations lay;
        And England's prophets hailed thee as their queen,
    In songs whose music cannot pass away,
        Though it must flow for ever; not unseen
Before the spirit-sighted countenance
    Of Milton didst thou pass, from the sad scene
    Beyond whose night he saw, with a dejected mien.

XI.

The eager hours and unreluctant years
    As on a dawn-illumined mountain stood,
Trampling to silence their loud hopes and fears,
    Darkening each other with their multitude,
And cried aloud, Liberty! Indignation
        Answered Pity from her cave;
        Death grew pale within the grave,
And Desolation howled to the destroyer, Save!
    When, like heaven's sun girt by the exhalation
        Of its own glorious light, thou didst arise,
    Chasing thy foes from nation unto nation
        Like shadows: as if day had cloven the skies
At dreaming midnight o'er the western wave,
    Men started, staggering with a glad surprise,
    Under the lightnings of thine unfamiliar eyes.

XII.

Thou heaven of earth! what spells could pall thee then,
    In ominous eclipse? a thousand years
Bred from the slime of deep oppression's den,
    Dyed all thy liquid light with blood and tears,

Till thy sweet stars could weep the stain away;
　　　How like Bacchanals of blood
　　　Round France, the ghastly vintage, stood
Destruction's sceptred slaves, and Folly's mitred brood!
　When one, like them, but mightier far than they,
　　The Anarch of thine own bewildered powers
　Rose: armies mingled in obscure array,
　　Like clouds with clouds, darkening the sacred bowers
Of serene heaven. He, by the past pursued,
　Rests with those dead, but unforgotten hours,
Whose ghosts scare victor kings in their ancestral towers.

XIII.

England yet sleeps: was she not called of old?
　Spain calls her now, as with its thrilling thunder
Vesuvius wakens Ætna, and the cold
　Snow-crags by its reply are cloven in sunder:
O'er the lit waves every Æolian isle
　　From Pithecusa to Pelorus
　　Howls, and leaps, and glares in chorus:
They cry, Be dim; ye lamps of heaven suspended o'er us.
　Her chains are threads of gold, she need but smile
　　And they dissolve: but Spain's were links of steel,
　Till bit to dust by virtue's keenest file.
　　Twins of a single destiny! appeal
To the eternal years enthroned before us,
　In the dim West: impress us from a seal.
All ye have thought and done! Time cannot dare conceal.

XIV.

Tomb of Arminius! render up thy dead
　Till, like a standard from a watch-tower's staff,
His soul may stream over the tyrant's head;
　Thy victory shall be his epitaph.

Wild Bacchanal of truth's mysterious wine,
    King-deluded Germany,
      His dead spirit lives in thee.
Why do we fear or hope? thou art already free!
  And thou, lost Paradise of this divine
    And glorious world! thou flowery wilderness!
  Thou island of eternity! thou shrine
    Where desolation clothed with loveliness,
Worships the thing thou wert! O Italy,
  Gather thy blood into thy heart; repress
  The beasts who make their dens thy sacred palaces.

XV.

O, that the free would stamp the impious name
  Of KING [1] into the dust! or write it there,
So that this blot upon the page of fame
  Were as a serpent's path, which the light air
Erases, and the flat sands close behind!
    Ye the oracle have heard:
    Lift the victory-flashing sword,
And cut the snaky knots of this foul gordian word,
  Which weak itself as stubble, yet can bind
    Into a mass, irrefragably firm,
  The axes and the rods which awe mankind;
    The sound has poison in it, 'tis the sperm
Of what makes life foul, cankerous, and abhorred;
  Disdain not thou, at thine appointed term,
  To set thine armèd heel on this reluctant worm.

XVI.

O, that the wise from their bright minds would kindle
  Such lamps within the dome of this dim world,

---

[1] In Shelley's and Mrs. Shelley's editions this word is omitted, and in its place are four asterisks, which have given rise to much discussion. *King* is the word in the extant fragment of the rough draft.—H. B. FORMAN.

That the pale name of PRIEST might shrink and dwindle[1]
  Into the hell from which it first was hurled,
A scoff of impious pride from fiends impure,
     Till human thoughts might kneel alone,
     Each before the judgment-throne
Of its own aweless soul, or of the power unknown!
  O, that the words which make the thoughts obscure
    From which they spring, as clouds of glimmering dew
  From a white lake blot heaven's blue portraiture,
    Were stript of their thin masks and various hue
And frowns and smiles and splendours not their own,
  Till in the nakedness of false and true
  They stand before their Lord, each to receive its due.

XVII.

He who taught man to vanquish whatsoever
  Can be between the cradle and the grave
Crowned him the King of Life. O vain endeavour!
  If on his own high will a willing slave,
He has enthroned the oppression and the oppressor.
     What if earth can clothe and feed
     Amplest millions at their need,
And power in thought be as the tree within the seed?
  O, what if Art, an ardent intercessor,
    Driving on fiery wings to Nature's throne,
  Checks the great mother stooping to caress her,
    And cries: Give me, thy child, dominion
Over all height and depth? if Life can breed
  New wants, and wealth from those who toil and groan
  Rend of thy gifts and hers a thousandfold for one.

----

[1] That he did to the last regard it (the Christian religion) as by all historical evidence the invariable accomplice of tyranny—as at once the constant shield and ready spear of force and fraud—his latest letters show as clearly as that he did no injustice to "the sublime human character" of its founder.—SWINBURNE.

XVIII.

Come Thou, but lead out of the inmost cave
  Of man's deep spirit, as the morning-star
Beckons the Sun from the Eoan wave,
  Wisdom. I hear the pennons of her car
Self-moving, like cloud charioted by flame;
        Comes she not, and come ye not,
        Rulers of eternal thought,
To judge, with solemn truth, life's ill-apportioned lot?
  Blind Love, and equal Justice, and the Fame
    Of what has been, the Hope of what will be?
  O, Liberty! if such could be thy name
    Wert thou disjoined from these, or they from thee:
If thine or theirs were treasures to be bought
  By blood or tears, have not the wise and free
  Wept tears, and blood like tears? The solemn harmony

XIX.

Paused, and the spirit of that mighty singing
  To its abyss was suddenly withdrawn;
Then, as a wild swan, when sublimely winging
  Its path athwart the thunder-smoke of dawn,
Sinks headlong through the aërial golden light
        On the heavy sounding plain,
        When the bolt has pierced its brain;
As summer clouds dissolve, unburthened of their rain;
  As a far taper fades with fading night,
    As a brief insect dies with dying day,
  My song, its pinions disarrayed of might,
    Drooped; o'er it closed the echoes far away
Of the great voice which did its flight sustain,
  As waves which lately paved his watery way
  Hiss round a drowner's head in their tempestuous play.
1820.]

ARETHUSA.

I.

Arethusa arose
From her couch of snows
In the Acroceraunian mountains,—
From cloud and from crag,
With many a jag,
Shepherding her bright fountains.
She leapt down the rocks,
With her rainbow locks
Streaming among the streams;—
Her steps paved with green
The downward ravine
Which slopes to the western gleams:
And gliding and springing
She went, ever singing,
In murmurs as soft as sleep;
The Earth seemed to love her,
And Heaven smiled above her,
As she lingered towards the deep.

II.

Then Alpheus bold,
On his glacier cold,
With his trident the mountains strook
And opened a chasm
In the rocks;—with the spasm
All Erymanthus shook.
And the black south wind
It concealed behind
The urns of the silent snow,

And earthquake and thunder
Did rend in sunder
The bars of the springs below:
The beard and the hair
Of the River-god were
Seen through the torrent's sweep,
As he followed the light
Of the fleet nymph's flight
To the brink of the Dorian deep.

III.

" Oh, save me! Oh, guide me!
And bid the deep hide me,
For he grasps me now by the hair! "
The loud Ocean heard,
To its blue depth stirred,
And divided at her prayer;
And under the water
The Earth's white daughter
Fled like a sunny beam:
Behind her descended
Her billows, unblended
With the brackish Dorian stream:—
Like a gloomy stain
On the emerald main
Alpheus rushed behind.—
As an eagle pursuing
A dove to its ruin
Down the streams of the cloudy wind.

IV.

Under the bowers
Where the Ocean Powers
Sit on their pearlèd thrones,
Through the coral woods

Of the weltering floods,
Over heaps of unvalued stones;
Through the dim beams
Which amid the streams
Weave a net-work of coloured light;
And under the caves,
Where the shadowy waves
Are as green as the forest's night:—
Outspeeding the shark,
And the sword-fish dark,
Under the ocean foam,
And up through the rifts
Of the mountain clifts
They past to their Dorian home.

V.

And now from their fountains
In Enna's mountains,
Down one vale where the morning basks,
Like friends once parted
Grown single-hearted,
They ply their watery tasks.
At sunrise they leap
From their cradles steep
In the cave of the shelving hill;
At noon-tide they flow
Through the woods below
And the meadows of Asphodel;
And at night they sleep
In the rocking deep
Beneath the Ortygian shore;—
Like spirits that lie
In the azure sky
When they love but live no more.

1820.]

HYMN OF APOLLO.

I.

The sleepless Hours who watch me as I lie,
　Curtained with star-inwoven tapestries,
From the broad moonlight of the sky,
　Fanning the busy dreams from my dim eyes.—
Waken me when their Mother, the grey Dawn,
Tells them that dreams and that the moon is gone.

II.

Then I arise, and climbing Heaven's blue dome,
　I walk over the mountains and the waves,
Leaving my robe upon the ocean foam:
　My footsteps pave the clouds with fire: the caves
Are filled with my bright presence, and the air
Leaves the green earth to my embraces bare.

III.

The sunbeams are my shafts, with which I kill
　Deceit, that loves the night and fears the day;
All men who do or even imagine ill
　Fly me, and from the glory of my ray
Good minds and open actions take new might,
Until diminished by the reign of night.

IV.

I feed the clouds, the rainbows and the flowers
　With their aethereal colours: the Moon's globe
And the pure stars in their eternal bowers
　Are cinctured with my power as with a robe;
Whatever lamps on Earth or Heaven may shine,
Are portions of one power, which is mine.

V.

I stand at noon upon the peak of Heaven,
  Then with unwilling steps I wander down
Into the clouds of the Atlantic even;
  For grief that I depart they weep and frown:
What look is more delightful than the smile
With which I soothe them from the western isle?

VI.

I am the eye with which the Universe
  Beholds itself and knows itself divine;
All harmony of instrument or verse,
  All prophecy, all medicine are mine,
All light of art or nature;—to my song,
Victory and praise in their own right belong.

1820.]

HYMN OF PAN.[1]

I.

From the forests and highlands
    We come, we come:
From the river-girt islands,
    Where loud waves are dumb
        Listening to my sweet pipings.
The wind in the reeds and the rushes,
    The bees on the bells of thyme,
The birds on the myrtle bushes,
    The cicale above in the lime,

---

[1] This and the former poem were written at the request of a friend, to be inserted
in a drama on the subject of Midas. Apollo and Pan contended before Tmolus for
the prize in music.—Mrs. Shelley.

And the lizards below in the grass,
Were as silent as ever old Tmolus was
    Listening to my sweet pipings.

II.

Liquid Peneus was flowing,
    And all dark Tempe lay
In Pelion's shadow, outgrowing
    The light of the dying day,
      Speeded by my sweet pipings.
The Sileni, and Sylvans, and Fauns,
    And the Nymphs of the woods and waves,
To the edge of the moist river-lawns,
    And the brink of the dewy caves,
And all that did then attend and follow,
Were silent with love, as you now, Apollo,
      With envy of my sweet pipings.

III.

I sang of the dancing stars,
    I sang of the dædal Earth,
And of Heaven—and the giant wars,
    And Love, and Death, and Birth,—
      And then I changed my pipings,—
Singing how down the vale of Menalus
    I pursued a maiden and clasped a reed:
Gods and men, we are all deluded thus!
    It breaks in our bosom and then we bleed:
All wept, as I think both ye now would,
If envy or age had not frozen your blood,
      At the sorrow of my sweet pipings.

1820.]

AUTUMN:

A DIRGE.

The warm sun is failing, the bleak wind is wailing,
The bare boughs are sighing, the pale flowers are dying,
   And the year
On the earth her death-bed, in a shroud of leaves dead,
   Is lying.
  Come, months, come away,
  From November to May,
  In your saddest array;
  Follow the bier
  Of the dead cold year,   10
And like dim shadows watch by her sepulchre.

The chill rain is falling, the nipped worm is crawling,
The rivers are swelling, the thunder is knelling
   For the year;
The blithe swallows are flown, and the lizards each gone
   To his dwelling:
  Come, months, come away;
  Put on white, black, and grey;
  Let your light sisters play—
  Ye, follow the bier   20
  Of the dead cold year,
And make her grave green with tear on tear.

1820.]

DIRGE FOR THE YEAR.

I.

Orphan hours, the year is dead,
  Come and sigh, come and weep!
Merry hours, smile instead,
  For the year is but asleep.
See, it smiles as it is sleeping,
Mocking your untimely weeping.

II.

As an earthquake rocks a corse
  In its coffin in the clay,
So White Winter, that rough nurse,
  Rocks the death-cold year to-day;
Solemn hours! wail aloud
For your mother in her shroud.

III.

As the wild air stirs and sways
  The tree-swung cradle of a child,
So the breath of these rude days
  Rocks the year:—be calm and mild,
Trembling hours, she will arise
With new love within her eyes.

IV.

January grey is here,
  Like a sexton by her grave;
February bears the bier,
  March with grief doth howl and rave,
And April weeps—but, O, ye hours,
Follow with May's fairest flowers.

1821.]

SONG.

I.

Rarely, rarely, comest thou,
    Spirit of Delight!
Wherefore hast thou left me now
    Many a day and night?
Many a weary night and day
'Tis since thou art fled away.

II.

How shall ever one like me
    Win thee back again?
With the joyous and the free
    Thou wilt scoff at pain.
Spirit false! thou hast forgot
All but those who need thee not.

III.

As a lizard with the shade
    Of a trembling leaf,
Thou with sorrow art dismayed;
    Even the sighs of grief
Reproach thee, that thou art not near,
And reproach thou wilt not hear.

IV.

Let me set my mournful ditty
    To a merry measure,
Thou wilt never come for pity,
    Thou wilt come for pleasure.
Pity then will cut away
Those cruel wings, and thou wilt stay.

V.

I love all that thou lovest,
   Spirit of Delight!
The fresh Earth in new leaves drest
   And the starry night;
Autumn evening, and the morn
When the golden mists are born.

VI.

I love snow, and all the forms
   Of the radiant frost:
I love waves, and winds, and storms,
   Everything almost
Which is Nature's, and may be
Untainted by man's misery.

VII.

I love tranquil solitude,
   And such society
As is quiet, wise, and good:
   Between thee and me
What difference? but thou dost possess
The things I seek, not love them less.

VIII.

I love Love—though he has wings,
   And like light can flee,
But above all other things,
   Spirit, I love thee—
Thou art love and life! O come,
Make once more my heart thy home.

1821.]

TO NIGHT.

I.

Swiftly walk o'er the western wave,
    Spirit of Night!
Out of the misty eastern cave,
Where all the long and lone daylight,
Thou wovest dreams of joy and fear,
Which make thee terrible and dear,—
    Swift be thy flight!

II.

Wrap thy form in a mantle grey,
    Star-inwrought!
Blind with thine hair the eyes of Day,
Kiss her until she be wearied out,
Then wander o'er city, and sea, and land,
Touching all with thine opiate wand—
    Come, long-sought!

III.

When I arose and saw the dawn,
    I sighed for thee;
When light rode high, and the dew was gone,
And noon lay heavy on flower and tree,
And the weary Day turned to his rest,
Lingering like an unloved guest,
    I sighed for thee.

IV.

Thy brother Death came, and cried,
    Wouldst thou me?
Thy sweet child Sleep, the filmy-eyed,

Murmured like a noon-tide bee,
Shall I nestle near thy side?
Wouldst thou me?—and I replied,
        No, not thee!

V.

Death will come when thou art dead,
        Soon; too soon—
Sleep will come when thou art fled;
Of neither would I ask the boon
I ask of thee, belovèd night,—
Swift be thy approaching flight,
        Come soon, soon!

1821.]

TO-MORROW.

Where art thou, beloved To-morrow?
    When young and old and strong and weak,
Rich and poor, through joy and sorrow,
    Thy sweet smiles we ever seek,—
In thy place—ah! well-a-day!
We find the thing we fled—To-day.

1821.]

WITH A GUITAR: TO JANE.

Ariel to Miranda.—Take
This slave of Music, for the sake
Of him who is the slave of thee,
And teach it all the harmony
In which thou canst, and only thou,
Make the delighted spirit glow,
Till joy denies itself again,

And, too intense, is turned to pain;
For by permission and command
Of thine own Prince Ferdinand,　　　　　　10
Poor Ariel sends this silent token
Of more than ever can be spoken;
Your guardian spirit, Ariel, who,
From life to life, must still pursue
Your happiness:—for thus alone
Can Ariel ever find his own.
From Prospero's enchanted cell,
As the mighty verses tell,
To the throne of Naples, he
Lit you o'er the trackless sea,　　　　　　20
Flitting on, your prow before,
Like a living meteor.
When you die, the silent Moon,
In her interlunar swoon,
Is not sadder in her cell
Than deserted Ariel.
When you live again on earth,
Like an unseen star of birth,
Ariel guides you o'er the sea
Of life from your nativity.　　　　　　30
Many changes have been run,
Since Ferdinand and you begun
Your course of love, and Ariel still
Has tracked your steps, and served your will;
Now, in humbler, happier lot,
This is all remembered not;
And now, alas! the poor sprite is
Imprisoned, for some fault of his,
In a body like a grave;—
From you he only dares to crave,　　　　　　40
For his service and his sorrow,
A smile to-day, a song to-morrow.

The artist who this idol wrought,
To echo all harmonious thought,
Felled a tree, while on the steep
The woods were in their winter sleep,
Rocked in that repose divine
On the wind-swept Apennine;
And dreaming, some of Autumn past,
And some of Spring approaching fast,　　50
And some of April buds and showers,
And some of songs in July bowers,
And all of love; and so this tree,—
O that such our death may be!—
Died in sleep, and felt no pain,
To live in happier form again:
From which, beneath Heaven's fairest star,
The artist wrought this loved Guitar,
And taught it justly to reply,
To all who question skilfully,　　60
In language gentle as thine own;
Whispering in enamoured tone
Sweet oracles of woods and dells,
And summer winds in sylvan cells;
For it had learnt all harmonies
Of the plains and of the skies,
Of the forests and the mountains,
And the many-voicéd fountains;
The clearest echoes of the hills,
The softest notes of falling rills,　　70
The melodies of birds and bees,
The murmuring of summer seas,
And pattering rain, and breathing dew,
And airs of evening: and it knew
That seldom-heard mysterious sound,
Which, driven on its diurnal round,
As it floats through boundless day,

Our world enkindles on its way—
All this it knows, but will not tell
To those who cannot question well   60
The spirit that inhabits it;
It talks according to the wit
Of its companions; and no more
Is heard than has been felt before,
By those who tempt it to betray
These secrets of an elder day:
But sweetly as its answers will
Flatter hands of perfect skill,
It keeps its highest, holiest tone
For our belovèd Jane alone.   90

1822.]

After a sketch by Severn.

JOHN KEATS.

staying a short time with Mrs
Brawne who lives in the House
which was Mrs Dilke's. I am ex-
cessively nervous. a person I am
not quite used to entering the
room half chokes me. 'Tis not
yet Consumption I believe, but
it would be mad of me to remain
in this climate all the Winter:
so I am thinking of either voyage-
ing or travelling to Italy. Yester-
day I received an invitation
from Mr Shelley, a Gentleman
residing at Pisa, to spend the
Winter with him: if I go I must
be away in a Month or even
less. I am glad you like the Poems

You must hope with me th[at]
time and health will pro[cure]
you some more. This is the first
morning I have been able to
sit to the paper and have many Letters to write if I can
manage them. God bless you
my dear Sister.

Your affectionate Bro[ther]
John.

SELECTIONS FROM KEATS

TO G. A. W.[1]

Nymph of the downward smile and sidelong glance,
   In what diviner moments of the day
   Art thou most lovely?—when gone far astray
Into the labyrinths of sweet utterance,
Or when serenely wand'ring in a trance
   Of sober thought?—or when starting away
   With careless robe to meet the morning ray
Thou spar'st the flowers in thy mazy dance?
Haply 'tis when thy ruby lips part sweetly,
   And so remain, because thou listenest:
But thou to please wert nurtured so completely
   That I can never tell what mood is best.
I shall as soon pronounce which Grace more neatly
   Trips it before Apollo than the rest.

December, 1816.]

TO SOLITUDE.

O Solitude! if I must with thee dwell,
   Let it not be among the jumbled heap
   Of murky buildings; climb with me to the steep,—
Nature's observatory—whence the dell,

Its flowery slopes, its river's crystal swell,
    May seem a span; let me thy vigils keep
    'Mongst boughs pavilion'd,[1] where the deer's swift leap
Startles the wild bee from the fox-glove bell.
But though I'll gladly trace these scenes with thee,
    Yet the sweet converse of an innocent mind,
    Whose words are images of thoughts refin'd,
Is my soul's pleasure; and it sure must be
    Almost the highest bliss of human-kind,
When to thy haunts two kindred spirits flee.

1816.]

ON FIRST LOOKING INTO CHAPMAN'S HOMER.

Much have I travell'd in the realms of gold,
    And many goodly states and kingdoms seen;
    Round many western islands have I been
Which bards in fealty to Apollo hold.
Oft of one wide expanse had I been told
    That deep-brow'd Homer ruled as his demesne;
    Yet did I never breathe its pure serene
Till I heard Chapman speak out loud and bold:
Then felt I like some watcher of the skies
    When a new planet swims into his ken;
Or like stout Cortez when with eagle eyes
    He star'd at the Pacific—and all his men
Look'd at each other with a wild surmise—
    Silent, upon a peak in Darien.

1816.]

---

[1] For verb forms in ed, the custom of Keats was to write 'd when the e was silent, ed where Shelley wrote èd, when the e was sounded. He did not, however, consistently follow his own rule.

ON THE GRASSHOPPER AND CRICKET.

The poetry of earth is never dead:
  When all the birds are faint with the hot sun,
  And hide in cooling trees, a voice will run
From hedge to hedge about the new-mown mead;
That is the Grasshopper's—he takes the lead
  In summer luxury,—he has never done
  With his delights; for when tired out with fun
He rests at ease beneath some pleasant weed.
The poetry of earth is ceasing never:
  On a lone winter evening, when the frost
    Has wrought a silence, from the stove there shrills
The Cricket's song, in warmth increasing ever,
  And seems to one in drowsiness half lost,
    The Grasshopper's among the grassy hills.

December 30, 1816.]

DEDICATION.

TO LEIGH HUNT, ESQ.[1]

Glory and loveliness have pass'd away:
  For if we wander out in early morn,
  No wreathed incense do we see upborne
Into the east, to meet the smiling day:
No crowd of nymphs soft-voic'd and young, and gay,
  In woven baskets bringing ears of corn,
  Roses, and pinks, and violets, to adorn
The shrine of Flora in her early May.

---

[1] Dedication to the first volume of poems, printed in 1817.

But there are left delights as high as these,
　And I shall ever bless my destiny,
That in a time, when under pleasant trees
　Pan is no longer sought, I feel a free
A leafy luxury, seeing I could please
　With these poor offerings, a man like thee.

THE OPENING STANZAS OF ENDYMION.[1]

A thing of beauty is a joy forever:
Its loveliness increases; it will never
Pass into nothingness; but still will keep
A bower quiet for us, and a sleep
Full of sweet dreams, and health, and quiet breathing.
Therefore, on every morrow, are we wreathing
A flowery band to bind us to the earth,
Spite of despondence, of the inhuman dearth
Of noble natures, of the gloomy days,
Of all the unhealthy and o'er-darkened ways　　10
Made for our searching: yes, in spite of all,
Some shape of beauty moves away the pall
From our dark spirits. Such the sun, the moon,
Trees old, and young, sprouting a shady boon
For simple sheep: and such are daffodils
With the green world they live in: and clear rills
That for themselves a cooling covert make
'Gainst the hot season: the mid forest brake,
Rich with a sprinkling of fair musk-rose blooms:
And such too is the grandeur of the dooms　　20

---

[1] In proof of the impression made by the genius and early death of Chatterton upon the poets who followed, see not only the "Monody on the Death of Chatterton," by Coleridge, and references by Shelley and Wordsworth, but also the dedication of "Endymion": "Inscribed, with every feeling of pride and regret, and with 'a bowed mind,' to the memory of the most English of poets except Shakspeare, Thomas Chatterton."

We have imagined for the mighty dead;
All lovely tales that we have heard or read:
An endless fountain of immortal drink,
Pouring unto us from the heaven's brink.

Nor do we merely feel these essences
For one short hour; no, even as the trees
That whisper round a temple become soon
Dear as the temple's self, so does the moon,
The passion poesy, glories infinite,
Haunt us till they become a cheering light   30
Unto our souls, and bound to us so fast,
That, whether there be shine, or gloom o'ercast,
They always must be with us, or we die.

Therefore, 'tis with full happiness that I
Will trace the story of Endymion.
The very music of the name has gone
Into my being, and each pleasant scene
Is growing fresh before me as the green
Of our own valleys: so I will begin
Now while I cannot hear the city's din;   40
Now while the early budders are just new,
And run in mazes of the youngest hue
About old forests; while the willow trails
Its delicate amber; and the dairy pails
Bring home increase of milk. And, as the year
Grows lush in juicy stalks, I'll smoothly steer
My little boat, for many quiet hours,
With streams that deepen freshly into bowers.
Many and many a verse I hope to write,
Before the daisies, vermeil rimm'd and white,   50
Hide in deep herbage: and ere yet the bees
Hum about globes of clover and sweet peas,
I must be near the middle of my story.

O may no wintry season, bare and hoary,
See it half finished: but let Autumn bold,
With universal tinge of sober gold,
Be all about me when I make an end.
And now at once, adventuresome, I send
My herald thought into a wilderness:
There let its trumpet blow, and quickly dress   60
My uncertain path with green, that I may speed
Easily onward, thorough flowers and weed.

    Upon the sides of Latmos was outspread
A mighty forest; for the moist earth fed
So plenteously all weed-hidden roots
Into o'er-hanging boughs, and precious fruits.
And it had gloomy shades, sequestered deep,
Where no man went; and if from shepherd's keep
A lamb strayed far a-down those inmost glens,
Never again saw he the happy pens   70
Whither his brethren, bleating with content,
Over the hills at every nightfall went.
Among the shepherds, 'twas believed ever,
That not one fleecy lamb which thus did sever
From the white flock, but pass'd unworried
By angry wolf, or pard with prying head,
Until it came to some unfooted plains
Where fed the herds of Pan: aye great his gains
Who thus one lamb did lose. Paths there were many,
Winding through palmy fern, and rushes fenny,   80
And ivy banks; all leading pleasantly
To a wide lawn, whence one could only see
Stems thronging all around between the swell
Of turf and slanting branches: who could tell
The freshness of the space of heaven above,
Edg'd round with dark tree tops? through which a dove
Would often beat its wings, and often too
A little cloud would move across the blue.

Full in the middle of this pleasantness
There stood a marble altar, with a tress   90
Of flowers budded newly; and the dew
Had taken fairy phantasies to strew
Daisies upon the sacred sward last eve,
And so the dawned light in pomp receive.
For 'twas the morn: Apollo's upward fire
Made every eastern cloud a silvery pyre
Of brightness so unsullied, that therein
A melancholy spirit well might win
Oblivion, and melt out his essence fine
Into the winds: rain-scented eglantine   100
Gave temperate sweets to that well-wooing sun;
The lark was lost in him: cold springs had run
To warm their chilliest bubbles in the grass;
Man's voice was on the mountains; and the mass
Of nature's lives and wonders puls'd tenfold,
To feel this sun-rise and its glories old.

1817.]

SONNET.

ON THE SEA.

It keeps eternal whisperings around
  Desolate shores, and with its mighty swell
  Gluts twice ten thousand caverns, till the spell
Of Hecate leaves them their old shadowy sound.
Often 'tis in such gentle temper found,
  That scarcely will the very smallest shell
  Be mov'd for days from whence it sometime fell.
When last the winds of heaven were unbound.
Oh ye! who have your eye-balls vex'd and tir'd,
  Feast them upon the wideness of the Sea;

Oh ye! whose ears are dinn'd with uproar rude,
Or fed too much with cloying melody,—
Sit ye near some old cavern's mouth, and brood
Until ye start, as if the sea-nymphs quir'd!

August, 1817.]

SONNET.

When I have fears that I may cease to be
Before my pen has glean'd my teeming brain,
Before high piled books, in charactry,
Hold like rich garners the full ripen'd grain;
When I behold, upon the night's starr'd face,
Huge cloudy symbols of a high romance,
And think that I may never live to trace
Their shadows, with the magic hand of chance;
And when I feel, fair creature of an hour,
That I shall never look upon thee more,
Never have relish in the faery power
Of unreflecting love;—then on the shore
Of the wide world I stand alone, and think
Till love and fame to nothingness do sink.

1817.]

FANCY.

Ever let the Fancy roam,
Pleasure never is at home:
At a touch sweet Pleasure melteth,
Like to bubbles when rain pelteth;
Then let winged Fancy wander
Through the thought still spread beyond her:
Open wide the mind's cage-door,
She'll dart forth, and cloudward soar.

O sweet Fancy! let her loose;
Summer's joys are spoilt by use, 10
And the enjoying of the Spring
Fades as does its blossoming;
Autumn's red-lipp'd fruitage too,
Blushing through the mist and dew,
Cloys with tasting: What do then?
Sit thee by the ingle, when
The sear faggot blazes bright,
Spirit of a winter's night;
When the soundless earth is muffled,
And the caked snow is shuffled 20
From the ploughboy's heavy shoon;
When the Night doth meet the Noon
In a dark conspiracy
To banish Even from her sky.
Sit thee there, and send abroad,
With a mind self-overaw'd,
Fancy, high-commission'd:—send her!
She has vassals to attend her:
She will bring, in spite of frost,
Beauties that the earth hath lost; 30
She will bring thee, all together,
All delights of summer weather;
All the buds and bells of May,
From dewy sward or thorny spray;
All the heaped Autumn's wealth,
With a still, mysterious stealth:
She will mix these pleasures up
Like three fit wines in a cup,
And thou shalt quaff it:—thou shalt hear
Distant harvest-carols clear; 40
Rustle of the reaped corn;
Sweet birds antheming the morn:
And, in the same moment—hark!

'Tis the early April lark.
Or the rooks, with busy caw,
Foraging for sticks and straw.
Thou shalt, at one glance, behold
The daisy and the marigold:
White-plum'd lilies, and the first
Hedge-grown primrose that hath burst; 50
Shaded hyacinth, alway
Sapphire queen of the mid-May:
And every leaf, and every flower
Pearled with the self-same shower.
Thou shalt see the field-mouse peep
Meagre from its celled sleep;
And the snake all winter-thin
Cast on sunny bank its skin;
Freckled nest-eggs thou shalt see
Hatching in the hawthorn-tree, 60
When the hen-bird's wing doth rest
Quiet on her mossy nest;
Then the hurry and alarm
When the bee-hive casts its swarm;
Acorns ripe down-pattering.
While the autumn breezes sing.

Oh, sweet Fancy! let her loose;
Everything is spoilt by use:
Where's the cheek that doth not fade,
Too much gaz'd at? Where's the maid 70
Whose lip mature is ever new?
Where's the eye, however blue,
Doth not weary? Where's the face
One would meet in every place?
Where's the voice, however soft
One would hear so very oft?
At a touch sweet Pleasure melteth

Like to bubbles when rain pelteth.
Let, then, winged Fancy find
Thee a mistress to thy mind: 80
Dulcet-eyed as Ceres' daughter,
Ere the God of Torment taught her
How to frown and how to chide;
With a waist and with a side
White as Hebe's, when her zone
Slipt its golden clasp, and down
Fell her kirtle to her feet,
While she held the goblet sweet,
And Jove grew languid.—Break the mesh
Of the Fancy's silken leash; 90
Quickly break her prison-string
And such joys as these she'll bring.—
Let the winged Fancy roam,
Pleasure never is at home.

1818.]

ODE.[1]

Bards of Passion and of Mirth,
Ye have left your souls on earth!
Have ye souls in heaven too,
Double-lived in regions new?
Yes, and those of heaven commune
With the spheres of sun and moon;
With the noise of fountains wond'rous,
And the parle of voices thund'rous;
With the whisper of heaven's trees
And one another, in soft ease 10

---

[1] Written in Beaumont and Fletcher's Tragi-Comedy, "The Fair Maid of the Inn," and hence, as Forman suggests, addressed, not to poets in general, but to Beaumont and Fletcher.

Seated on Elysian lawns
Brows'd by none but Dian's fawns;
Underneath large blue-bells tented,
Where the daisies are rose-scented,
And the rose herself has got
Perfume which on earth is not;
Where the nightingale doth sing
Not a senseless, tranced thing,
But divine melodious truth;
Philosophic numbers smooth;   20
Tales and golden histories
Of heaven and its mysteries.

    Thus ye live on high, and then
On the earth ye live again:
And the souls ye left behind you
Teach us, here, the way to find you,
Where your other souls are joying.
Never slumber'd, never cloying.
Here, your earth-born souls still speak
To mortals, of their little week;   30
Of their sorrows and delights;
Of their passions and their spites;
Of their glory and their shame;
What doth strengthen and what maim.
Thus ye teach us, every day,
Wisdom, though fled far away.

    Bards of Passion and of Mirth,
Ye have left your souls on earth!
Ye have souls in heaven too,
Double-lived in regions new!   40

LINES ON THE MERMAID TAVERN.[1]

Souls of Poets dead and gone,
What Elysium have ye known,
Happy field or mossy cavern,
Choicer than the Mermaid Tavern?
Have ye tippled drink more fine
Than mine host's Canary wine?
Or are fruits of Paradise
Sweeter than those dainty pies
Of venison? O generous food!
Drest as though bold Robin Hood   10
Would, with his maid Marian,
Sup and bowse from horn and can.

I have heard that on a day
Mine host's sign-board flew away,
Nobody knew whither, till
An astrologer's old quill
To a sheepskin gave the story,
Said he saw you in your glory,
Underneath a new old-sign
Sipping beverage divine,   20
And pledging with contented smack
The Mermaid in the Zodiac.

Souls of Poets dead and gone,
What Elysium have ye known,
Happy field or mossy cavern,
Choicer than the Mermaid Tavern?

1818.]

---

[1] The meeting-place of Shakspere and the other poets of his time.

ODE TO A NIGHTINGALE.[1]

1.

My heart aches, and a drowsy numbness pains
 My sense, as though of hemlock I had drunk,
Or emptied some dull opiate to the drains
 One minute past, and Lethe-wards had sunk:
'Tis not through envy of thy happy lot,
 But being too happy in thine happiness,—
  That thou, light-winged Dryad of the trees,
   In some melodious plot
 Of beechen green, and shadows numberless,
  Singest of summer in full-throated ease.

2.

O, for a draught of vintage! that hath been
 Cool'd a long age in the deep-delved earth,
Tasting of Flora and the country green,
 Dance, and Provençal song, and sunburnt mirth!
O for a beaker full of the warm South,
 Full of the true, the blushful Hippocrene,
  With beaded bubbles winking at the brim,
   And purple-stained mouth:
That I might drink, and leave the world unseen,
 And with thee fade away into the forest dim:

3.

Fade far away, dissolve, and quite forget
 What thou among the leaves hast never known,
The weariness, the fever, and the fret
 Here, where men sit and hear each other groan;

---

[1] Written during the depression caused by the death of Keats's brother, Tom, and his own illness.

Where palsy shakes a few, sad, last gray hairs,
  Where youth grows pale, and spectre-thin, and dies;
    Where but to think is to be full of sorrow
      And leaden-eyed despairs,
  Where Beauty cannot keep her lustrous eyes,
    Or new Love pine at them beyond to-morrow.

4.

Away! away! for I will fly to thee,
  Not charioted by Bacchus and his pards,
But on the viewless wings of Poesy,
  Though the dull brain perplexes and retards:
Already with thee! tender is the night,
  And haply the Queen-Moon is on her throne,
    Cluster'd around by all her starry Fays;
      But here there is no light,
  Save what from heaven is with the breezes blown
    Through verdurous glooms and winding mossy ways.

5.

I cannot see what flowers are at my feet,
  Nor what soft incense hangs upon the boughs,
But, in embalmed darkness, guess each sweet
  Wherewith the seasonable month endows
The grass, the thicket, and the fruit-tree wild;
  White hawthorn, and the pastoral eglantine;
    Fast fading violets cover'd up in leaves;
      And mid-May's eldest child,
  The coming musk-rose, full of dewy wine,
    The murmurous haunt of flies on summer eves.

6.

Darkling I listen: and, for many a time
  I have been half in love with easeful Death,

Call'd him soft names in many a mused rhyme,
  To take into the air my quiet breath;
Now more than ever seems it rich to die,
  To cease upon the midnight with no pain,
    While thou art pouring forth thy soul abroad
      In such an ecstasy!
  Still wouldst thou sing, and I have ears in vain—
    To thy high requiem become a sod.

7.

Thou wast not born for death, immortal Bird!
  No hungry generations tread thee down;
The voice I hear this passing night was heard
  In ancient days by emperor and clown:
Perhaps the self-same song that found a path
  Through the sad heart of Ruth, when, sick for home,
    She stood in tears amid the alien corn;
      The same that oft-times hath
  Charm'd magic casements, opening on the foam
    Of perilous seas, in faery lands forlorn.

8.

Forlorn! the very word is like a bell
  To toll me back from thee to my sole self!
Adieu! the fancy cannot cheat so well
  As she is fam'd to do, deceiving elf.
Adieu! adieu! thy plaintive anthem fades
  Past the near meadows, over the still stream,
    Up the hillside; and now 'tis buried deep
      In the next valley-glades:
  Was it a vision, or a waking dream?
    Fled is that music:—Do I wake or sleep?

May, 1819.]

ODE ON A GRECIAN URN.

1.

Thou still unravish'd bride of quietness,
    Thou foster-child of silence and slow time,
Sylvan historian, who canst thus express
    A flowery tale more sweetly than our rhyme:
What leaf-fring'd legend haunts about thy shape
    Of deities or mortals, or of both,
        In Tempe or the dales of Arcady?
    What men or gods are these? What maidens loth?
What mad pursuit? What struggle to escape?
    What pipes and timbrels? What wild ecstasy?

2.

Heard melodies are sweet, but those unheard
    Are sweeter; therefore, ye soft pipes, play on;
Not to the sensual ear, but, more endear'd,
    Pipe to the spirit ditties of no tone:
Fair youth, beneath the trees, thou canst not leave
    Thy song, nor ever can those trees be bare;
        Bold Lover, never, never canst thou kiss,
Though winning near the goal—yet, do not grieve;
    She cannot fade, though thou hast not thy bliss,
        For ever wilt thou love, and she be fair!

3.

Ah, happy, happy boughs! that cannot shed
    Your leaves, nor ever bid the Spring adieu;
And, happy melodist, unwearied,
    For ever piping songs for ever new;

More happy love! more happy, happy love!
  For ever warm and still to be enjoy'd,
    For ever panting, and for ever young;
All breathing human passion far above,
  That leaves a heart high-sorrowful and cloy'd,
    A burning forehead, and a parching tongue.

4.

Who are these coming to the sacrifice?
  To what green altar, O mysterious priest,
Lead'st thou that heifer lowing at the skies,
  And all her silken flanks with garlands drest?
What little town by river or sea shore,
  Or mountain-built with peaceful citadel,
    Is emptied of this folk, this pious morn?
And, little town, thy streets for evermore
  Will silent be; and not a soul to tell
    Why thou art desolate, can e'er return.

5.

O Attic shape! Fair attitude! with brede
  Of marble men and maidens overwrought,
With forest branches and the trodden weed;
  Thou, silent form, dost tease us out of thought
As doth eternity: Cold Pastoral!
  When old age shall this generation waste,
    Thou shalt remain, in midst of other woe
Than ours, a friend to man, to whom thou say'st,
  " Beauty is truth, truth beauty,"—that is all
    Ye know on earth, and all ye need to know.

1819.]

ODE TO PSYCHE.

O Goddess! hear these tuneless numbers, wrung
  By sweet enforcement and remembrance dear,
And pardon that thy secrets should be sung
  Even into thine own soft-conched ear:
Surely I dreamt to-day, or did I see
  The winged Psyche with awaken'd eyes?
I wander'd in a forest thoughtlessly,
  And, on the sudden, fainting with surprise,
Saw two fair creatures, couched side by side
  In deepest grass, beneath the whisp'ring roof   10
Of leaves and trembled blossoms, where there ran
      A brooklet, scarce espy'd:

'Mid hush'd, cool-rooted flowers, fragrant-eyed,
  Blue, silver-white, and budded Tyrian,
They lay calm-breathing, on the bedded grass;
  Their arms embraced, and their pinions too:
  Their lips touch'd not, but had not bade adieu,
As if disjoined by soft-handed slumber,
And ready still past kisses to outnumber
  At tender eye-dawn of aurorean love: 20
      The winged boy I knew:
  But who wast thou, O happy, happy dove?
      His Psyche true!

O latest born and loveliest vision far
  Of all Olympus' faded hierarchy!
Fairer than Phœbe's sapphire-region'd star,
  Or Vesper, amorous glow-worm of the sky:
Fairer than these, though temple thou hast none,
      Nor altar heap'd with flowers;

Nor virgin-choir to make delicious moan   30
    Upon the midnight hours;
No voice, no lute, no pipe, no incense sweet
  From chain-swung censer teeming;
No shrine, no grove, no oracle, no heat
  Of pale-mouth'd prophet dreaming.

O brightest! though too late for antique vows,
  Too, too late for the fond believing lyre,
When holy were the haunted forest boughs,
  Holy the air, the water, and the fire;
Yet even in these days so far retir'd   40
  From happy pieties, thy lucent fans,
  Fluttering among the faint Olympians,
I see, and sing, by my own eyes inspir'd.
So let me be thy choir, and make a moan
    Upon the midnight hours;
Thy voice, thy lute, thy pipe, thy incense sweet
  From swinged censer teeming;
Thy shrine, thy grove, thy oracle, thy heat
  Of pale-mouth'd prophet dreaming.

Yes, I will be thy priest, and build a fane   50
  In some untrodden region of my mind,
Where branched thoughts, new grown with pleasant pain,
  Instead of pines shall murmur in the wind:
Far, far around shall those dark-cluster'd trees
  Fledge the wild-ridged mountains steep by steep;
And there by zephyrs, streams, and birds, and bees,
  The moss-lain Dryads shall be lull'd to sleep;
And in the midst of this wide quietness
A rosy sanctuary will I dress
With the wreath'd trellis of a working brain,   60
  With buds, and bells, and stars without a name,
With all the gardener Fancy e'er could feign,

Who breeding flowers, will never breed the same:
And there shall be for thee all soft delight
   That shadowy thought can win,
A bright torch, and a casement ope at night,
   To let the warm Love in!

April, 1819.]

TO AUTUMN.

1.

Season of mists and mellow fruitfulness,
   Close bosom-friend of the maturing sun;
Conspiring with him how to load and bless
   With fruit the vines that round the thatch-eves run;
To bend with apples the moss'd cottage-trees,
   And fill all fruit with ripeness to the core;
      To swell the gourd, and plump the hazel shells
With a sweet kernel; to set budding more,
   And still more, later flowers for the bees,
   Until they think warm days will never cease,
      For Summer has o'er-brimm'd their clammy cells.

2.

Who hath not seen thee oft amid thy store?
   Sometimes whoever seeks abroad may find
Thee sitting careless on a granary floor,
   Thy hair soft-lifted by the winnowing wind;
Or on a half-reap'd furrow sound asleep,
   Drows'd with the fume of poppies, while thy hook
      Spares the next swath and all its twined flowers:
And sometimes like a gleaner thou dost keep
   Steady thy laden head across a brook;
   Or by a cyder-press, with patient look,
      Thou watchest the last oozings hours by hours.

3.

Where are the songs of Spring? Ay, where are they?
  Think not of them, thou hast thy music too,—
While barred clouds bloom the soft-dying day,
  And touch the stubble-plains with rosy hue;
Then in a wailful choir the small gnats mourn
  Among the river sallows, borne aloft
    Or sinking as the light wind lives or dies;
And full-grown lambs loud bleat from hilly bourn;
  Hedge-crickets sing; and now with treble soft
  The red-breast whistles from a garden-croft;
    And gathering swallows twitter in the skies.

September, 1819.]

ODE ON MELANCHOLY.

1.

No, no, go not to Lethe, neither twist
  Wolf's-bane, tight-rooted, for its poisonous wine;
Nor suffer thy pale forehead to be kiss'd
  By nightshade, ruby grape of Proserpine;
Make not your rosary of yew-berries,
  Nor let the beetle, nor the death-moth be
    Your mournful Psyche, nor the downy owl
A partner in your sorrow's mysteries;
  For shade to shade will come too drowsily,
    And drown the wakeful anguish of the soul.

2.

But when the melancholy fit shall fall
  Sudden from heaven like a weeping cloud,
That fosters the droop-headed flowers all,
  And hides the green hill in an April shroud;

Then glut thy sorrow on a morning rose,
  Or on the rainbow of the salt sand-wave,
    Or on the wealth of globed peonies;
Or if thy mistress some rich anger shows,
  Emprison her soft hand, and let her rave,
    And feed deep, deep upon her peerless eyes.

3.

She dwells with Beauty—Beauty that must die;
  And Joy, whose hand is ever at his lips
Bidding adieu: and aching Pleasure nigh,
  Turning to poison while the bee-mouth sips:
Ay, in the very temple of Delight
  Veil'd Melancholy has her sovran shrine,
    Though seen of none save him whose strenuous tongue
Can burst Joy's grape against his palate fine;
  His soul shall taste the sadness of her might,
    And be among her cloudy trophies hung.

THE EVE OF ST. AGNES.[1]

I.

St. Agnes' Eve—Ah, bitter chill it was!
The owl, for all his feathers, was a-cold;
The hare limp'd trembling through the frozen grass,
And silent was the flock in woolly fold:
Numb were the Beadsman's fingers, while he told

---

[1] January 20th.
  For a running commentary on the poem, see Leigh Hunt's "Imagination and Fancy," page 300. [Smith & Elder, 1883.]
  For variant readings, see Forman's edition of Keats.

His rosary, and while his frosted breath,
Like pious incense from a censer old,
Seem'd taking flight for heaven, without a death,
Past the sweet Virgin's picture, while his prayer he saith.

II.

His prayer he saith, this patient, holy man;
Then takes his lamp, and riseth from his knees,
And back returneth, meagre, barefoot, wan,
Along the chapel aisle by slow degrees:
The sculptur'd dead, on each side, seem to freeze,
Emprison'd in black, purgatorial rails:
Knights, ladies, praying in dumb orat'ries,
He passeth by; and his weak spirit fails
To think how they may ache in icy hoods and mails.

III.

Northward he turneth through a little door,
And scarce three steps, ere Music's golden tongue
Flatter'd to tears this aged man and poor:
But no—already had his deathbell rung:
The joys of all his life were said and sung:
His was harsh penance on St. Agnes' Eve:
Another way he went, and soon among
Rough ashes sat he for his soul's reprieve,
And all night kept awake, for sinners' sake to grieve.

IV.

That ancient Beadsman heard the prelude soft;
And so it chanc'd, for many a door was wide,
From hurry to and fro. Soon, up aloft,
The silver, snarling trumpets 'gan to chide:
The level chambers, ready with their pride,

Were glowing to receive a thousand guests:
The carved angels, ever eager-eyed,
Star'd, where upon their heads the cornice rests,
With hair blown back, and wings put cross-wise on their
       breasts.

V.

At length burst in the argent revelry,
With plume, tiara, and all rich array,
Numerous as shadows haunting faerily
The brain, new stuff'd, in youth, with triumphs gay
Of old romance. These let us wish away,
And turn, soul-thoughted, to one Lady there,
Whose heart had brooded, all that wintry day,
On love, and wing'd St. Agnes' saintly care,
As she had heard old dames full many times declare.

VI.

They told her how, upon St. Agnes' Eve,
Young virgins might have visions of delight,
And soft adorings from their loves receive
Upon the honey'd middle of the night,
If ceremonies due they did aright;
As, supperless to bed they must retire,
And couch supine their beauties, lily white;
Nor look behind, nor sideways, but require
Of Heaven with upward eyes for all that they desire.

VII.

Full of this whim was thoughtful Madeline:
The music, yearning like a God in pain,
She scarcely heard: her maiden eyes divine,
Fix'd on the floor, saw many a sweeping train

Pass by—she heeded not at all: in vain
Came many a tiptoe, amorous cavalier,
And back retir'd; not cool'd by high disdain,
But she saw not: her heart was otherwhere:
She sigh'd for Agnes' dreams, the sweetest of the year.

VIII.

She danc'd along with vague, regardless eyes,
Anxious her lips, her breathing quick and short:
The hallow'd hour was near at hand: she sighs
Amid the timbrels, and the throng'd resort
Of whisperers in anger, or in sport:
'Mid looks of love, defiance, hate, and scorn,
Hoodwink'd with faery fancy; all amort,
Save to St. Agnes and her lambs unshorn,[1]
And all the bliss to be before to-morrow morn.

IX.

So, purposing each moment to retire,
She linger'd still. Meantime, across the moors,
Had come young Porphyro, with heart on fire
For Madeline. Beside the portal doors,
Buttress'd from moonlight, stands he, and implores
All saints to give him sight of Madeline,
But for one moment in the tedious hours,
That he might gaze and worship all unseen:
Perchance speak, kneel, touch, kiss—in sooth such things
          have been.

---

[1] The offering to St. Agnes was two unshorn lambs; the wool was afterwards carded and spun by the nuns. Cf. Stanza XIII., lines 7 9.

X.

He ventures in: let no buzz'd whisper tell:
All eyes be muffled, or a hundred swords
Will storm his heart, Love's fev'rous citadel:
For him, those chambers held barbarian hordes,
Hyena foemen, and hot-blooded lords,
Whose very dogs would execrations howl
Against his lineage: not one breast affords
Him any mercy, in that mansion foul,
Save one old beldame, weak in body and in soul.

XI.

Ah, happy chance! the aged creature came,
Shuffling along with ivory-headed wand,
To where he stood, hid from the torch's flame,
Behind a broad hall-pillar, far beyond
The sound of merriment and chorus bland:
He startled her; but soon she knew his face,
And grasp'd his fingers in her palsied hand,
Saying, " Mercy, Porphyro! hie thee from this place:
" They are all here to-night, the whole blood-thirsty race!

XII.

" Get hence! get hence! there's dwarfish Hildebrand;
" He had a fever late, and in the fit
" He cursed thee and thine, both house and land:
" Then there's that old Lord Maurice, not a whit
" More tame for his gray hairs—Alas me! flit!
" Flit like a ghost away."—" Ah, Gossip dear,
" We're safe enough; here in this arm-chair sit,
" And tell me how "—" Good Saints! Not here, not
        here;
" Follow me, child, or else these stones will be thy bier."

XIII.

He follow'd through a lowly arched way,
Brushing the cobwebs with his lofty plume,
And as she mutter'd " Well-a— well-a-day! "
He found him in a little moonlight room,
Pale, lattic'd, chill, and silent as a tomb.
" Now tell me where is Madeline," said he,
" O tell me, Angela, by the holy loom
" Which none but secret sisterhood may see,
" When they St. Agnes' wool are weaving piously."

XIV.

" St. Agnes! Ah! it is St. Agnes' Eve—
" Yet men will murder upon holy days:
" Thou must hold water in a witch's sieve,
" And be liege-lord of all the Elves and Fays,
" To venture so: it fills me with amaze
" To see thee, Porphyro!— St. Agnes' Eve!
" God's help! my lady fair the conjuror plays
" This very night: good angels her deceive!
" But let me laugh awhile, I've mickle time to grieve."

XV.

Feebly she laugheth in the languid moon,
While Porphyro upon her face doth look,
Like puzzled urchin on an aged crone
Who keepeth clos'd a wond'rous riddle-book,
As spectacled she sits in chimney nook.
But soon his eyes grew brilliant, when she told
His lady's purpose: and he scarce could brook
Tears, at the thought of those enchantments cold,
And Madeline asleep in lap of legends old.

XVI.

Sudden a thought came like a full-blown rose,
Flushing his brow, and in his pained heart
Made purple riot: then doth he propose
A stratagem, that makes the beldame start:
" A cruel man and impious thou art:
" Sweet lady, let her pray, and sleep, and dream
" Alone with her good angels, far apart
" From wicked men like thee. Go, go!—I deem
" Thou canst not surely be the same that thou didst seem."

XVII.

" I will not harm her, by all saints I swear,"
Quoth Porphyro: " O may I ne'er find grace
" When my weak voice shall whisper its last prayer,
" If one of her soft ringlets I displace,
" Or look with ruffian passion in her face:
" Good Angela, believe me by these tears;
" Or I will, even in a moment's space,
" Awake, with horrid shout, my foemen's ears,
" And beard them, though they be more fang'd than wolves
and bears."

XVIII.

" Ah! why wilt thou affright a feeble soul?
" A poor, weak, palsy-stricken, churchyard thing,
" Whose passing-bell may ere the midnight toll:
" Whose prayers for thee, each morn and evening,
" Were never miss'd."—Thus plaining, doth she bring
A gentler speech from burning Porphyro;
So woful, and of such deep sorrowing,
That Angela gives promise she will do
Whatever he shall wish, betide her weal or woe.

XIX.

Which was, to lead him, in close secrecy,
Even to Madeline's chamber, and there hide
Him in a closet, of such privacy
That he might see her beauty unespied,
And win perhaps that night a peerless bride,
While legion'd faeries pac'd the coverlet,
And pale enchantment held her sleepy-eyed.
Never on such a night have lovers met,
Since Merlin paid his Demon all the monstrous debt.[1]

XX.

" It shall be as thou wishest," said the Dame:
" All cates and dainties shall be stored there
" Quickly on this feast-night: by the tambour frame
" Her own lute thou wilt see: no time to spare,
" For I am slow and feeble, and scarce dare
" On such a catering trust my dizzy head.
" Wait here, my child, with patience: kneel in prayer
" The while: Ah! thou must needs the lady wed,
" Or may I never leave my grave among the dead."

XXI.

So saying, she hobbled off with busy fear.
The lover's endless minutes slowly pass'd:
The dame return'd, and whisper'd in his ear
To follow her: with aged eyes aghast
From fright of dim espial. Safe at last,
Through many a dusky gallery, they gain
The maiden's chamber, silken, hush'd, and chaste;
Where Porphyro took covert, pleas'd amain.
His poor guide hurried back with agues in her brain.

---

[1] Cf. Tennyson's " Vivian."

XXII.

Her falt'ring hand upon the balustrade,
Old Angela was feeling for the stair,
When Madeline, St. Agnes' charmed maid,
Rose, like a mission'd spirit, unaware:
With silver taper's light, and pious care,
She turn'd, and down the aged gossip led
To a safe level matting. Now prepare,
Young Porphyro, for gazing on that bed;
She comes, she comes again, like ring-dove fray'd and fled

XXIII.

Out went the taper as she hurried in;
Its little smoke, in pallid moonshine, died:
She clos'd the door, she panted, all akin
To spirits of the air, and visions wide:
No uttered syllable, or, woe betide!
But to her heart, her heart was voluble,
Paining with eloquence her balmy side;
As though a tongueless nightingale should swell
Her throat in vain, and die, heart-stifled, in her dell.

XXIV.

A casement high and triple-arch'd there was,
All garlanded with carven imag'ries
Of fruits, and flowers, and bunches of knot-grass,
And diamonded with panes of quaint device,
Innumerable of stains and splendid dyes,
As are the tiger-moth's deep-damask'd wings;
And in the midst, 'mong thousand heraldries,
And twilight saints, and dim emblazonings,
A shielded scutcheon blush'd with blood of queens and
          kings.

XXV.

Full on this casement shone the wintry moon,
And threw warm gules on Madeline's fair breast,[1]
As down she knelt for heaven's grace and boon;
Rose-bloom fell on her hands, together prest,
And on her silver cross soft amethyst,
And on her hair a glory, like a saint:
She seem'd a splendid angel, newly drest,
Save wings, for heaven:—Porphyro grew faint:
She knelt, so pure a thing, so free from mortal taint.

XXVI.

Anon his heart revives: her vespers done,
Of all its wreathed pearls her hair she frees;
Unclasps her warmed jewels one by one;
Loosens her fragrant boddice: by degrees
Her rich attire creeps rustling to her knees:
Half-hidden, like a mermaid in sea-weed,
Pensive awhile she dreams awake, and sees,
In fancy, fair St. Agnes in her bed,
But dares not look behind, or all the charm is fled.

XXVII.

Soon, trembling in her soft and chilly nest,
In sort of wakeful swoon, perplex'd she lay,
Until the poppied warmth of sleep oppress'd
Her soothed limbs, and soul fatigued away;

---

[1] The fact that the light of the moon is not strong enough to cast colored shadows does not make this stanza a blemish upon the poem; nor is it necessary to resort to Foreman's expedient of regarding the phenomenon as a miracle performed by St. Agnes. There is poetic if not scientific truth in it.

Flown, like a thought, until the morrow-day;
Blissfully haven'd both from joy and pain;
Clasp'd like a missal where swart Paynims pray;
Blinded alike from sunshine and from rain,
As though a rose should shut, and be a bud again.

XXVIII.

Stol'n to this paradise, and so entranced,
Porphyro gazed upon her empty dress,
And listen'd to her breathing, if it chanced
To wake into a slumberous tenderness;
Which when he heard, that minute did he bless,
And breath'd himself: then from the closet crept,
Noiseless as fear in a wide wilderness,
And over the hush'd carpet, silent, stept,
And 'tween the curtains peep'd, where, lo!—how fast she
    slept.

XXIX.

Then by the bed-side, where the faded moon
Made a dim, silver twilight, soft he set
A table, and, half anguish'd, threw thereon
A cloth of woven crimson, gold, and jet:—
O for some drowsy Morphean amulet!
The boisterous, midnight, festive clarion,
The kettle-drum, and far-heard clarionet,
Affray his ears, though but in dying tone:—
The hall door shuts again, and all the noise is gone.

XXX.

And still she slept an azure-lidded sleep,
In blanched linen, smooth, and lavender'd,
While he from forth the closet brought a heap
Of candied apple, quince, and plum, and gourd;

With jellies soother than the creamy curd,
And lucent syrops, tinct with cinnamon;
Manna and dates, in argosy transferr'd
From Fez; and spiced dainties, every one,
From silken Samarcand to cedar'd Lebanon.

XXXI.

These delicates he heap'd with glowing hand
On golden dishes and in baskets bright
Of wreathed silver: sumptuous they stand
In the retired quiet of the night,
Filling the chilly room with perfume light.—
" And now, my love, my seraph fair, awake!
" Thou art my heaven, and I thine eremite:
" Open thine eyes, for meek St. Agnes' sake,
" Or I shall drowse beside thee, so my soul doth ache."

XXXII.

Thus whispering, his warm, unnerved arm
Sank in her pillow. Shaded was her dream
By the dusk curtains:—'twas a midnight charm
Impossible to melt as iced stream:
The lustrous salvers in the moonlight gleam;
Broad golden fringe upon the carpet lies:
It seem'd he never, never could redeem
From such a stedfast spell his lady's eyes:
So mus'd awhile, entoil'd in woofed phantasies.

XXXIII.

Awakening up, he took her hollow lute,—
Tumultuous,—and, in chords that tenderest be,
He play'd an ancient ditty, long since mute,
In Provence call'd, " La belle dame sans mercy: "

Close to her ear touching the melody:—
Wherewith disturb'd, she utter'd a soft moan:
He ceased—she panted quick—and suddenly
Her blue affrayed eyes wide open shone:
Upon his knees he sank, pale as smooth-sculptured stone.

XXXIV.

Her eyes were open, but she still beheld,
Now wide awake, the vision of her sleep:
There was a painful change, that nigh expell'd
The blisses of her dream so pure and deep
At which fair Madeline began to weep,
And moan forth witless words with many a sigh;
While still her gaze on Porphyro would keep;
Who knelt, with joined hands and piteous eye,
Fearing to move or speak, she look'd so dreamingly.

XXXV.

" Ah, Porphyro! " said she, " but even now
" Thy voice was at sweet tremble in mine ear.
" Made tuneable with every sweetest vow;
" And those sad eyes were spiritual and clear:
" How chang'd thou art! how pallid, chill, and drear!
" Give me that voice again, my Porphyro,
" Those looks immortal, those complainings dear!
" Oh leave me not in this eternal woe,
" For if thou diest, my love, I know not where to go."

XXXVI.

Beyond a mortal man impassion'd far
At these voluptuous accents, he arose,
Ethereal, flush'd, and like a throbbing star
Seen mid the sapphire heaven's deep repose:

Into her dream he melted, as the rose
Blendeth its odour with the violet,—
Solution sweet: meantime the frost-wind blows
Like Love's alarum pattering the sharp sleet
Against the window-panes; St. Agnes' moon hath set.

XXXVII.

'Tis dark: quick pattereth the flaw-blown sleet:
" This is no dream, my bride, my Madeline! "
'Tis dark: the iced gusts still rave and beat:
" No dream, alas! alas! and woe is mine!
" Porphyro will leave me here to fade and pine.—
" Cruel! what traitor could thee hither bring?
" I curse not, for my heart is lost in thine,
" Though thou forsakest a deceived thing:—
" A dove forlorn and lost with sick unpruned wing."

XXXVIII.

" My Madeline! sweet dreamer! lovely bride!
" Say, may I be for aye thy vassal blest?
" Thy beauty's shield, heart-shap'd and vermeil dyed?
" Ah, silver shrine, here will I take my rest
" After so many hours of toil and quest,
" A famish'd pilgrim,—saved by miracle.
" Though I have found, I will not rob thy nest
" Saving of thy sweet self: if thou think'st well
" To trust, fair Madeline, to no rude infidel.

XXXIX.

" Hark! 'tis an elfin-storm from faery land,
" Of haggard seeming, but a boon indeed:
" Arise—arise! the morning is at hand:—
" The bloated wassailers will never heed:—

" Let us away, my love, with happy speed;
" There are no ears to hear, or eyes to see,—
" Drown'd all in Rhenish and the sleepy mead:
" Awake! arise! my love, and fearless be,
" For o'er the southern moors I have a home for thee."

XL.

She hurried at his words, beset with fears,
For there were sleeping dragons all around,
At glaring watch, perhaps, with ready spears—
Down the wide stairs a darkling way they found.—
In all the house was heard no human sound.
A chain-droop'd lamp was flickering by each door;
The arras, rich with horseman, hawk, and hound,
Flutter'd in the besieging wind's uproar;
And the long carpets rose along the gusty floor.

XLI.

They glide, like phantoms, into the wide hall;
Like phantoms, to the iron porch, they glide;
Where lay the Porter, in uneasy sprawl,
With a huge empty flagon by his side:
The wakeful bloodhound rose, and shook his hide,
But his sagacious eye an inmate owns:
By one, and one, the bolts full easy slide:—
The chains lie silent on the footworn stones:—
The key turns, and the door upon its hinges groans.

XLII.

And they are gone: ay, ages long ago
These lovers fled away into the storm.
That night the Baron dreamt of many a woe,
And all his warrior-guests, with shade and form

Of witch, and demon, and large coffin-worm,
Were long be-nightmar'd. Angela the old
Died palsy-twitch'd, with meagre face deform;
The Beadsman, after thousand aves told,
For aye unsought for slept among his ashes cold.

LA BELLE DAME SANS MERCI.

1.

Ah, what can ail thee, wretched wight,[1]
  Alone and palely loitering;
The sedge is wither'd from the lake,
  And no birds sing.

2.

Ah, what can ail thee, wretched wight,[1]
  So haggard and so woe-begone?
The squirrel's granary is full,
  And the harvest's done.

3.

I see a lily on thy brow,
  With anguish moist and fever dew;
And on thy cheek a fading rose
  Fast withereth too.

4.

I met a lady in the meads
  Full beautiful, a faery's child;
Her hair was long, her foot was light,
  And her eyes were wild.

---

[1] This is the reading in *The Indicator* for May 10, 1820 (published by Leigh Hunt).
Lord Houghton's copy reads : O what can ail thee, knight-at-arms   For other variations consult Forman's Keats.

5.

I set her on my pacing steed,
   And nothing else saw all day long;
For sideways would she lean, and sing
   A faery's song.

6.

I made a garland for her head,
   And bracelets too, and fragrant zone;
She look'd at me as she did love,
   And made sweet moan.

7.

She found me roots of relish sweet,
   And honey wild, and manna dew;
And sure in language strange she said,
   I love thee true.

8.

She took me to her elfin grot,[1]
   And there she gazed and sighed deep,
And there I shut her wild sad eyes
   So kiss'd to sleep.

9.

And there we slumber'd on the moss,
   And there I dream'd, ah woe betide,
The latest dream I ever dream'd
   On the cold hillside.

---

[1] Lord Houghton's version reads:

    She took me to her elfin grot,
      And there she wept, and sigh'd full sore,
    And there I shut her wild, wild eyes
      With kisses four.

13

10.

I saw pale kings, and princes too,
   Pale warriors, death-pale were they all;
Who cry'd—" La belle Dame sans merci
   Hath thee in thrall! "

11.

I saw their starv'd lips in the gloom
   With horrid warning gaped wide,
And I awoke, and found me here
   On the cold hillside.

12.

And this is why I sojourn here
   Alone and palely loitering,
Though the sedge is wither'd from the lake,
   And no birds sing.

SONNET.[1]

Bright star, would I were stedfast as thou art—
   Not in lone splendour hung aloft the night
And watching, with eternal lids apart,
   Like nature's patient, sleepless Eremite,
The moving waters at their priestlike task
   Of pure ablution round earth's human shores,
Or gazing on the new soft-fallen mask
   Of snow upon the mountains and the moors—

[1] Written on a page facing "A Lover's Complaint," in a copy of Shakspere given by John Hamilton Reynolds to Keats, and by him to Severn. Composed in Dorsetshire, where Keats and Severn had landed on their way to Italy. They are the last lines known to have been written by Keats.

No—yet still stedfast, still unchangeable,
  Pillow'd upon my fair love's ripening breast,
To feel for ever its soft fall and swell,
  Awake for ever in a sweet unrest,
Still, still to hear her tender-taken breath,
  And so live ever—or else swoon to death.

September (?), 1820.]

LORD BYRON.

And — but for that sad shrouded eye
    That fires not — pleads not — weeps not — now —
blank — but for that cold chilling brow
            pale
Whose touch tells of " Mortality
And curdles to the Gazer's heart
As if to him it could impart
The doom he only looks upon —
Yes — but for these & these alone —
A moment — yet — a little hour
We still might doubt the tyrant's power
So fair — so calm — so softly sealed
The first — last look — by Death revealed!

LORD BYRON.

Fac-simile of lines 80-91 of " The Giaour," according to the original draft, 1813.

SELECTIONS FROM BYRON

"SHE WALKS IN BEAUTY."

She walks in beauty, like the night
  Of cloudless climes and starry skies;
And all that's best of dark and bright
  Meet in her aspect and her eyes:
Thus mellow'd to that tender light
  Which heaven to gaudy day denies.

One shade the more, one ray the less,
  Had half impair'd the nameless grace
Which waves in every raven tress,
  Or softly lightens o'er her face;
Where thoughts serenely sweet express
  How pure, how dear their dwelling-place.

And on that cheek, and o'er that brow,
  So soft, so calm, so eloquent,
The smiles that win, the tints that glow,
  But tell of days in goodness spent,
A mind at peace with all below,
  A heart whose love is innocent!

1814(?)]

THE DESTRUCTION OF SENNACHERIB.[1]

The Assyrian came down like the wolf on the fold,
And his cohorts were gleaming in purple and gold;
And the sheen of their spears was like stars on the sea,
When the blue wave rolls nightly on deep Galilee.

Like the leaves of the forest when Summer is green,
That host with their banners at sunset were seen:
Like the leaves of the forest when Autumn hath blown,
That host on the morrow lay wither'd and strown.

For the angel of death spread his wings on the blast,	10
And breathed in the face of the foe as he pass'd;
And the eyes of the sleepers wax'd deadly and chill,
And their hearts but once heav'd and forever grew still!

And there lay the steed with his nostril all wide,
But through it there roll'd not the breath of his pride:
And the foam of his gasping lay white on the turf,
And cold as the spray of the rock-beating surf.

And there lay the rider distorted and pale,
With the dew on his brow and the rust on his mail;
And the tents were all silent, the banners alone,
The lances unlifted, the trumpet unblown.	20

And the widows of Ashur are loud in their wail,
And the idols are broke in the temples of Baal;
And the might of the Gentile, unsmote by the sword,
Hath melted like snow in the glance of the Lord!

Published 1815.]

---

[1] See "Isaiah" xxxvii. 14-36.

STANZAS FOR MUSIC.

There be none of Beauty's daughters
  With a magic like thee;
And like music on the waters
  Is thy sweet voice to me:
When, as if its sound were causing
The charmed ocean's pausing
The waves lie still and gleaming,
And the lull'd winds seem dreaming.

And the midnight moon is weaving
  Her bright chain o'er the deep;
Whose breast is gently heaving,
  As an infant's sleep:
So the spirit bows before thee,
To listen and adore thee;
With a full but soft emotion,
Like the swell of Summer's ocean.

STANZAS TO AUGUSTA.[1]

Though the day of my destiny's over,
  And the star of my fate hath declined,
Thy soft heart refused to discover
  The faults which so many could find;
Though thy soul with my grief was acquainted,
  It shrunk not to share it with me,
And the love which my spirit hath painted
  It never hath found but in *thee*.

[1] Byron's half sister, the Honorable Mrs. Leigh, for whom Byron always felt the deepest affection, and who was with him during his trouble with Lady Byron.

Then when nature around me is smiling,
   The last smile which answers to mine, 10
I do not believe it beguiling,
   Because it reminds me of thine;
And when winds are at war with the ocean,
   As the breasts I believed in with me,
If their billows excite an emotion,
   It is that they bear me from *thee*.

Though the rock of my last hope is shiver'd,
   And its fragments are sunk in the wave,
Though I feel that my soul is deliver'd
   To pain—it shall not be its slave. 20
There is many a pang to pursue me:
   They may crush, but they shall not contemn—
They may torture, but shall not subdue me—
   'Tis of *thee* that I think—not of them.

Though human, thou didst not deceive me,
   Though woman, thou didst not forsake,
Though loved, thou forborest to grieve me,
   Though slander'd, thou never couldst shake,—
Though trusted, thou didst not disclaim me,
   Though parted, it was not to fly, 30
Though watchful, 'twas not to defame me,
   Nor, mute, that the world might belie.

Yet I blame not the world, nor despise it,
   Nor the war of the many with one;
If my soul was not fitted to prize it,
   'Twas folly not sooner to shun:
And if dearly that error hath cost me,
   And more than I once could foresee,
I have found that, whatever it lost me,
   It could not deprive me of *thee*. 40

From the wreck of the past, which hath perish'd,
　Thus much I at least may recall,
It hath taught me that what I most cherish'd
　Deserved to be dearest of all:
In the desert a fountain is springing,
　In the wide waste there still is a tree,
And a bird in the solitude singing,
　Which speaks to my spirit of *thee*.

July 24, 1816.]

THE DREAM.[1]

I.

Our life is twofold: Sleep hath its own world,
A boundary between the things misnamed
Death and existence: Sleep hath its own world,
And a wide realm of wild reality.
And dreams in their developement have breath,
And tears, and tortures, and the touch of joy;
They leave a weight upon our waking thoughts,
They take a weight from off our waking toils,
They do divide our being; they become
A portion of ourselves as of our time, 10
And look like heralds of eternity;
They pass like spirits of the past,—they speak
Like sibyls of the future: they have power—
The tyranny of pleasure and of pain:
They make us what we were not—what they will,
And shake us with the vision that's gone by.
The dread of vanish'd shadows—Are they so?
Is not the past all shadow? What are they?

---

[1] Byron's imagination was fired by his love for Mary Chaworth, for their union would have healed a family feud. Moore says that "The Dream" "cost him many a tear in writing." It was written in Switzerland, in the summer of 1816, when he was still suffering from the deadly attacks of Lady Byron's friends.

Creations of the mind?—The mind can make
Substance, and people planets of its own   20
With beings brighter than have been, and give
A breath to forms which can outlive all flesh.
I would recall a vision which I dream'd
Perchance in sleep—for in itself a thought,
A slumbering thought, is capable of years,
And curdles a long life into one hour.

II.

I saw two beings in the hues of youth
Standing upon a hill, a gentle hill,
Green and of mild declivity, the last
As 't were the cape of a long ridge of such,   30
Save that there was no sea to lave its base,
But a most living landscape, and the wave
Of woods and cornfields, and the abodes of men
Scatter'd at intervals, and wreathing smoke
Arising from such rustic roofs:—the hill
Was crown'd with a peculiar diadem
Of trees,[1] in circular array, so fix'd,
Not by the sport of nature, but of man:
These two, a maiden and a youth, were there
Gazing—the one on all that was beneath   40
Fair as herself—but the boy gazed on her:
And both were young, and one was beautiful:
And both were young—yet not alike in youth.
As the sweet moon on the horizon's verge,
The maid was on the eve of womanhood;
The boy had fewer summers, but his heart
Had far outgrown his years, and to his eye
There was but one beloved face on earth,

[1] The "diadem of trees" has long ceased to stand; in a fit of jealous anger at the poem, Mr Musters levelled the place with the ground. Elze's "Byron," p. 48.

And that was shining on him: he had look'd
Upon it till it could not pass away;   50
He had no breath, no being, but in hers:
She was his voice; he did not speak to her,
But trembled on her words; she was his sight,
For his eye follow'd hers, and saw with hers,
Which colour'd all his objects:—he had ceased
To live within himself; she was his life,
The ocean to the river of his thoughts,
Which terminated all: upon a tone,
A touch of hers, his blood would ebb and flow,
And his cheek change tempestuously—his heart   60
Unknowing of its cause of agony.
But she in these fond feelings had no share:
Her sighs were not for him; to her he was
Even as a brother—but no more; 'twas much,
For brotherless she was, save in the name
Her infant friendship had bestow'd on him;
Herself the solitary scion left
Of a time-honour'd race.—It was a name
Which pleased him, and yet pleased him not—and why?
Time taught him a deep answer—when she loved   70
Another; even *now* she loved another,
And on the summit of that hill she stood
Looking afar if yet her lover's steed
Kept pace with her expectancy, and flew.

III.

A change came o'er the spirit of my dream.
There was an ancient mansion, and before
Its walls there was a steed caparison'd:
Within an antique Oratory stood
The Boy of whom I spake:—he was alone,
And pale, and pacing to and fro: anon   80

He sate him down, and seized a pen, and traced
Words which I could not guess of; then he lean'd
His bow'd head on his hands, and shook as 'twere
With a convulsion—then arose again,
And with his teeth and quivering hands did tear
What he had written, but he shed no tears.
And he did calm himself, and fix his brow
Into a kind of quiet: as he paused,
The Lady of his love re-enter'd there;
She was serene and smiling then, and yet   90
She knew she was by him beloved,—she knew,
For quickly comes such knowledge, that his heart
Was darken'd with her shadow, and she saw
That he was wretched, but she saw not all.
He rose, and with a cold and gentle grasp
He took her hand; a moment o'er his face
A tablet of unutterable thoughts
Was traced, and then it faded, as it came;
He dropp'd the hand he held, and with slow steps
Retired, but not as bidding her adieu,   100
For they did part with mutual smiles: he pass'd
From out the massy gate of that old Hall,
And mounting on his steed he went his way:
And ne'er repass'd that hoary threshold more.

IV.

A change came o'er the spirit of my dream.
The Boy was sprung to manhood: in the wilds
Of fiery climes he made himself a home,
And his soul drank their sunbeams: he was girt
With strange and dusky aspects: he was not
Himself like what he had been; on the sea   110
And on the shore he was a wanderer;
There was a mass of many images

Crowded like waves upon me, but he was
A part of all; and in the last he lay
Reposing from the noontide sultriness,
Couch'd among fallen columns, in the shade
Of ruin'd walls that had survived the names
Of those who rear'd them; by his sleeping side
Stood camels grazing, and some goodly steeds
Were fasten'd near a fountain; and a man   120
Clad in a flowing garb did watch the while,
While many of his tribe slumber'd around:
And they were canopied by the blue sky,
So cloudless, clear, and purely beautiful,
That God alone was to be seen in Heaven.

V.

A change came o'er the spirit of my dream.
The Lady of his love was wed with One
Who did not love her better:—in her home,
A thousand leagues from his,—her native home,
She dwelt, begirt with growing Infancy,   130
Daughters and sons of Beauty,—but behold!
Upon her face there was the tint of grief,
The settled shadow of an inward strife,
And an unquiet drooping of the eye,
As if its lid were charged with unshed tears.
What could her grief be?—she had all she loved,
And he who had so loved her was not there
To trouble with bad hopes, or evil wish,
Or ill-repress'd affliction, her pure thoughts.
What could her grief be?—she had loved him not,   140
Nor given him cause to deem himself beloved,
Nor could he be a part of that which prey'd
Upon her mind—a spectre of the past.

VI.

A change came o'er the spirit of my dream.
The Wanderer was return'd.—I saw him stand
Before an Altar—with a gentle bride;
Her face was fair, but was not that which made
The Starlight of his Boyhood:—as he stood
Even at the altar, o'er his brow there came
The selfsame aspect, and the quivering shock　　　150
That in the antique Oratory shook
His bosom in its solitude; and then—
As in that hour—a moment o'er his face
The tablet of unutterable thoughts
Was traced—and then it faded as it came.
And he stood calm and quiet, and he spoke
The fitting vows, but heard not his own words,
And all things reel'd around him; he could see
Not that which was, nor that which should have been—
But the old mansion, and the accustom'd hall,　　　160
And the remember'd chambers, and the place,
The day, the hour, the sunshine, and the shade,
All things pertaining to that place and hour,
And her who was his destiny, came back
And thrust themselves between him and the light:
What business had they there at such a time?

VII.

A change came o'er the spirit of my dream.
The Lady of his love:—Oh! she was changed,[1]
As by the sickness of the soul: her mind
Had wander'd from its dwelling, and her eyes　　　170
They had not their own lustre, but the look
Which is not of the earth; she was become

---

[1] Miss Chaworth was not happy in her marriage with Mr. Musters, and her mind
gave way. She and her husband were separated.

The queen of a fantastic realm; her thoughts
Were combinations of disjointed things;
And forms impalpable and unperceived
Of others' sight familiar were to hers.
And this the world calls frenzy: but the wise
Have a far deeper madness, and the glance
Of melancholy is a fearful gift;
What is it but the telescope of truth?   80
Which strips the distance of its phantasies,
And brings life near in utter nakedness,
Making the cold reality too real!

VIII.

A change came o'er the spirit of my dream.
The Wanderer was alone as heretofore.
The beings which surrounded him were gone,
Or were at war with him; he was a mark
For blight and desolation, compass'd round
With Hatred and Contention: Pain was mix'd
In all which was served up to him, until,   190
Like to the Pontic monarch of old days,
He fed on poisons, and they had no power,
But were a kind of nutriment: he lived
Through that which had been death to many men,
And made him friends of mountains: with the stars
And the quick Spirit of the Universe
He held his dialogues! and they did teach
To him the magic of their mysteries;
To him the book of Night was open'd wide,
And voices from the deep abyss reveal'd   200
A marvel and a secret—Be it so.

IX.

My dream was past: it had no further change.
It was of a strange order, that the doom

Of these two creatures should be thus traced out
Almost like a reality—the one
To end in madness—both in misery.

Diodati, July, 1816.]

TO THOMAS MOORE.[1]

My boat is on the shore,
    And my bark is on the sea;
But, before I go, Tom Moore,
    Here's a double health to thee!

Here's a sigh to those who love me,
    And a smile to those who hate;
And, whatever sky's above me,
    Here's a heart for every fate.

Though the ocean roar around me,
    Yet it still shall bear me on;
Though a desert should surround me,
    It hath springs that may be won.

Were't the last drop in the well,
    As I gasp'd upon the brink,
Ere my fainting spirit fell,
    'Tis to thee that I would drink.

With that water, as this wine,
    The libation I would pour
Should be—peace with thine and mine,
    And a health to thee, Tom Moore.[2]

[1] Byron's poetry is full of his admiration and affection for Moore.
[2] This should have been written fifteen moons ago: the first stanza was.—"Lord Byron to Moore," July 10, 1817.

CHILDE HAROLD.

CANTO THE THIRD.[1]

(WATERLOO.)

XXI.

There was a sound of revelry by night,
And Belgium's capital had gathered then
Her Beauty and her Chivalry, and bright
The lamps shone o'er fair women and brave men;
A thousand hearts beat happily; and when
Music arose with its voluptuous swell,
Soft eyes looked love to eyes which spake again,
And all went merry as a marriage bell;
But hush! hark! a deep sound strikes like a rising knell!

XXII.

Did ye not hear it?—No; 'twas but the wind,
Or the car rattling o'er the stony street;
On with the dance! let joy be unconfined;
No sleep till morn, when Youth and Pleasure meet
To chase the glowing Hours with flying feet—
But hark!—that heavy sound breaks in once more
As if the clouds its echo would repeat;
And nearer, clearer, deadlier than before!
Arm! arm! it is—it is—the cannon's opening roar!

---

[1] Two cantos of "Childe Harold" were written during Byron's first travels through
the Mediterranean countries. The last two, less personal and less morbid, form part
of the harvest of the years 1816–1817. They are the record of the thoughts which rose
in Byron's mind in connection with the various places he visited as he travelled or
rested, on his way southward from England; they are specially remarkable for their
brilliant descriptions and for the strong historic sympathies which they display.

For this edition it has been deemed best to consider these cantos as made up of
separate poems, as indeed they properly are, and to make selections from among the
poems, rather than to insert a continuous section of either canto.

XXIII.

Within a windowed niche of that high hall
Sate Brunswick's fated chieftain; he did hear
That sound the first amidst the festival,
And caught its tone with Death's prophetic ear;
And when they smiled because he deemed it near,
His heart more truly knew that peal too well
Which stretched his father on a bloody bier,
And roused the vengeance blood alone could quell:
He rushed into the field, and, foremost fighting, fell.

XXIV.

Ah! then and there was hurrying to and fro,
And gathering tears, and tremblings of distress,
And cheeks all pale, which but an hour ago
Blushed at the praise of their own loveliness;
And there were sudden partings, such as press
The life from out young hearts, and choking sighs
Which ne'er might be repeated: who could guess
If ever more should meet those mutual eyes,
Since upon night so sweet such awful morn could rise!

XXV.

And there was mounting in hot haste: the steed,
The mustering squadron, and the clattering car,
Went pouring forward with impetuous speed,
And swiftly forming in the ranks of war:
And the deep thunder peal on peal afar;
And near, the beat of the alarming drum
Roused up the soldier ere the morning star;
While thronged the citizens with terror dumb,
Or whispering, with white lips—"The foe! They come!
    they come!"

XXVI.

And wild and high the " Cameron's gathering " rose!
The war-note of Lochiel, which Albyn's hills
Have heard, and heard, too, have her Saxon foes:—
How in the noon of night that pibroch thrills,
Savage and shrill! But with the breath which fills
Their mountain-pipe, so fill the mountaineers
With the fierce native daring which instils
The stirring memory of a thousand years,
And Evan's, Donald's fame rings in each clansman's ears!

XXVII.

And Ardennes waves above them her green leaves,
Dewy with Nature's tear-drops, as they pass,
Grieving, if aught inanimate e'er grieves,
Over the unreturning brave,—alas!
Ere evening to be trodden like the grass
Which now beneath them, but above shall grow
In its next verdure, when this fiery mass
Of living valour, rolling on the foe
And burning with high hope, shall moulder cold and low.

XXVIII.

Last noon beheld them full of lusty life,
Last eve in Beauty's circle proudly gay.
The midnight brought the signal-sound of strife,
The morn the marshalling in arms,—the day
Battle's magnificently stern array!
The thunder-clouds close o'er it. which when rent
The earth is covered thick with other clay,
Which her own clay shall cover. heaped and pent.
Rider and horse,—friend. foe.—in one red burial blent!

(DRACHENFELS.)

1.

The castled crag of Drachenfels
Frowns o'er the wide and winding Rhine,
Whose breast of waters broadly swells
Between the banks which bear the vine,
And hills all rich with blossomed trees,
And fields which promise corn and wine,
And scattered cities crowning these,
Whose far white walls along them shine,
Have strew'd a scene, which I should see
With double joy wert *thou*[1] with me.

2.

And peasant girls, with deep blue eyes,
And hands which offer early flowers,
Walk smiling o'er this paradise;
Above, the frequent feudal towers
Through green leaves lift their walls of grey,
And many a rock which steeply lowers,
And noble arch in proud decay,
Look o'er this vale of vintage bowers;
But one thing want these banks of Rhine,—
Thy gentle hand to clasp in mine!

3.

I send the lilies given to me;
Though long before thy hand they touch,
I know that they must wither'd be,
But yet reject them not as such;

---

[1] Byron's sister.

For I have cherish'd them as dear,
Because they yet may meet thine eye,
And guide thy soul to mine even here,
When thou behold'st them drooping nigh,
And know'st them gather'd by the Rhine,
And offer'd from my heart to thine!

4.

The river nobly foams and flows,
The charm of this enchanted ground,
And all its thousand turns disclose
Some fresher beauty varying round:
The haughtiest breast its wish might bound
Through life to dwell delighted here;
Nor could on earth a spot be found
To Nature and to me so dear,
Could thy dear eyes in following mine
Still sweeten more these banks of Rhine!

(LAKE GENEVA.)

LXXXV.

Clear, placid Leman! thy contrasted lake,
With the wild world I dwelt in, is a thing
Which warns me, with its stillness, to forsake
Earth's troubled waters for a purer spring.
This quiet sail is as a noiseless wing
To waft me from distraction: once I loved
Torn ocean's roar, but thy soft murmuring
Sounds sweet as if a Sister's voice reproved.
That I with stern delights should e'er have been so
moved.

LXXXVI.

It is the hush of night, and all between
Thy margin and the mountains, dusk, yet clear,
Mellowed and mingling, yet distinctly seen,
Save darken'd Jura, whose capt heights appear
Precipitously steep; and drawing near,
There breathes a living fragrance from the shore,
Of flowers yet fresh with childhood: on the ear
Drops the light drip of the suspended oar,
Or chirps the grasshopper one good-night carol more;

LXXXVII.

He is an evening reveller, who makes
His life an infancy, and sings his fill;
At intervals, some bird from out the brakes
Starts into voice a moment, then is still.
There seems a floating whisper on the hill,
But that is fancy, for the starlight dews
All silently their tears of love instil,
Weeping themselves away, till they infuse
Deep into Nature's breast the spirit of her hues.

LXXXVIII.

Ye stars! which are the poetry of heaven!
If in your bright leaves we would read the fate
Of men and empires,—'tis to be forgiven,
That in our aspirations to be great,
Our destinies o'erleap their mortal state,
And claim a kindred with you: for ye are
A beauty and a mystery, and create
In us such love and reverence from afar,
That fortune, fame, power, life, have named themselves a
      star.

LXXXIX.

All heaven and earth are still—though not in sleep,
But breathless, as we grow when feeling most;
And silent, as we stand in thoughts too deep:—
All heaven and earth are still: From the high host
Of stars, to the lull'd lake and mountain-coast,
All is concenter'd in a life intense,
Where not a beam, nor air, nor leaf is lost,
But hath a part of being, and a sense
Of that which is of all Creator and defence.

XC.

Then stirs the feeling infinite, so felt
In solitude, where we are *least* alone;
A truth, which through our being then doth melt,
And purifies from self: it is a tone,
The soul and source of music, which makes known
Eternal harmony, and sheds a charm,
Like to the fabled Cytherea's zone,
Binding all things with beauty;—'twould disarm
The spectre Death, had he substantial power to harm.

XCI.

Not vainly did the early Persian make
His altar the high places and the peak
Of earth-o'ergazing mountains, and thus take
A fit and unwalled temple, there to seek
The Spirit, in whose honour shrines are weak,
Upreared of human hands. Come, and compare
Columns and idol-dwellings, Goth or Greek,
With Nature's realms of worship, earth and air,
Nor fix on fond abodes to circumscribe thy pray'r!

XCII.

The sky is changed!—and such a change! Oh night,
And storm, and darkness, ye are wondrous strong,
Yet lovely in your strength, as is the light
Of a dark eye in woman! Far along,
From peak to peak, the rattling crags among
Leaps the live thunder! Not from one lone cloud,
But every mountain now hath found a tongue,
And Jura answers, through her misty shroud,
Back to the joyous Alps, who call to her aloud!

XCIII.

And this is in the night:—Most glorious night!
Thou wert not sent for slumber! let me be
A sharer in thy fierce and far delight,—
A portion of the tempest and of thee!
How the lit lake shines, a phosphoric sea,
And the big rain comes dancing to the earth!
And now again 'tis black,—and now, the glee
Of the loud hills shakes with its mountain-mirth,
As if they did rejoice o'er a young earthquake's birth.

XCIV.

Now, where the swift Rhone cleaves his way between
Heights which appear as lovers who have parted
In hate, whose mining depths so intervene,
That they can meet no more, though broken-hearted:
Though in their souls, which thus each other thwarted,
Love was the very root of the fond rage
Which blighted their life's bloom, and then departed:—
Itself expired, but leaving them an age
Of years all winters,—war within themselves to wage.

XCV.

Now, where the quick Rhone thus hath cleft his way,
The mightiest of the storms hath ta'en his stand;
For here, not one, but many, make their play,
And fling their thunderbolts from hand to hand,
Flashing and cast around: of all the band,
The brightest through these parted hills hath fork'd
His lightnings,—as if he did understand,
That in such gaps as desolation work'd,
There the hot shaft should blast whatever therein lurk'd.

XCVI.

Sky, mountains, river, winds, lake, lightnings! ye!
With night, and clouds, and thunder, and a soul
To make these felt and feeling, well may be
Things that have made me watchful; the far roll
Of your departing voices, is the knoll
Of what in me is sleepless,—if I rest.
But where of ye, O tempests! is the goal?
Are ye like those within the human breast?
Or do ye find, at length, like eagles, some high nest?

CANTO THE FOURTH.

(VENICE.)

I.

I stood in Venice, on the Bridge of Sighs;
A palace and a prison on each hand:
I saw from out the wave her structures rise
As from the stroke of the enchanter's wand:
A thousand years their cloudy wings expand
Around me, and a dying Glory smiles

O'er the far times, when many a subject land
Look'd to the winged Lion's marble piles,
Where Venice sate in state, throned on her hundred isles!

II.

She looks a sea Cybele, fresh from ocean,
Rising with her tiara of proud towers
At airy distance, with majestic motion,
A ruler of the waters and their powers:
And such she was;—her daughters had their dowers
From spoils of nations, and the exhaustless East
Pour'd in her lap all gems in sparkling showers.
In purple was she robed, and of her feast
Monarchs partook, and deem'd their dignity increased.

III.

In Venice, Tasso's echoes are no more,[1]
And silent rows the songless gondolier;
Her palaces are crumbling to the shore,
And music meets not always now the ear:
Those days are gone—but Beauty still is here.
States fall, arts fade—but Nature doth not die,
Nor yet forget how Venice once was dear,
The pleasant place of all festivity,
The revel of the earth, the masque of Italy!

IV.

But unto us she hath a spell beyond
Her name in story, and her long array
Of mighty shadows, whose dim forms despond
Above the dogeless city's vanish'd sway;

[1] The Gondoliers used formerly to sing a Venetian version of Tasso's "Gerusalemme Liberata," answering each other in alternate stanzas, sometimes from a long distance.

Ours is a trophy which will not decay
With the Rialto; Shylock and the Moor,
And Pierre,[1] cannot be swept or worn away—
The keystones of the arch! though all were o'er,
For us repeopled were the solitary shore.

*   *   *   *   *   *   *

XI.

The spouseless Adriatic mourns her lord;
And, annual marriage now no more renew'd,
The Bucentaur lies rotting unrestored,
Neglected garment of her widowhood!
St. Mark yet sees his lion where he stood
Stand, but in mockery of his wither'd power,
Over the proud Place where an Emperor sued,
And monarchs gazed and envied in the hour
When Venice was a queen with an unequall'd dower.

XII.

The Suabian [2] sued, and now the Austrian reigns—
An Emperor tramples where an Emperor knelt:
Kingdoms are shrunk to provinces, and chains
Clank over sceptred cities; nations melt
From power's high pinnacle, when they have felt
The sunshine for a while, and downward go
Like lauwine loosen'd from the mountain's belt:
Oh for one hour of blind old Dandolo!
Th' octogenarian chief, Byzantium's conquering foe.

XIII.

Before St. Mark still glow his steeds of brass,
Their gilded collars glittering in the sun;

---

[1] The hero of Otway's tragedy, "Venice Preserved." In Byron's time the character was a favorite on the stage. [2] Frederic Barbarossa.

But is not Doria's menace come to pass?
Are they not *bridled?*—Venice, lost and won,
Her thirteen hundred years of freedom done,
Sinks, like a seaweed, into whence she rose!
Better be whelm'd beneath the waves, and shun,
Even in destruction's depth, her foreign foes,
From whom submission wrings an infamous repose.[1]

XIV.

In youth she was all glory,—a new Tyre;
Her very byword sprung from victory,
The " Planter of the Lion," which through fire
And blood she bore o'er subject earth and sea:
Though making many slaves, herself still free,
And Europe's bulwark 'gainst the Ottomite;
Witness Troy's rival, Candia! Vouch it, ye
Immortal waves that saw Lepanto's fight!
For ye are names no time nor tyranny can blight.

XV.

Statues of glass—all shiver'd—the long file
Of her dead Doges are declined to dust:
But where they dwelt, the vast and sumptuous pile
Bespeaks the pageant of their splendid trust:
Their sceptre broken, and their sword in rust,
Have yielded to the stranger: empty halls,
Thin streets, and foreign aspects, such as must
Too oft remind her who and what enthrals,
Have flung a desolate cloud o'er Venice' lovely walls.

---

[1] The enforced subjection of Venice to Austria from 1797–1866 was the theme of mourning or indignation for many a poet.

XVI.

When Athens' armies fell at Syracuse,
And fetter'd thousands bore the yoke of war,
Redemption rose up in the Attic Muse,
Her voice their only ransom from afar:
See! as they chant the tragic hymn, the car
Of the o'ermaster'd victor stops, the reins
Fall from his hands—his idle scimitar
Starts from its belt—he rends his captive's chains,
And bids him thank the bard for freedom and his strains.

XVII.

Thus, Venice, if no stronger claim were thine,
Were all thy proud historic deeds forgot,
Thy choral memory of the Bard divine,
Thy love of Tasso, should have cut the knot
Which ties thee to thy tyrants; and thy lot
Is shameful to the nations,—most of all,
Albion! to thee: the Ocean queen should not
Abandon Ocean's children; in the fall
Of Venice think of thine, despite thy watery wall.

XVIII.

I loved her from my boyhood; she to me
Was as a fairy city of the heart,
Rising like water-columns from the sea,
Of joy the sojourn. and of wealth the mart:
And Otway, Radcliffe, Schiller. Shakspeare's art,
Had stamp'd her image in me, and even so,
Although I found her thus. we did not part,
Perchance even dearer in her day of woe,
Than when she was a boast, a marvel, and a show.

(SUNSET IN THE RHÆTIAN ALPS.)

XXVII.

The moon is up, and yet it is not night—
Sunset divides the sky with her—a sea
Of glory streams along the Alpine height
Of blue Friuli's mountains; Heaven is free
From clouds, but of all colours seems to be,—
Melted to one vast Iris of the West,—
Where the Day joins the past Eternity;
While, on the other hand, meek Dian's crest
Floats through the azure air—an island of the blest!

XXVIII.

A single star is at her side, and reigns
With her o'er half the lovely heaven; but still
Yon sunny sea heaves brightly, and remains
Roll'd o'er the peak of the far Rhætian hill,
As Day and Night contending were, until
Nature reclaim'd her order:—gently flows
The deep-dyed Brenta, where their hues instil
The odorous purple of a new-born rose,
Which streams upon her stream, and glass'd within it
    glows,

XXIX.

Fill'd with the face of heaven, which, from afar,
Comes down upon the waters: all its hues,
From the rich sunset to the rising star,
Their magical variety diffuse:
And now they change: a paler shadow strews
Its mantle o'er the mountains; parting day
Dies like the dolphin, whom each pang imbues
With a new colour as it gasps away,
The last still loveliest, till—'tis gone—and all is gray.

(ARQUA.)

XXX.

There is a tomb in Arqua;—rear'd in air,
Pillar'd in their sarcophagus, repose
The bones of Laura's lover: here repair
Many familiar with his well-sung woes,
The pilgrims of his genius. He arose
To raise a language, and his land reclaim
From the dull yoke of her barbaric foes:
Watering the tree which bears his lady's name
With his melodious tears, he gave himself to fame.

XXXI.

They keep his dust in Arqua, where he died;
The mountain-village where his latter days
Went down the vale of years; and 'tis their pride—
An honest pride—and let it be their praise,
To offer to the passing stranger's gaze
His mansion and his sepulchre: both plain
And venerably simple. such as raise
A feeling more accordant with his strain
Than if a pyramid form'd his monumental fane.

XXXII.

And the soft quiet hamlet where he dwelt
Is one of that complexion which seems made
For those who their mortality have felt,
And sought a refuge from their hopes decay'd
In the deep umbrage of a green hill's shade.
Which shows a distant prospect far away
Of busy cities. now in vain display'd.
For they can lure no further: and the ray
Of a bright sun can make sufficient holiday,

XXXIII.

Developing the mountains, leaves, and flowers,
And shining in the brawling brook, where-by,
Clear as its current, glide the sauntering hours
With a calm languor, which, though to the eye
Idlesse it seem, hath its morali'y.
If from society we learn to live,
'Tis solitude should teach us how to die;
It hath no flatterers; vanity can give
No hollow aid; alone—man with his God must strive.

(ITALY.)

XLII.

Italia! Oh Italia! thou who hast
The fatal gift of beauty, which became
A funeral dower of present woes and past,
On thy sweet brow is sorrow plough'd by shame,
And annals graved in characters of flame.
Oh, God! that thou wert in thy nakedness
Less lovely or more powerful, and couldst claim
Thy right, and awe the robbers back, who press
To shed thy blood, and drink the tears of thy distress;

XLIII.

Then might'st thou more appal; or, less desired,
Be homely and be peaceful, undeplored
For thy destructive charms; then, still untired,
Would not be seen the armed torrents pour'd
Down the deep Alps; nor would the hostile horde
Of many-nationed spoilers from the Po
Quaff blood and water; nor the stranger's sword
Be thy sad weapon of defence, and so,
Victor or vanquish'd, thou the slave of friend or foe.

(SANTA CROCE.)

LIV.

In Santa Croce's holy precincts lie
Ashes which make it holier, dust which is
Even in itself an immortality,
Though there were nothing save the past, and this,
The particle of those sublimities
Which have relapsed to chaos:—here repose
Angelo's, Alfieri's bones, and his,
The starry Galileo, with his woes;
Here Machiavelli's earth return'd to whence it rose.

LV.

These are four minds, which, like the elements,
Might furnish forth creation:—Italy!
Time, which hath wrong'd thee with ten thousand rents
Of thine imperial garment, shall deny,
And hath denied, to every other sky,
Spirits which soar from ruin:—thy decay
Is still impregnate with divinity,
Which gilds it with revivifying ray;
Such as the great of yore, Canova is to-day.

LVI.

But where repose the all Etruscan three—
Dante, and Petrarch, and, scarce less than they,
The Bard of Prose, creative spirit! he
Of the Hundred Tales of love—where did they lay
Their bones, distinguish'd from our common clay
In death as life? Are they resolved to dust,
And have their country's marbles nought to say?
Could not her quarries furnish forth one bust?
Did they not to her breast their filial earth entrust?

LVII.

Ungrateful Florence! Dante sleeps afar,
Like Scipio, buried by the upbraiding shore:
Thy factions, in their worse than civil war,
Proscribed the bard whose name for evermore
Their children's children would in vain adore
With the remorse of ages; and the crown
Which Petrarch's laureate brow supremely wore,
Upon a far and foreign soil had grown,
His life, his fame, his grave, though rifled—not thine own.

LVIII.

Boccaccio to his parent earth bequeath'd
His dust,—and lies it not her Great among,
With many a sweet and solemn requiem breathed
O'er him who form'd the Tuscan's siren tongue?
That music in itself, whose sounds are song,
The poetry of speech? No;—even his tomb
Uptorn, must bear the hyæna bigot's wrong,
No more amidst the meaner dead find room,
Nor claim a passing sigh, because it told for *whom!*

LIX.

And Santa Croce wants their mighty dust;
Yet for this want more noted, as of yore
The Cæsar's pageant, shorn of Brutus' bust,
Did but of Rome's best Son remind her more:
Happier Ravenna! on thy hoary shore,
Fortress of falling empire! honour'd sleeps
The immortal exile;—Arqua, too, her store
Of tuneful relics proudly claims and keeps,
While Florence vainly begs her banish'd dead and weeps.

LX.

What is her pyramid of precious stones?
Of porphyry, jasper, agate, and all hues
Of gem and marble, to encrust the bones
Of merchant-dukes? the momentary dews
Which, sparkling to the twilight stars, infuse
Freshness in the green turf that wraps the dead,
Whose names are mausoleums of the Muse,
Are gently prest with far more reverent tread
Than ever paced the slab which paves the princely head.

(VELINO.)

LXIX.

The roar of waters!—from the headlong height
Velino cleaves the wave-worn precipice;
The fall of waters! rapid as the light
The flashing mass foams shaking the abyss;
The hell of waters! where they howl and hiss,
And boil in endless torture; while the sweat
Of their great agony, wrung out from this
Their Phlegethon, curls round the rocks of jet
That gird the gulf around, in pitiless horror set,

LXX.

And mounts in spray the skies, and thence again
Returns in an unceasing shower, which round,
With its unemptied cloud of gentle rain,
Is an eternal April to the ground,
Making it all one emerald:—how profound
The gulf! and how the giant element
From rock to rock leaps with delirious bound,
Crushing the cliffs, which, downward worn and rent
With his fierce footsteps, yield in chasms a fearful vent

LXXI.

To the broad column which rolls on, and shows
More like the fountain of an infant sea
Torn from the womb of mountains by the throes
Of a new world, than only thus to be
Parent of rivers, which flow gushingly,
With many windings, through the vale:—Look back!
Lo! where it comes like an eternity,
As if to sweep down all things in its track,
Charming the eye with dread,—a matchless cataract,

LXXII.

Horribly beautiful! but on the verge,
From side to side, beneath the glittering morn,
An Iris sits, amidst the infernal surge,
Like Hope upon a deathbed, and, unworn
Its steady dyes, while all around is torn
By the distracted waters, bears serene
Its brilliant hues with all their beams unshorn:
Resembling, mid the torture of the scene,
Love watching Madness with unalterable mien.

(ROME.)

LXXVIII.

Oh Rome! [1] my country! city of the soul!
The orphans of the heart must turn to thee,
Lone mother of dead empires! and control
In their shut breasts their petty misery.
What are our woes and sufferance? Come and see

---

[1] "I have been some days in Rome the Wonderful. I am delighted with Rome. As a whole—ancient and modern, it beats Greece, Constantinople, everything at least that I have ever seen."—"Byron Letters," May, 1817.

The cypress, hear the owl, and plod your way
O'er steps of broken thrones and temples, Ye!
Whose agonies are evils of a day—
A world is at our feet as fragile as our clay.

LXXIX.

The Niobe of nations! there she stands,
Childless and crownless, in her voiceless woe;
An empty urn within her wither'd hands,
Whose holy dust was scatter'd long ago;
The Scipios' tomb [1] contains no ashes now;
The very sepulchres lie tenantless
Of their heroic dwellers: dost thou flow,
Old Tiber! through a marble wilderness?
Rise, with thy yellow waves, and mantle her distress!

LXXX.

The Goth, the Christian, Time, War, Flood, and Fire,
Have dealt upon the seven-hilled city's pride;
She saw her glories star by star expire,
And up the steep barbarian monarchs ride,
Where the car climb'd the capitol: far and wide
Temple and tower went down, nor left a site:—
Chaos of ruins! who shall trace the void,
O'er the dim fragments cast a lunar light,
And say, " here was, or is," where all is doubly night?

LXXXI.

The double night of ages, and of her,
Night's daughter, Ignorance, hath wrapt, and wrap

All round us; we but feel our way to err:
The ocean hath his chart, the stars their map,
And Knowledge spreads them on her ample lap;
But Rome is as the desert, where we steer
Stumbling o'er recollections; now we clap
Our hands, and cry, " Eureka! " it is clear—
When but some false mirage of ruin rises near.

LXXXII.

Alas! the lofty city! and alas!
The trebly hundred [1] triumphs! and the day
When Brutus made the dagger's edge surpass
The conqueror's sword in bearing fame away!
Alas, for Tully's voice, and Virgil's lay,
And Livy's pictured page!—But these shall be
Her resurrection; all beside—decay.
Alas, for Earth, for never shall we see
That brightness in her eye she bore when Rome was free!

(THE COLISEUM.)

CXXVIII.

Arches on arches! as it were that Rome,
Collecting the chief trophies of her line,
Would build up all her triumphs in one dome,
Her Coliseum stands: the moonbeams shine
As 'twere its natural torches, for divine
Should be the light which streams here, to illume
This long-explored but still exhaustless mine
Of contemplation: and the azure gloom
Of an Italian night, where the deep skies assume

---

[1] It is recorded that Roman generals " triumphed " three hundred and twenty times
in honor of victories over foreign nations.

CXXIX.

Hues which have words, and speak to ye of heaven,
Floats o'er this vast and wondrous monument,
And shadows forth its glory. There is given
Unto the things of earth, which Time hath bent,
A spirit's feeling, and where he hath leant
His hand, but broke his scythe, there is a power
And magic in the ruin'd battlement,
For which the palace of the present hour
Must yield its pomp, and wait till ages are its dower.

.   .   .   .

CXXXIX.

And here the buzz of eager nations ran,
In murmur'd pity, or loud-roar'd applause,
As man was slaughter'd by his fellow-man.
And wherefore slaughter'd? wherefore, but because
Such were the bloody Circus' genial laws,
And the imperial pleasure.—Wherefore not?
What matters where we fall to fill the maws
Of worms—on battle-plains or listed spot?
Both are but theatres where the chief actors rot.

CXL.

I see before me the Gladiator[1] lie:
He leans upon his hand—his manly brow
Consents to death, but conquers agony,
And his droop'd head sinks gradually low—
And through his side the last drops, ebbing slow
From the red gash, fall heavy, one by one,
Like the first of a thunder-shower; and now

---

[1] Now generally known as the Dying Gaul, a work of the third century B. C. See Lübke's "History of Sculpture," I., p. 244.

The arena swims around him—he is gone,
Ere ceased the inhuman shout which hail'd the wretch who
    won.

CXLI.

He heard it, but he heeded not—his eyes
Were with his heart, and that was far away;
He reck'd not of the life he lost nor prize,
But where his rude hut by the Danube lay,
There were his young barbarians all at play,
There was their Dacian mother—he, their sire,
Butcher'd to make a Roman holiday—
All this rush'd with his blood—Shall he expire
And unavenged?—Arise! ye Goths, and glut your ire!

CXLII.

But here, where Murder breathed her bloody steam;
And here, where buzzing nations choked the ways,
And roar'd or murmur'd like a mountain stream
Dashing or winding as its torrent strays;
Here, where the Roman million's blame or praise
Was death or life, the playthings of a crowd,[1]
My voice sounds much—and fall the stars' faint rays
On the arena void—seats crushed—walls bow'd—
And galleries, where my steps seem echoes strangely loud.

CXLIII.

A ruin—yet what ruin! from its mass
Walls, palaces, half-cities, have been rear'd;
Yet oft the enormous skeleton ye pass
And marvel where the spoil could have appear'd.

---

[1] Perhaps everyone knows that a Roman audience decided the fate of a wounded
gladiator, by turning their thumbs up or down. Thumbs down meant death.

Hath it indeed been plunder'd, or but clear'd?
Alas! developed, opens the decay,
When the colossal fabric's form is near'd:
It will not bear the brightness of the day,
Which streams too much on all years, man, have reft
    away.

CXLIV.

But when the rising moon begins to climb
Its topmost arch, and gently pauses there;
When the stars twinkle through the loops of time,
And the low night-breeze waves along the air
The garland-forest, which the gray walls wear,
Like laurels on the bald first Cæsar's head;
When the light shines serene but doth not glare,
Then in this magic circle raise the dead:
Heroes have trod this spot—'tis on their dust ye tread.

CXLV.

" While stands the Coliseum, Rome shall stand;
" When falls the Coliseum, Rome shall fall;
" And when Rome falls—the World." From our own
    land
Thus spake the pilgrims o'er this mighty wall
In Saxon times, which we are wont to call
Ancient; and these three mortal things are still
On their foundations, and unalter'd all:
Rome and her Ruin past Redemption's skill,
The World, the same wide den—of thieves, or what ye
    will.

(APOLLO BELVIDERE.)

CLXI.

Or view the Lord of the unerring bow,
The God of life, and poesy, and light—
The Sun in human limbs array'd, and brow
All radiant from his triumph in the fight;
The shaft hath just been shot—the arrow bright
With an immortal's vengeance; in his eye
And nostril beautiful disdain, and might,
And majesty, flash their full lightnings by,
Developing in that one glance the Deity.

CLXII.

But in his delicate form—a dream of Love,
Shaped by some solitary nymph, whose breast
Long'd for a deathless lover from above,
And madden'd in that vision—are exprest
All that ideal beauty ever bless'd
The mind within its most unearthly mood,
When each conception was a heavenly guest—
A ray of immortality—and stood,
Starlike, around, until they gather'd to a god!

CLXIII.

And if it be Prometheus stole from Heaven
The fire which we endure, it was repaid
By him to whom the energy was given
Which this poetic marble hath array'd
With an eternal glory—which, if made
By human hands, is not of human thought;
And Time himself hath hallow'd it, nor laid
One ringlet in the dust—nor hath it caught
A tinge of years, but breathes the flame with which 'twas
    wrought.

(DIRGE FOR THE PRINCESS CHARLOTTE.)

CLXVII.

Hark! forth from the abyss a voice proceeds,[1]
A long, low distant murmur of dread sound,
Such as arises when a nation bleeds
With some deep and immedicable wound;
Through storm and darkness yawns the rending ground,
The gulf is thick with phantoms, but the chief
Seems royal still, though with her head discrown'd,
And pale, but lovely, with maternal grief
She clasps a babe, to whom her breast yields no relief.

CLXVIII.

Scion of chiefs and monarchs, where art thou?
Fond hope of many nations, art thou dead?
Could not the grave forget thee, and lay low
Some less majestic, less beloved head?
In the sad midnight, while thy heart still bled,
The mother of a moment, o'er thy boy,
Death hush'd that pang for ever: with thee fled
The present happiness and promised joy
Which fill'd the imperial isles so full it seem'd to cloy.

CLXIX.

Peasants bring forth in safety.—Can it be,
Oh thou that wert so happy, so adored!
Those who weep not for kings shall weep for thee,
And Freedom's heart, grown heavy, cease to hoard
Her many griefs for ONE; for she had pour'd

---

[1] The Princess Charlotte was almost the only member of the royal family who was beloved by the nation, and her early death, in 1817, made a deep impression upon all Englishmen.

Her orisons for thee, and o'er thy head
Beheld her Iris.—Thou, too, lonely lord,[1]
And desolate consort—vainly wert thou wed!
The husband of a year! the father of the dead!

CLXX.

Of sackcloth was thy wedding garment made;
Thy bridal's fruit is ashes: in the dust
The fair-hair'd Daughter of the Isles is laid,
The love of millions! How we did entrust
Futurity to her! and, though it must
Darken above our bones, yet fondly deem'd
Our children should obey her child, and bless'd
Her and her hoped-for seed, whose promise seem'd
Like stars to shepherd's eyes:—'twas but a meteor beam'd.

CLXXI.

Woe unto us, not her; for she sleeps well:
The fickle reek of popular breath, the tongue
Of hollow counsel, the false oracle,
Which from the birth of monarchy hath rung
Its knell in princely ears, till the o'erstung
Nations have arm'd in madness, the strange fate
Which tumbles mightiest sovereigns, and hath flung
Against their blind omnipotence a weight
Within the opposing scale, which crushes soon or late,—

CLXXII.

These might have been her destiny; but no,
Our hearts deny it: and so young, so fair,

---

[1] Leopold, afterwards King of Belgium.

Good without effort, great without a foe;
But now a bride and mother—and now *there!*
How many ties did that stern moment tear!
From thy Sire's to his humblest subject's breast
Is link'd the electric chain of that despair,
Whose shock was as an earthquake's, and opprest
The land which loved thee so that none could love thee best.

(THE OCEAN.)

CLXXV.

But I forget.—My Pilgrim's shrine is won,
And he and I must part,—so let it be,—
His task and mine alike are nearly done;
Yet once more let us look upon the sea;
The midland ocean breaks on him and me,
And from the Alban Mount we now behold
Our friend of youth, that ocean, which when we
Beheld it last by Calpe's rock unfold
Those waves, we follow'd on till the dark Euxine roll'd

CLXXVI.

Upon the blue Symplegades: long years—
Long, though not very many, since have done
Their work on both: some suffering and some tears
Have left us nearly where we had begun:
Yet not in vain our mortal race hath run,
We have had our reward—and it is here;
That we can yet feel gladden'd by the sun,
And reap from earth, sea, joy almost as dear
As if there were no man to trouble what is clear.

CLXXVII.

Oh! that the Desert were my dwelling-place,
With one fair Spirit for my minister,
That I might all forget the human race,
And, hating no one, love but only her!
Ye Elements!—in whose ennobling stir
I feel myself exalted—Can ye not
Accord me such a being?   Do I err
In deeming such inhabit many a spot?
Though with them to converse can rarely be our lot.

CLXXVIII.

There is a pleasure in the pathless woods,
There is a rapture on the lonely shore,
There is society, where none intrudes,
By the deep Sea, and music in its roar:
I love not Man the less, but Nature more,
From these our interviews, in which I steal
From all I may be, or have been before,
To mingle with the Universe, and feel
What I can ne'er express, yet cannot all conceal.

CLXXIX.

Roll on, thou deep and dark blue ocean—roll!
Ten thousand fleets sweep over thee in vain;
Man marks the earth with ruin—his control
Stops with the shore;—upon the watery plain
The wrecks are all thy deed, nor doth remain
A shadow of man's ravage, save his own,
When, for a moment, like a drop of rain,
He sinks into thy depths with bubbling groan,
Without a grave, unknell'd, uncoffin'd, and unknown.

CLXXX.

His steps are not upon thy paths,—thy fields
Are not a spoil for him,—thou dost arise
And shake him from thee; the vile strength he wields
For earth's destruction thou dost all despise,
Spurning him from thy bosom to the skies,
And send'st him, shivering in thy playful spray
And howling, to his Gods, where haply lies
His petty hope in some near port or bay,
And dashest him again to earth:—there let him lay.

CLXXXI.

The armaments which thunderstrike the walls
Of rock-built cities, bidding nations quake,
And monarchs tremble in their capitals,
The oak leviathans, whose huge ribs make
Their clay creator the vain title take
Of lord of thee, and arbiter of war:
These are thy toys, and, as the snowy flake,
They melt into thy yeast of waves, which mar
Alike the Armada's pride, or spoils of Trafalgar.

CLXXXII.

Thy shores are empires, changed in all save thee—
Assyria, Greece, Rome, Carthage, what are they?
Thy waters wash'd them power while they were free,
And many a tyrant since: their shores obey
The stranger, slave, or savage: their decay
Has dried up realms to deserts:—not so thou,
Unchangeable save to thy wild waves' play—
Time writes no wrinkle on thine azure brow—
Such as creation's dawn beheld, thou rollest now.

CLXXXIII.

Thou glorious mirror, where the Almighty's form
Glasses itself in tempests; in all time,
Calm or convulsed—in breeze, or gale, or storm,
Icing the pole, or in the torrid clime
Dark-heaving;—boundless, endless, and sublime—
The image of Eternity—the throne
Of the Invisible; even from out thy slime
The monsters of the deep are made; each zone
Obeys thee; thou goest forth, dread, fathomless, alone.

CLXXXIV.

And I have loved thee, Ocean![1] and my joy
Of youthful sports was on thy breast to be
Borne, like thy bubbles, onward: from a boy
I wanton'd with thy breakers—they to me
Were a delight: and if the freshening sea
Made them a terror—'twas a pleasing fear,
For I was as it were a child of thee,
And trusted to thy billows far and near,
And laid my hand upon thy mane—as I do here.

---

[1] From his boyhood, Byron loved the grandeur both of the mountains and of the sea. In later life he often referred to the impression made upon him at the age of eight by the Scotch Highlands; and his intercourse with the wild solemnity of the northern ocean during his childhood had a profound influence upon his whole life. Cf. "Childe Harold," III., 72-75, "The Island," XII., etc.

THE ISLES OF GREECE.

1.

The isles of Greece, the isles of Greece!
  Where burning Sappho loved and sung,
Where grew the arts of war and peace,—
  Where Delos rose, and Phœbus sprung!
Eternal summer gilds them yet,
But all, except their sun, is set.

2.

The Scian [1] and the Teian [2] muse,
  The hero's harp, the lover's lute,
Have found the fame your shores refuse:
  Their place of birth alone is mute
To sounds which echo further west
Than your sires' " Islands of the Blest."

3.

The mountains look on Marathon—
  And Marathon looks on the sea;
And musing there an hour alone,
  I dream'd that Greece might still be free;
For standing on the Persians' grave,
I could not deem myself a slave.

4.

A king sat on the rocky brow
  Which looks o'er sea-born Salamis;
And ships, by thousands, lay below,
  And men in nations;—all were his!

---

[1] Homer.   [2] Anacreon.

He counted them at break of day—
And when the sun set where were they?

5.

And where are they? and where art thou,
　My country? On thy voiceless shore
The heroic lay is tuneless now—
　The heroic bosom beats no more!
And must thy lyre, so long divine,
Degenerate into hands like mine?

6.

'Tis something, in the dearth of fame,
　Though link'd among a fetter'd race,
To feel at least a patriot's shame,
　Even as I sing, suffuse my face;
For what is left the poet here?
For Greeks a blush—for Greece a tear.

7.

Must *we* but weep o'er days more blest?
　Must *we* but blush?—Our fathers bled.
Earth! render back from out thy breast
A remnant of our Spartan dead!
Of the three hundred grant but three,
To make a new Thermopylæ!

8.

What, silent still? and silent all?
　Ah! no:—the voices of the dead
Sound like a distant torrent's fall,
　And answer, " Let one living head,
But one arise,—we come, we come! "
'Tis but the living who are dumb.

9.

In vain—in vain: strike other chords;
　Fill high the cup with Samian wine!
Leave battles to the Turkish hordes,
　And shed the blood of Scio's vine!
Hark! rising to the ignoble call—
How answers each bold Bacchanal!

10.

You have the Pyrrhic dance as yet,
　Where is the Pyrrhic phalanx gone?
Of two such lessons, why forget
　The nobler and the manlier one?
You have the letters Cadmus gave—
Think ye he meant them for a slave?

11.

Fill high the bowl with Samian wine!
　We will not think of themes like these!
It made Anacreon's song divine:
　He served—but served Polycrates—
A tyrant: but our masters then
Were still, at least, our countrymen.

12.

The tyrant of the Chersonese
　Was freedom's best and bravest friend;
That tyrant was Miltiades!
　Oh! that the present hour would lend
Another despot of the kind!
Such chains as his were sure to bind.

13.

Fill high the bowl with Samian wine!
    On Suli's rock, and Parga's shore,
Exists the remnant of a line
    Such as the Doric mothers bore;
And there, perhaps, some seed is sown,
The Heracleidan blood might own.

14.

Trust not for freedom to the Franks—
    They have a king who buys and sells:
In native swords, and native ranks,
    The only hope of courage dwells;
But Turkish force, and Latin fraud,
Would break your shield, however broad.

15.

Fill high the bowl with Samian wine!
    Our virgins dance beneath the shade—
I see their glorious black eyes shine;
    But gazing on each glowing maid,
My own the burning tear-drop laves,
To think such breasts must suckle slaves.

16.

Place me on Sunium's marbled steep,
    Where nothing, save the waves and I,
May hear our mutual murmurs sweep:
    There, swan-like, let me sing and die:
A land of slaves shall ne'er be mine—
Dash down yon cup of Samian wine!

" Don Juan," Canto III., 1819.]

TO MR. MURRAY.

For Oxford [1] and for Waldegrave [2]
You gave much more than me you gave;
Which is not fairly to behave,
                    My Murray.

Because if a live dog, 't is said,
Be worth a lion fairly sped,
A *live lord* must be worth *two* dead,
                    My Murray.

And if, as the opinion goes,
Verse hath a better sale than prose,—
Certes, I should have more than those,[3]
                    My Murray.

But now this sheet is nearly cramm'd,
So, if *you will*, *I* shan't be shamm'd,
And if you *won't*, *you* may be damn'd,[4]
                    My Murray.

1821.]

---

[1] " Memoirs of the Last Ten Years of the Reign of George II ," by Horace Walpole.

[2] Memoirs by James Earl Waldegrave.

[3] When Byron began to write he refused payment ; later he drove hard bargains.

[4] Byron discovered his genius for satire only when he took up the stanza of " Don Juan." "The Vision of Judgment," written in the same metre, gives in moderate compass the best idea of his mastery of the satiric vein.

STANZAS WRITTEN ON THE ROAD BETWEEN FLORENCE AND PISA.[1]

Oh, talk not to me of a name great in story;
The days of our youth are the days of our glory;
And the myrtle and ivy of sweet two-and-twenty
Are worth all your laurels, though ever so plenty.

What are garlands and crowns to the brow that is wrinkled?
'Tis but as a dead-flower with May-dew besprinkled.
Then away with all such from the head that is hoary!
What care I for the wreaths that can *only* give glory?

Oh, FAME!—if I e'er took delight in thy praises,
'Twas less for the sake of thy high-sounding phrases,
Than to see the bright eyes of the dear one discover
The thought that I was not unworthy to love her.

There chiefly I sought thee, *there* only I found thee:
Her glance was the best of the rays that surround thee;
When it sparkled o'er aught that was bright in my story,
I knew it was love, and I felt it was glory.

---

[1] I composed these stanzas (except the fourth, added now) a few days ago, on the road from Florence to Pisa.— Byron's "Diary." November 6, 1821.

ON THIS DAY I COMPLETE MY THIRTY-SIXTH YEAR.[1]

MISSOLONGHI, January 22, 1824.

'Tis time this heart should be unmoved,
  Since others it hath ceased to move:
Yet, though I cannot be beloved,
      Still let me love!

My days are in the yellow leaf;
  The flowers and fruits of love are gone;
The worm, the canker, and the grief
      Are mine alone!

The fire that on my bosom preys
  Is lone as some volcanic isle;
No torch is kindled at its blaze—
      A funeral pile.

The hope, the fear, the jealous care,
  The exalted portion of the pain
And power of love, I cannot share,
      But wear the chain.

But 'tis not *thus*—and 'tis not *here*—
  Such thoughts should shake my soul, nor *now*,
Where glory decks the hero's bier,
      Or binds his brow.

---

[1] Byron wrote these stanzas upon the complaint of his friends that he had ceased to write poetry. They are his last verses.

The sword, the banner, and the field,
   Glory and Greece, around me see!
The Spartan, borne upon his shield,
     Was not more free.

Awake! (not Greece—she *is* awake!)
   Awake, my spirit! Think through *whom*
Thy life-blood tracks its parent lake,
     And then strike home!

Tread those reviving passions down,
   Unworthy manhood!—unto thee
Indifferent should the smile or frown
     Of beauty be.

If thou regrett'st thy youth, *why live?*
   The land of honourable death
Is here:—up to the field, and give
     Away thy breath!

Seek out—less often sought than found—
   A soldier's grave, for thee the best;
Then look around, and choose thy ground,
     And take thy rest.

INDEXES

INDEX OF FIRST LINES

INDEX OF POEMS

SELECTIONS FROM WORDSWORTH.

SELECTIONS FROM COLERIDGE.

SELECTIONS FROM SHELLEY.

SELECTIONS FROM KEATS.